SUFFICIENT MAGIC

JAMES A EGGEBEEN

PROLOGUE

Garyll stood quietly at the foot of the hill. The shaking of his knees put a lie to his confident stance. In moments, the fate of the wizarding world was going to be decided. Either the small magic would remain available to everyone, or it would be diverted for the exclusive use of Adrylt and his triad.

The burden of what Garyll had undertaken weighed down on him as he prepared to take the only action possible. He must form his own triad. Even though it was forbidden and would probably cost him everything.

Endwa's fingers slid between his own, trembling as they grasped his. She nodded almost imperceptibly, signaling her commitment to his plan.

Garyll gave her hand a brief squeeze, hoping to instill a confidence in her that he himself lacked, and waited for Sama to complete the circle and activate the spell he wished they had not been forced to use.

Sama spoke the words that bound them together, joining their magic for life.

The power came awake, flaring to life like the rising of the sun. It shot through Garyll.

The earth itself distorted.

Every cell in Garyll's body joined in the awakened state. The blood in his veins ran hot, like molten lead. The hair on his head and arms stood straight, uncounted follicles pinching him like the jaws of an army of ants.

The wild magic surged, a thing alive.

Starting as a single stream, like lava from the fire mountains, it spiraled upward from the depths of the earth, splitting into three.

One stream leaped from Garyll.

One from Sama.

And one from Endwa.

Three founts of molten fire wrapped themselves around one another as they jetted for Adrylt.

Across the field, Adrylt raised his hand and screamed. A bolt of lightning struck his hand, leaving Garyll momentarily blind. When his vision cleared, the lightning was gone, but in its place, Adrylt gripped a fiery blade. Three spans in length, the great blade shimmered with an internal light that accentuated the myriad folds of the iron forged by some ancient smith. The guard shone gold, catching the rays of the afternoon sun.

It was true then. Adrylt had let the wild magic corrupt him. Had taken it for his own, robbing others of its benefit. If Garyll could not stop Adrylt and his triad, they would soon be unstoppable.

This had to end now.

Garyll recovered his senses and drove the wild magic toward Adrylt, guiding a mighty serpent straight for his enemy's heart.

Adrylt leveled the point of the sword at Garyll.

A maelstrom of pain engulfed Garyll. It was as if the sword had slashed him uncounted times leaving a myriad of tiny cuts across his flesh that seared with pain. He fought back the pain. There was no time for self-pity. He stepped forward, but lost his footing, dropping to his knees.

Beside him, Endwa raised her arm, guiding her own magic against Adrylt.

"No. Endwa. It's too dangerous," Garyll choked out between clenched teeth.

Endwa ignored him, pressing her magic forward with a speed that even Garyll could not match.

But it was not fast enough.

Adrylt swung his sword. The blade contacted Endwa's magic with a shriek that split the air as it slid effortlessly through the fiery serpent, severing its head.

Endwa shrieked.

Adrylt screamed.

The two remaining serpents rushed past Adrylt and struck his cohorts.

A great flash erupted behind Adrylt as one of his triad turned to ashes and vanished.

Garyll felt a surge of satisfaction, but his elation quickly turned to concern.

Endwa's fingers slid from his own, and he felt the wild magic fade.

It was over.

Both triads were broken.

The wild magic was safe.

At least, until another triad arose to take possession of it once more.

Garyll knelt beside Endwa.

Her still face was almost peaceful, but the crimson scar that ran along her arm toward her heart told him she had fallen. He knew that already. He'd felt the life drain out of her. Felt the wild magic subside. She was gone — paid the price he had hoped would not be levied against them.

He knelt beside her.

"Endwa?" He lifted her head, cradling it in his lap.

"Endwa?"

But she didn't respond.

She would never respond.

As if in celebration, the clouds parted and sunlight streamed down to bathe the meadow behind the trio. The grass waved in the gentle breeze that flowed across the great canyon where the academy of magic floated.

Garyll saw none of this.

He only had eyes for Endwa.

He let his tears wash across her still face as if they had the power to reanimate her flesh.

They didn't.

Finally, he bent his lips to her ear and whispered. "Endwa. We won."

1

INSUFFICIENT MAGIC
KEEREE

The ancient oak stood beside the overgrown path, its gnarled roots reaching deep into the earth. All the way to the wild magic, some said. The trunk was twisted as if a giant had grasped it in a fit of rage, attempting to rip it from the ground. Failing that, it had smashed it. Halfway up the trunk, a clock ticked a steady metronome beat. Its face was scarred by generations of woodpeckers until the numbers were barely visible. It was said to mark the days since the creation of magic, and someday, when the clock struck midnight, the era of wizards would end. Surely the magic that had created such a thing would be available to Keeree if she dared approach. Yet there was danger. Rumor had it that the tree had devoured more than one unworthy soul who dared draw too near.

Keeree swallowed her fears, bit her lip, and took a step closer, feeling the moss-covered roots beneath her bare feet. It was her time. She had reached her sixteenth name day, and that was the age when magic came awake, except when it didn't. But now was not the time for doubt. She pushed the nagging insecurity away and stepped forward. As she approached them, the gnarled roots shifted and writhed. It was as if a nest of serpents had entangled itself around the tree, their girth almost as thick as Keeree's legs. Her heart beat wildly as she struggled to control her breathing, waiting while the undulating mass formed an opening in the base of the tree.

She heaved a sigh of relief.

It had accepted her.

She dropped to her knees and crawled inside. Snug and safe within the mighty oak, she settled onto a floor of dried leaves, her back resting against the rough wood. For a moment, she thought she sensed the presence of another with strong magic. Today, of all days, she wished for complete secrecy. No witnesses. She brushed off the feeling and drew a breath, taking in the odor of decaying leaves recently washed by rain. The forest was quiet with only the sound of rustling leaves, and far off, the call of a mourning dove. No. She was alone. No one would witness what she was about to attempt.

Tomorrow was the examination, and she wasn't ready. It had been three moons since her name-day. Surely enough time for the magic to come awake in her. If it were up to her, she might have waited another summer, given the magic time to fully come upon her, but her mother had pushed her to try now. She refused to explain herself. She said Keeree's magic was plenty powerful and her time was now.

So why did she feel this way? She was no great wizard. She was a misfit. A damp-wick. People told her to accept her lot in life, but she knew she was meant for bigger things.

Keeree shuddered, recalling how her mother had pulled her aside on her name-day and given her *the talk*. Keeree had paid it little heed, getting lost in her own thoughts when her mother informed her that soon her magic would awaken. Beyond that, Sama had been reluctant to explain much. She assured Keeree that when the time came, she would understand. But the magic had not come. Only the dreams. The confusing dreams and waking visions. Keeree was still waiting for the day when she would finally call up her magic. The day she would prove herself worthy of an education. The day she would take the first step on her journey to become a powerful wizard, revered and respected across the land, wielding magic for the benefit of the downtrodden and poor. Yes, she would be one of those. A white wizard. An itinerant. A wise woman who was welcomed and respected wherever she went.

She reached into the pocket of her homespun trousers and pulled out a freshly dipped candle. She'd made it with her own hands, collecting the fat and rendering it down over a fire built of wood gathered from this very forest. It was a trick she'd been told of. A way to help the magic come to life. To make it more personal. She hoped it was true.

She held the candle before her, gaze fixed firmly on the wick, as if staring down an unruly bull. Never let your gaze waver. Never show fear.

Her vision shimmered, and everything changed. It was as if she had stepped outside of her own body. It was strange to behold the change in the world around her. Thin lines of vermillion coursed through the air, rising from the twisted grains in the rough wood that wrapped around her, almost as if the tree itself was coming to life with magic. A strange and wild magic, untamed, ferocious. The magic spoke to her in a muted voice that reminded her of her mother. Whispers of unfamiliar words that left afterimages in her mind. The words were in a foreign language, familiar sounds strung together in a strange manner, yet beneath the words, she felt power. As if the words themselves directed power that she had no access to.

Then the voice was gone.

The colors muted.

The bands of vermillion faded.

Once more she sat alone in the interior of the grand tree.

She blinked.

It was time. What had the voice said? Strange words echoed in her head. Had it given her the words she needed? She had seen others use magic to light a candle. It was so common, no one paid it much attention. It was like walking. Something so simple, everyone did it. Yet it was the source of so much frustration for children who had yet to master the skill.

"Incendio ignius!" she spat the unfamiliar words.

A tiny spark appeared at the end of the wick and quickly

vanished. A spindly thread of white smoke rose to dwindle in the air. The wick poking from the tallow turned away from her as if spurning her desire.

"Cow flop," she muttered.

Maybe it was all in her head. She'd heard that too. That magic was more in the practitioner's mind than anything else. Maybe she needed to imagine the fire. She could do that.

She focused her gaze on the wick. In her mind's eye, she saw the threads of magic touch the wick, encouraging it to bring forth the thing she desired most. A tiny red ember would glow at the tip for just a heartbeat until a lone strand of the braided cord turned a brilliant red. A single twisting line of smoke would rise from that tiny spark and dance its way into the air. That was it. That was what she desired above all else, yet it stubbornly refused to appear. It was as if someone was blowing out the spark just as it touched the wick.

No one could interfere with her magic, could they? She was alone. She'd made certain of that. Yet she could not shake the feeling that someone was watching her. Witnessing her attempts. Laughing.

She pinched her eyes shut. Ignore it. Once more, she reached for the flame. Her stomach churned. She grew light-headed. Something was hindering her, preventing her from performing this spell. She could sense it.

A slight pressure wrapped her chest as if a heavy leather belt had been drawn tight around her. There was a dampness in the air she hadn't sensed earlier. Was someone trying to prevent her from succeeding? She would not let *that* happen. She reached for the fire, pushing aside the feeling. No one would keep her from doing this. The flame was hers. She reached for it again; her imagined hand impervious to the flame. In her mind's eye, the tongue of flame touched the candlewick. It burst to life, a brilliant orange flame filling the shadows beneath the tree with its flickering yellow light.

"Yes!" Keeree shouted.

She opened her eyes, but the shadows still clung to the dried leaves.

The candle remained cold and dark.

She had failed.

She knew it. She wasn't cut out for this. She should have listened when they told her she would never be able to master even the simplest spell. Almost everyone could light a candle. Why not her? Her parents were both damp-wicks. Did that mean that there was no hope for her?

Her eyes stung as she blinked back tears and took a calming breath.

Thankfully, no one had seen her embarrass herself. She would have died if they had. She could always claim that she wasn't interested, that getting accepted into the Academy of Magic wasn't something she wanted. That she preferred the life of a mundane. Who would know that such a simple thing as a candle had crushed her dreams? But who was she fooling? She was a failure. A damp-wick. Someone who couldn't even raise a candle flame in a place where magic was plentiful.

How was she going to do it tomorrow in the square with everyone watching? It would be a disaster. They would laugh at her. They would all know. If she hadn't already signed up for the exam, she could claim her magic hadn't come upon her yet, that she was waiting another summer before attempting it, but she *had* given her name. She was stuck. No backing out, no matter how bad it looked. Backing out was worse than failing. It was admitting defeat without even trying.

She took a deep breath to calm herself and backed from beneath the ancient oak.

She stood up and brushed the leaves from her trousers and shirt.

The feeling that she wasn't alone grew stronger.

Slowly, she turned.

The forest was much the same as when she'd entered the tree, the same leaves fluttered about in the light breeze, the same branches swayed overhead, their leaves blocking out the afternoon sun. Everything was as it had been, even the hands on the clock had remained where they were. Or had they? She wished she'd paid more attention. Still, she could not shake the feeling that someone was there.

Once again, a distant whisper offered words. Strange words that somehow felt right. She waved her hand in the air. "Ostende te." As she spoke, a tingle spread along her arm as if something had risen from the soles of her bare feet, threaded its way through her heart, and rushed out her fingertips.

The surrounding air shivered, growing distorted in spots as if it were being bent around something. Half a dozen somethings.

"Ostende te statim." Once again, the tingling spread through her, this time wrapping itself in a ball inside her chest, pausing as if gathering strength, then once more racing out of her fingertips.

Half a dozen student wizards appeared in a ring surrounding the tree. They ranged in size from slightly shorter than Keeree to taller than her father. Each one wore the traditional dark-blue robe adorned with stars to represent the skills the student had mastered. Most of them bore at least a dozen stars. But one, less than a handful.

"Horse apples," she said. "What are you doing here?"

"We came to see a damp-wick firsthand." The boy who spoke was a summer older than Keeree. His sandy blond hair was cut short in the academy's style. He was the one with only a few stars. He wasn't a very promising student.

Keeree turned to the boy. "Stuff yourself, Socha." She shoved him out of the way. "I'm no damp-wick."

"You were trying to light that candle. I can see the bulge in your pocket." He jutted his chin at her trousers.

The rest of the students snickered, some covering their mouths as if they retained a shred of decency. Most laughed openly.

She stepped closer to Socha. He had half a head on her, but he was a villager, not a farmer. She could take him.

"Stay back." Socha held up his hands, thumbs crossed, fingers twisted into strange shapes. As his hands moved, a dim violet glow rose to coat his flesh. It made the hair on Keeree's arms stand on end. Was this what magic felt like? It differed from what she'd felt only moments before when she commanded the students to show themselves. She tried to savor the feeling. Maybe if she could recall it later, it would help her bring forth fire. She grew so wrapped up in trying to understand what magic felt like, that for a moment, she forgot herself.

She was in danger.

Socha was preparing to use magic against her. But would he? Truly? He was a fool, but not that foolish.

"You won't use magic on me," Keeree said. "Not in front of witnesses."

Socha hesitated. He glanced around at the other students, then lowered his hands. The violet glow died away. "You're not worth it. You're a lackwit and a damp-wick, and you're ugly." He balled his fists and pressed them against his thighs. "Did anyone ever tell you that? That you're ugly? I've seen toads more attractive than you."

He shoved her, and she lost her balance, landing hard on the dirt.

"Lizard snot," she muttered. Why hadn't she seen *that* coming? She must look like a fool. She should have just walked away. Her father always said her tongue would be her undoing. But what was she supposed to do? Just take it?

Someday she would put Socha in his place. Most students had acquired at least a dozen stars by the end of their first summer, but Socha was struggling. He was falling behind. One day, they would declare him a damp-wick and push him out. When that happened, he'd probably take his anger out on her, as if she had anything to do with what went on at the academy. She'd never even seen the place, and she probably never would.

Not if today's performance was any indication.

2

UNEXPECTED MAGIC
PHYR

Phyr sat back and tried to relax. The chair was hard despite its luxurious leather upholstery. The room was chilly even though a fire burned in the hearth behind him. It felt gloomy even though the afternoon sun streamed in the open windows. His stomach growled. His legs cramped. His head ached, and he had to make water. These were the distractions that could trip him up. Using magic in front of his mother might just expose the secret he'd been hiding from her ever since he'd discovered it. Issur and Teil were wizards. They had command of not only the small magic, but the more powerful magic that few possessed. But Phyr had touched something else. Something forbidden.

He swallowed the bile that rose in his throat and turned to face the crackling energy that played between the crystals before him. All his life, he'd been fascinated by the wild magic. It was pulled from the earth and arced back and forth between the jewels set at the tips of the intricately carved horns of alabaster marble. Horns that rose from the floor and arched over. They channeled the raw power, filtered the wild magic, cooled it, made it safe for those who wished to wield it. Touching the wild magic in its pure form was dangerous. He knew that. Everyone did, but he was drawn to it, compelled to touch it.

He knew better. Yet, it still called to him, and in the quiet of his room, he *had* touched it. Drawn it forth and shaped it to his will. No one had ever told him outright that it was forbidden, but his parents had made it clear that it was frowned upon. Phyr's own father was charged with protecting the wizarding world from those who went rogue and wielded the wild magic. What would he think if he knew what Phyr had done?

Issur, his mother, interrupted his thoughts. "You can do this."

She placed a single pure white taper into the golden candlestick that had been used by her, her mother before her, and her grandfather before that. Phyr's guts twisted. He had mastered this spell long ago, but since he'd touched the wild magic, that had become his sole focus. Could he do what was asked of him without revealing his dark secret?

"*My* mother used to rub my neck when I practiced," Issur whispered. "Do you want me to do that?"

If he lost his focus and she saw what he was capable of, she would be furious with him. "No, mother. It distracts me."

Phyr concentrated on the spell he had been taught. Ignored the itching, nagging, call of the wild magic. He closed his eyes, allowing only the image of the candle floating free in the air to remain. He carefully erased the image of the chair that sat beside him, edited out the table and the ornate candlestick. He even banished the image of his mother as she stood behind him. Gone, the brilliant red jewel set in gold that hung around her neck. Gone, the shimmering headband that bore the brilliant garnet that carried magic with her wherever she went. Gone, the sea of silver stars embroidered on her robe. Gone, her shoulder-length black hair. Gone, her confident and reassuring smile.

"Concentrate," she said.

Phyr blocked out the sound of her voice, focusing on the candle, permitting his imagination to contain only what he required for this spell. He tried to ignore the sound of the fountain as the wild magic coursed through it, calling to him. Just a touch, it said. That was all. Just a taste to get things started.

He pushed it away.

No. The small magic. That was what he needed. The filtered, watered-down power that everyone had access to. The cleansed and stunted magic that flowed between the arching jewels set in the fount.

He focused his thoughts on the candle.

For the longest moment, nothing happened. As Phyr directed his thoughts toward the candle, his chest tightened. It was as if something hardened beneath his ribs. Something crowded out his heart, making it strain inside his chest. He panicked. Was he dying? Had he done something wrong? Had the wild magic contaminated him somehow?

He calmed himself and let his thoughts reach out to the tamed magic. He lifted a tiny flame from the passive energy and brought it to the candle wick. For a moment, wild magic flared, but he fought it. His heart raced. Did she suspect? Could she tell?

Fingers gripped Phyr's shoulder. "Open your eyes."

He did.

The candle before him cast a brilliant light into the room.

"I did it!" He glanced at Issur, alert to any sign that she saw the truth of what he'd almost done.

She seemed genuinely happy.

"Of course, you did. Again." Issur raised an eyebrow at the candle and the flame extinguished. Not a spark remained, not even a thread of smoke. It was as if the candle were newly dipped and had yet to be lit for the first time.

"I did it." If he feigned excitement, would she think his success was what drove his heart thumping in his chest? Would one success be enough to convince her he had control of the small magic? He would rather not risk exposing his unorthodox methods again.

"I saw you. I felt you. I heard you." Issur said. "You called up magic, but there's plenty of magic here to harness. On the morrow, you will be called upon to perform this spell in the square. The magic there will be artificially depleted. Barely any will be available for your use."

His father had told him that sometimes during the examination, a candidate was distracted at the worst possible moment. He said that a wizard must be able to conjure, no matter what was happening around him. Be wary, he'd said. A cough from the crowd, a crying child, a barking dog, someone laughing, an unexpected word. Any of these might happen at any moment. Phyr needed to concentrate. What if that happened to him on the morrow? What if he forgot or became distracted and touched the wild magic in the square? In front of everyone?

"This time," Issur was saying. "I will block off your access to the magic of the fount. You need to know what it feels like to wrest power from the earth rather than have it flow into you unbidden." Issur opened a hollowed-out book and withdrew a silver medallion inset with a crimson jewel. The silver filigree had been expertly wrought in patterns that defied the eye's attempts to trace them. They seemed to shift and squirm, making Phyr's eyes water even as he attempted to follow their path.

"Hold still," Issur lifted the talisman and placed the ribbon around Phyr's neck.

He shuddered as the weight of it settled against his chest. The same place the tightness had been when he'd wrestled with the magic. He wondered what it would be like to live in a world where magic was scarce or even non-existent.

He didn't have long to wonder.

The world around him turned a flat sepia. It was as if the color had suddenly ceased to exist. The air tasted of copper and smelled of smoke. The temperature dropped, and the energy flowing between the stones ceased.

"Is this what it will be like?" Phyr asked.

"Yes. Try now. You must reach for the magic. You're used to having it come to you. The talisman is damping out the magic in the room. It's almost non-existent, just as it will be tomorrow. You must summon it. Grasp it. Call it to do your bidding."

"How do I do that?" Phyr asked. The small magic was indeed gone. But, the wild magic had been unaffected by the talisman. If anything, it was even stronger. She wasn't expecting him to use that, was she? Certainly not.

Phyr calmed himself, slowing his breathing and waiting for his heart to settle into the rhythm he was accustomed to. He closed his eyes and focused on the candle. This time, he added brilliant colors to the image, as if in defiance of the sepia of the world around him. He recalled what the magic had felt like when his mother placed her hand on his neck. No, not that. Another source, then. The wild magic coursed deep beneath the ground. The fount drew it forth like water from a well. It called to him.

Maybe he could cleanse it before he wielded it. He imagined an earthen shaft dug deep into the ground beneath him. He would lower his pail and draw the magic forth just as one drew water from a well.

He envisioned it.

A wooden bucket — staves carefully planed smooth, bound with slightly tarnished brass bands.

The bucket disappeared into his imaginary well to return moments later, half filled with a shimmering silver fluid.

He grasped the bucket, preparing to fling the magic at the candle, but he stopped short. This was pure wild magic. In his mind's eye, he dipped his hand into the silver liquid and drew forth the tiniest bit, flicking a drop toward the candle.

The magic flared.

His chest throbbed with fire.

It was as if *he* had been ignited, not the candle.

He panicked.

What had he done? Had he somehow misdirected the magic? Was it even now consuming his flesh? His hand flew to his chest. No, no flames. He wasn't on fire. It just felt like it.

"Phyr!" His mother gasped.

Phyr opened his eyes.

The world was back to normal.

The sepia color was gone.

The candle was gone.

All that remained of it was a puddle of wax congealing rapidly as it flowed across the tabletop. In the middle of the puddle of hardening wax, floated the remnant of the candle wick. Dancing above it, a flame no bigger than his little finger.

"That was a bit much, don't you think?" Issur yanked the talisman from around his neck and shoved it back into the hollowed-out book.

Phyr shivered. Had she seen it? Did she know what he'd done? How could she not?

She looked at him with an expression he had never seen before.

It was somewhere between fear and shock.

She *had* witnessed his shame.

She knew.

She drew a breath as if to speak, but she did not. Not for the longest time. When she finally did speak, her voice came in a shaky whisper. "Do — not — let — your — father — know." She spun on her heels and fled.

As the door closed, Phyr was almost certain he heard her crying.

3

UNACCEPTABLE MAGIC
DARAYA

*D*araya rubbed her back where the switch had landed. She'd chosen one that was smooth and wouldn't leave too much of a mark, but that never seemed to matter. Adrylt had a way with a switch that left her in pain for days every time he delivered one of his *reminders*. No matter. Tomorrow Daraya would be chosen, and that would be the end of it. No more Adrylt. No more beatings. No more admonishment about the evils of magic. She would be a student at the Academy of Magic, and with that title came rights and privileges that would prevent Adrylt from ever laying a hand on her again. She would take up residency at the academy with the rest of those who were selected. She could almost feel the warmth of bodies flowing around her, a gaggle of dark-blue robed, like-minded students making their way down the hallowed halls of that prestigious institute as they purposefully strode from one center of learning to the next.

It would be a whole new life for her. The one she had now would fade silently into her past. She would not miss it. Not really. Sure, she would miss her mother, and little Arria, but not Adrylt. And not really her mother. Daraya and Tailke had grown apart after the magic came awake in her. One afternoon, Tailke had seen Daraya light a candle despite her best efforts to hide it. Tailke burst into tears and moaned that Daraya had ruined their family. She proclaimed that Daraya was no longer her daughter, and made a great show of turning her back.

How could she say such a thing? Of course, Daraya was still her daughter. A little thing like magic wasn't going to change that.

But it had.

Ever since that day, Daraya noticed that Tailke was spending more time with Arria than her, as if Daraya no longer mattered, as if she was no longer part of the family. Daraya wanted to run off, to run away from her horrid family, but she hadn't. She'd stuck around, hoping things would get better.

But they hadn't.

When Adrylt caught her using magic to light the stove for the morning meal, he'd beaten her until blood ran down her back. Adrylt, who played the part of a respected merchant. One who traveled the land in search of exotic spices on behalf of the wealthy. How would those wealthy clients feel about him if they knew what he did to his own daughter? This time he had crossed the line from strict discipline into sadistic torture.

Next time, he would kill her.

He was *that* angry.

Enough was enough. The sun was up, and it would soon be warm. She would be expected to complete her chores even after such a beating. It was leave now or put it off one more day.

She made up her mind.

Leave now.

She looked around her room one last time. The bed that had been hers would be handed down to her younger sister, as would her clothes. She would not need them. She'd wear the robes of a student and when her time at the academy was complete, the robes of a wizard. She had no need of anything from her old life and no desire to be reminded of the place she had once called home. She was done.

She crept into the bedroom where her sister lay sleeping. The tiny face bore a slight smile. "I'll be back for you, little one. When the magic comes upon you, look for me. I won't let them do to you what they did to me."

She bent down, kissed the babe's forehead, and whispered. "I've not been such a great big sister, but I won't forget. I'll be back for you. When it's safe."

She gently touched a rosy cheek and turned from the cradle. That was it. There would never be a time like the present. Tomorrow she would be safe at the academy, but she wouldn't forget her sister.

She crawled out the window and ran, glancing back occasionally on the off chance that someone cared and would call out to her to stay.

No one did.

No one cared about her. Not since Rodaso died. Her father's sister had been the only one who ever understood her. Rodaso had secretly taught Daraya how to read the wizards' script and how magic truly worked. All in secret, of course. Rodaso would have taken her in, but that route was closed. Daraya was alone.

Where to go?

She had no genuine friends. Those few who said they were, whispered behind her back when they thought she wasn't listening. They had drawn away from her when they learned that her father had no love for magic. They all had dreams of becoming wizards. They were all going to be accepted into the academy. At least that was what they thought. Didn't everyone? Daraya tried to think which of her friends might offer her a room for the night. She couldn't come up with a single name. No, they weren't really her friends.

Without thinking, she found herself on the road that led out of town. Why had she chosen this path? She stopped herself, wondering where she was headed. She had no idea. She really hadn't thought it through. She was simply following her gut. So what next? Stop at one of the farms? Offer to help with the beasts and the children in exchange for a bed for the night?

She made her way to the first farm she reached and knocked. The woman who answered was sunburned and wrinkled despite being younger than Daraya's own mother.

"I'm in need of a place to stay. I can help with the housework and the children if you would be so kind as to put me up for the night." Daraya hated to beg, but she had little choice.

"You're Adrylt's girl, aren't you?" The woman squinted at her.

"Yes, ma'am."

"We don't need that sort of trouble." She stepped back and closed the door in Daraya's face.

Things were not going the way Daraya had hoped. There were more farms along the road. Maybe they had not all heard tales of her father.

But they had.

By the middle of the day, she started to worry. The sun beat down on her with an angry heat that she couldn't escape. Yet, she would not give up. She would not go back. She walked along, hoping for inspiration, letting her tears fall, and her thoughts wander. The road she was on was little more than a lane, not as well traveled as some, but more than a trail. It showed signs of recent use by a wagon if the horse-droppings in the roadway were any indication. The wind whipped dust in her face as she trudged along.

Her stomach growled.

She paused to pick wild berries from a raspberry bush that grew beside the road. She gently nudged the berries off the stalks, popped them into her mouth, and let the tart sweetness linger on her tongue for just a moment before swallowing each one. She was hungry. She'd avoided the kitchen where Tailke labored and Adrylt lingered, on her way out. She was starting to think that was a foolish idea — leaving without preparation. But she'd had enough. She could survive a day without food if she had to. No one died of starvation in just one day.

She reached for another berry but stopped. The air felt prickly. Gooseflesh rose on her arms. What was it? Lightning? She turned her gaze back toward town, and the feeling subsided. How strange. She reached out for more berries and the feeling rose up once more. She backed away. The feeling subsided. Even more strange.

She brushed past the wild raspberry bush and took a step toward the ditch that separated the lane from the field, careful to step over the water that trickled along the bottom from the previous evening's rain.

As her foot touched the alfalfa, the feeling of electricity grew stronger. Was this magic? She searched her memory. It felt a little like it had when she'd called fire, but not quite the same. This was subtler yet more powerful, as if it were masked or covered. She took another step. The path beneath her feet was visible, if faint. It was as if someone had trod these hills not long ago, a sole individual. The alfalfa was barely disturbed.

Where did it lead, and why did it set her hair standing on end? All thoughts of hunger vanished as she cautiously stepped along the path. She had barely gone half a dozen steps when the surrounding air thinned. It was as if the world had been stretched out, each step taking her a league from where she'd begun.

She glanced down at her feet.

No, the land was much the same, yet the feeling that she was moving a great distance was hard to shake.

She took another step.

Again, the sensation that she had gone a great distance washed over her.

Another step.

She froze, feeling her heart pound in her chest.

She looked down.

Her foot was at the edge of a cliff that dropped away farther than her eye could see.

She blinked to clear her vision, and everything came into sharp focus. Spread out before her was a great canyon, its far wall so distant it was shrouded in mist. She leaned over the edge, her head spinning with the great depths. She had never heard of a great canyon.

Just where was she?

She stepped back and gazed across the canyon. Hovering in the center was an island bearing the strangest structure she'd ever seen. But it was not the structure that caught her eye. The island was formed of solid rock, and it was floating in midair. Streamers of vines and vegetation trailed from the edges of the great rock and lost themselves in the depths of the canyon.

How was that even possible? She knew of the small magic. Everyone could levitate the tiniest of objects. It was the rare mother who didn't, at one time or another, entertain a babe by levitating a coin or a toy for their amusement, but this was on a whole other scale. The island was massive, solid rock, half a league in length. It just floated. There shouldn't be enough magic anywhere to do something like that.

She squinted at the island. With her eyes pinched almost shut, she saw the ghostly image of the magic that supported the great rock. Lightning bolts of scarlet arose from the base of the canyon far below. Flashing bolts struck the massive stone again and again. She felt, more than heard, crackling as the magic poured from the canyon and into the great hovering rock. It was breathtaking. And just a bit frightening. Even stranger was the castle that occupied nearly the entire surface of the floating rock. It was not the sort of castle she'd read about, tall and proud with imposing walls to keep out intruders. Rather, this was low and sprawling. The walls were only man-height as they stretched between squat towers with rough crenellations. Smoke rising from chimneys abruptly vanished in the still air as if it had been eaten by some unseen monster. And, gliding gracefully in the air above the castle, was that a gryphon?

What was this place?

How was such a thing so near her own home and she had never heard of it? This could only be the Academy of Magic. It had to be. But the academy was hidden from the mundane world, so how was she seeing it? Was this her newfound magic at work? She must finally possess magic sufficient to see it. That meant they would surely choose her. She would be accepted. Her future was secure.

She was a wizard.

She searched for a way to reach the floating island, but there was nothing apparent. No bridge, no great span of rock. How did the students cross the canyon then? No matter. On the morrow, she would pass the examination and then all the secrets this place hid would be revealed. But until then, she needed a place to sleep.

Not far along the edge of the canyon was an outbuilding. Little more than a large caretaker's cottage. Was it also a gatekeeper's abode? Would there be someone who might allow her to pass over the great canyon? If not, then perhaps she could still beg a bed for the night. It never hurt to ask.

Things were looking up.

She approached the cottage. The brick walls stood perfectly straight. Each joint of the beams that supported the roof was in perfect form. The roof itself was not thatch but deep-red tile. Each tile had been placed with perfect precision. This place had been built by no craftsman. It was a thing made by magic, powerful magic, yet it stood open and inviting.

The path leading to the cottage was paved with polished marble laid out in strange squares. Each square was bordered in gold with eight tiles arranged in rows of three. In each square, the final row had one tile missing, as if they were meant to be rearranged like a child's puzzle. Engraved in the tiles were symbols that Daraya had never seen before. She considered the puzzle for a moment, then abandoned the thought of trying to solve it. Things of magic did not always follow normal aesthetics, and she had no idea where to start.

"Hello?" she called out.

No one was home.

She crept inside and took a seat on a couch that faced a cold fireplace. Whoever lived here hadn't been around in a while. Everything was covered in dust. She could sleep here, then on the morrow, she would show them. She'd been practicing. The spell she had in mind was impressive, to say the least.

She held out her hand, slowly turning her palm up.

She'd practiced the gesture until it was second nature.

"Incendio," she whispered.

Whispering helped, but it was not needed.

She would not use her words on the morrow.

A brilliant white flame appeared wavering in the air half a digit above her outstretched hand. The flame flickered, shedding a light strong enough to cast a shadow.

"Dance for me."

Daraya sang a song she'd learned as a child. It was a tune Tailke used to sing to her when Daraya was small, an enchanting tune about a mother hen and her chicks. But Daraya had changed the words as she grew older. Her mother would not have recognized the song. It was Daraya's song now. She'd made it her own, and that pleased her.

The magic liked it too. The flame was especially bright today. As she watched it dance, a tightness grew inside her. In her chest, near her heart. For a moment she panicked. Had she done something wrong? She steeled herself to run for help, but the tightness settled down to a warmth that pulsed in time with her singing. The shadows the flame cast on the far wall of the cottage formed themselves into the shape of a man and a woman. The man wore a sword and dagger. The woman was dressed in the finest gown, and wore a crown on her head. Her skirt flowed around her as she twirled in time with the man. It was a display sure to impress, but it was best not to waste any magic.

Daraya let the shadows dance for a dozen heartbeats then closed her hand, extinguishing the flame.

How could they not select her when she had mastered such a spell as this?

She leaned back, congratulating herself.

She would be selected.

She knew it.

But her joy was short-lived.

As she settled into the couch, pain stabbed her in the back. She reached around to feel the cuts that Adrylt had gifted her with, on what she was certain, was his final beating.

Her hand came away with blood.

That would never do.

She made her way to the kitchen and worked the gleaming iron pump, hoping it had not lost its prime. Of course it hadn't. This was a place of magic, wasn't it?

She let out a sigh as water gushed to fill the sink.

It was warm.

She took a cloth and swished it in the water, wrung it out, and gently dabbed at her back. It stung where the water contacted her raw flesh. Thoughts of Adrylt and his switch surfaced, but she pushed them back down. That part of her life was over.

Someone coughed.

Daraya yanked her shirt down and turned to look.

Standing in the doorway was a young man barely a summer older than Daraya. He had short blond hair and wore a dark-blue robe with a smattering of white stars sewn on it. "How did you get here?" he demanded.

"I walked." Daraya flinched. Was she about to be punished for trespassing?

"Not *how* you got here, but how you got *here*." The boy placed his fists on his hips in a gesture Daraya knew all too well.

Her stomach churned. "I walked — from town — just followed the path until I saw this place and decided to drop in. I didn't know anyone was here. I need a place to stay for the night. I was hoping to find one here."

"How did you get through the wards?" the boy demanded.

"Wards?"

"You're on academy grounds. Not even students are allowed here. How did you even *see* the path? Why didn't the wards stop you?"

If students were not allowed, why was he here? "Aren't you a student?" she asked.

The boy stared at her, arms tensed at his sides. The twist of his face told Daraya he was less than happy to be challenged. His face grew red. He glanced off to one side as if seeking guidance from someone Daraya could not see. "We're not talking about me. I felt your presence, and I came here to investigate. Why are you here?" He sounded unsure of himself.

"I was lost," she lied. "I need a place to stay. I never noticed any wards."

"You're not supposed to be here."

"I just needed a place to stay." Daraya stood, ready to flee.

"Why?"

She hesitated. She wasn't about to reveal her shame before some strange boy.

He looked askance at her. "You're Adrylt's girl. It was your father, wasn't it?" The boy jutted his chin at her. "He's the one who gave you those."

"Gave me what?"

"Those stripes. I saw you cleaning them. Your father did that to you."

Daraya's hand went to her back. The scars and welts were a source of shame. They marked her as a disobedient daughter. Incorrigible, according to Adrylt. She had never shown them to anyone, and she wasn't about to start now. "There's nothing to see."

The boy's expression softened. "Those stripes will leave a scar, and one of them is already corrupted. If you don't get that looked at by a proper healer, the corruption will spread, and you'll die."

"I've survived worse."

"Then you've been lucky." The boy glanced toward the open door once again. He held out his hand and motioned Daraya to come closer. "I can heal you. It won't hurt. I promise."

Daraya craned her neck. Was there someone just outside the door that wished to remain unseen? A guard perhaps, or an instructor from the academy?

"I don't need help," she said.

"Yes, you do — especially if you want to be a wizard. They won't select you with switch marks."

"Why not?"

"Shows that you have an unstable family. How would it look for the academy to have it known that one of their students was regularly beaten by her own father?"

"He can't touch me. There are rules." Even as Daraya spoke, her heart sank. What if the boy was right? What if even being accepted to the academy would not protect her? What then?

"There are rules, but who really follows them?" he asked.

Daraya folded her arms across her chest. She didn't want any help. But what if the offer was genuine? What if the boy was right? What if the stripes would cost her the examination? What then? "I'll take my chances."

The boy took a step closer. "Let me help."

"Don't touch me." Daraya had no intention of letting some stranger touch her.

"Fine. I don't need to touch you to heal you." He gestured for her to turn her back. "It won't hurt at all, especially not here. You're fortunate to have run into me at a nexus."

"What's a nexus?" She wanted to steer the discussion away from her back, even though it hurt her just standing still. Maybe he could help her, but could she trust him?

"Never mind. Just relax." The boy raised his hand.

Daraya backed away but stopped. If what he said was true, her chances of being accepted would be much greater if she let him heal her.

She turned her back, closed her eyes, and steeled herself against the anticipated pain. Every healer said their ministrations would not hurt. Every healer lied. It was just a way to get their patients to relax. Even Rodaso had told this lie. Daraya had come to expect it.

A low humming erupted from behind the boy.

Warmth flowed over her flesh, caressing her skin where it touched her, raising a tiny shock as it explored her wounds. It was soothing, almost relaxing, but at one point, it flared into pain. The scab was loose there and the skin tender. So, the boy *had* lied.

She bit her tongue and let him continue. The touch grew warm, then hot. Then came the sound. Daraya listened intently. The boy was whispering. Why? Wasn't vocalizing a spell considered crude?

Daraya listened closely, trying to make out what he was saying.

"Industria, fluxus et sana," came the words, but they were not uttered by the boy as she at first thought. They were in a deep, baritone voice that lulled her into complacency. She felt compelled to sit and listen to that voice. It could go on all day and she would not grow tired of listening to it.

"Vade et malos." As the voice spoke the words, a pleasant sensation washed over her. It was as if she'd been gently lowered into a tub of warm water. The voice buoyed her up, supported her, cradled her in its soothing ripples. She let the feeling wash over her. It was going to be all right. The morning would come. She would be selected. She would be a student, just like the boy whose magic caressed her. What harm could come of a little healing?

When she had called up the fire, the magic had coursed through her, focusing in her chest, then spreading out to her hand to drive the fire, almost as if she were channeling it. This time it came from outside of her, as if the magic were being drawn from the foundations of the caretaker's cottage. Strange. She thought magic was magic. Could there be more than one way to wield it? Never mind. This was heaven. The warmth filled her and carried her thoughts away once more. She felt herself fall into a deep sleep but woke when the tone of the voice changed abruptly.

Gone was the soothing baritone.

It had been replaced by a deep growl. "Inde tollere atmet," it shouted.

Daraya's chest wrenched as if something were being torn from her. Right beside her heart. Where she'd felt the magic earlier.

Fire erupted.

Pain flared.

She screamed.

The fading words of the mysterious voice were all Daraya heard as the darkness took her. "You foolish girl."

4

CONTESTED MAGIC
KEEREE

*K*eeree took in the sights. The square looked nothing like it usually did. Gone were the stalls of merchants and vendors wowing the children with feats of small magic. Gone, the hanging slabs of swine, kine, and poultry. Gone, the merchants covered in blood. Gone, the stalls draped with brilliantly colored scarves, and rugs. Gone, the patrons who visited them, hoping the products would improve their chances of landing the right sort of mate. Gone, the heaps of vegetables, breads, and small tools for cooking or carpentry. This late in the morning, the place was usually packed, but not today. Today, the square contained only one structure. A dais. It had been created during the night by students of the academy using magic. Magic that would no longer fill the square to give a prospective student a leg up. Half as high as Keeree was tall, the platform stood on the backs of four ornately carved jade elephants. The dais itself sported three thrones, for what else would you call a chair so intricately carved and upholstered other than a throne? And they floated. Each throne hovered half a span above the surface of the dais, gently bobbing in the mid-morning breeze.

Stretching over the thrones, a pair of glimmering crystal arches glowed with power. Lightning arced back and forth between tips that tapered down to needle-sharp points where emeralds glowed with a light almost too bright to look at. The crystals absorbed the free magic that usually permeated the square, preventing anyone from accessing it directly. The academy maintained that in a land where every milk-maiden and washerwoman was able to call fire into existence, the true test of a wizard's ability was how they fared handling magic when it was scarce. And scarce it was this day. Every ounce of magic in the square had been funneled through those crystals. The crackling of that energy set the hair on Keeree's arms standing on end.

"Do you really want to do this?" Her father, Garyll, placed his hand on her shoulder. He squeezed gently. It was meant to remind her he would think no less of her should she choose to abandon her quest. He'd made that clear.

She shook the hand off. "They'll take me. You'll see." She was not the sort of girl to disagree with her father, but this was important, and he didn't understand how much it meant to her.

She scanned the square, planning her path away from her father and his lack of belief. Leading up to the dais from the square were three sets of stairs. This was how prospective students were to ascend and be judged. Three sets to represent the classes of society the students were drawn from.

On either side of the dais, was another set of stairs. These two represented either success or failure and symbolized the merging of the three paths. The Academy of Magic recognized no class, no heritage, no lineage. Every student left the dais either as a wizard of equal standing or not a wizard at all.

Keeree didn't believe *that* for a moment.

Loitering by the stairs that represented failure were a handful of blue-robed students. Most had an impressive number of stars, save one. Socha. Of course he would be there to witness her failure. Well, she would show him. She would be accepted. She would be a wizard, and soon she would have more stars than he did.

"Don't be disappointed if they reject you," Garyll told her. "Not everyone is cut out for magic. I wouldn't be shocked if they failed you just to hurt me."

"They won't reject me," Keeree said. "They're fair. Impartial."

"That's what *they* say." Garyll shook his head.

Keeree signed. "I'm not going home, not without trying. I'm not going to spend my life as a mundane."

"I don't want you to get hurt, that's all," Garyll said.

"I'm going to be a wizard, a powerful wizard. *If* I fail, and I won't, *then* I'll worry about what to do with my life." Keeree shuddered. If only she believed her own words.

Garyll squeezed her shoulder and sighed. "Do well."

She reached up and patted her father's hand. "I will." She turned toward the dais. For a moment, the air before her wavered and her visions shifted. It was the same square, but different. The dais appeared less festive, more menacing.

A chill washed over her.

A distant memory of standing on that dais poked at the back of her thoughts, but when she reached for it, it vanished, like a soap bubble drifting away on the breeze.

The square shimmered once more, and everything returned to normal. Keeree brushed aside the memory, crossed the square, and joined the crowd milling before the rightmost staircase, the one that was reserved for those of limited means. The offspring of farmers and serfs. The middle stair was for the townsfolk of moderate means, and the leftmost for those who came from families of wealth, or the children of powerful wizards.

She glanced from anxious face to anxious face. She recognized some of them from her infrequent visits to town, but most were unfamiliar. Those who lived on the land only went to town for essentials. It was rare that they gathered with anyone other than close family, and Keeree had no family. She was on her own.

"They're here," a girl with startlingly blue eyes and shimmering white hair pointed to the stage.

A trumpet flared with a fanfare, each note crisp and clear in the morning air, announcing the commencement of the examinations.

Three wizards ascended the platform using the wide stairs to the side, the one reserved for successful challengers. The ones Keeree hoped to use after she was accepted.

First was an elderly gentleman. Bannwor. He was thin, and tall, despite the crook in his back. He wore a robe almost white with stars. So thick were they, that the dark blue was barely visible beneath them. His face was clean shaven, and his eyes deep set. He strolled across the dais and raised his arm. The thrones slowly lowered themselves to the platform. He took the seat to the left and nodded to the next wizard.

The second wizard, Charyl, was short and round, with a close-cropped grey beard and a bald pate. His eyes were too close together, and he wore thick spectacles that kept sliding down his nose. His robe was almost as well adorned with stars as Bannwor's, but the blue still made it look like the sky on a dark summer's night. He sat on the center throne and scanned the crowd. As his gaze landed on Keeree, he smiled and winked, as if he recognized her.

A shiver ran down her spine.

Thankfully, he broke his gaze and nodded to the next wizard.

The final wizard, Issur, the head of the academy, was a woman not much older than her own mother. Her black hair was cut to her shoulders. She wore a headband of gold with a glowing jewel in the center that did little to draw Keeree's gaze away from the deep red of her eyes. When *her* gaze landed on the crowd, she smiled, unlike the other wizards. She floated to the seat on the right and settled in.

Silence fell over the assembled crowd for half a hand of heart-beats before she nodded to a page who ascended the broad stairs and stepped to the front of the platform.

"The annual examination for entry into the Academy of Magic is hereby commenced." He glanced at the three sets of stairs before him, then the assembled crowd. "Please form a single line by the appro-priate stairs when your name is called."

As the page called out names, Keeree fretted. She had made the application as required, conveying her name to the scribe the moon before. He wrote notes in the wizard's tongue on a small piece of parchment, and handed her a copy, but she was at a loss to read it. She had attempted to learn the wizards' script, but her father discouraged it. Said it would only confuse her. She worried that perhaps the scribe had only been placating her. It was hard to believe the academy wanted a farm-girl. Even one with powers. Powers that Keeree had yet to demonstrate.

Her guts churned. For a moment, she imagined rushing from the line and losing herself in the crowd. No one would think it was because she had lost her courage, not until she had already vanished, but, that would do no good. There was always tomorrow, and the others would taunt her no less for running away than for failing. She crossed her fingers. Maybe the scribe had forgotten to pass her name on. Maybe she wouldn't have to face the humiliation. Maybe things would sort themselves out.

"Keeree," the page called.

Her pulse quickened. She was committed. No backing out now. She stepped in line. It was long, and she was close to the last. She fell in behind the girl she'd seen earlier, the one with the white hair and deep-blue eyes. Keeree felt uncomfortable standing behind her. She was obviously from a well-to-do family, with fine garments and well-crafted shoes, even though she was in the line reserved for the less well-off. Keeree's homespun clothes were rough but clean. Her bare feet marked her as someone who lived on the land. She knew what the townsfolk thought of people like her. But the academy would change all that. Everyone there wore the same blue robe, and only the number of white stars varied from student to student.

"Turtle turds," Keeree said. "We're last. The magic will be gone before we get there. How are we supposed to raise fire when the magic's gone?"

The girl shrugged. "It's part of the test."

"Aren't you worried?"

"Not me. I have a show planned for them. I've been practicing."

"I've been practicing, too." Keeree lied. She should have waited another summer. Let her power come fully awake, mastered a few spells, and then applied. She shouldn't be here. Not now.

The girl jutted her chin to the left throne. "Look at him."

Standing before the wizard Bannwor was a boy about their age. He wore a gray robe with gold trim. That attire told the world that his parents were important and influential wizards. Not that it did him any good. He appeared to be struggling.

"He'll get in," the girl said. "He's the son of the head of the academy."

"I don't think so," Keeree said. "He keeps glancing over at Issur. He's terrified. I think he's going to make water right there."

The boy's face scrunched up as if he were about to relieve himself. He squatted a bit to give credence to that image. His face turned red as he stretched a hand out, but there was no fire. Nothing.

"He *is* about to soil himself," the girl said.

"Why is he struggling?" Keeree asked.

"Probably a damp-wick," the girl said.

Even though the name was not aimed at her, Keeree flinched. Damp-wick. Someone for whom even the small magic would not work. They called it that because the person could not even raise fire. It was as if their candle had a damp wick.

"What if that happens to us?" Keeree's guts clenched. If the son of a prominent wizard family was struggling, what made her think she would succeed?

"Won't happen to me. I'm ready. Just yesterday, I called up fire and made the shadows dance for me. Surely that will be enough to impress them."

"I wish I had your confidence." Keeree glanced at the stage. The boy in the gray robe was descending the narrow stairs on the left, head hung in shame, shoulders slumped. He'd failed. How much worse was it going to be for her?

She shifted her weight from one foot to the other as candidate after candidate ascended the stairs to present themselves before the judges. Few were accepted. A young girl had just left the stage in tears when the page called out. "Ersama!"

The girl ascended the stairs and positioned herself before Issur.

Keeree tried to get a look at her, but her back was turned.

A mighty whoosh.

A fiery gryphon appeared in the air above the girl.

"Showoff," the girl in line ahead of Keeree said.

Keeree's mouth had fallen open at the appearance of the gryphon. She slowly closed it and said, "That's pretty impressive." She had never seen anything like it. The gryphon was nearly the size of the girl, the body of a lion formed of brilliant crimson sparks that chased one another around as if alive. Its eagle head peered directly at Issur, beak open soundlessly, sparks shedding from its body to land on the dais around the girl like a waterfall.

"Look." The girl poked Keeree. "Issur is not impressed. The girl is only trying to curry favor with Charyl. He has a gryphon familiar named Theored. It goes everywhere he does. A great hulking thing filled with molten fire. Puts hers to shame. You'll see it some day, if you're lucky enough. Don't let it frighten you. It's mostly harmless."

Issur raised a hand, flicked her fingers at the girl, and the gryphon vanished. She leaned in and spoke quietly to the girl who turned and descended the wide stairs reserved for successful candidates.

The display of power made Keeree's stomach twist even tighter.

"Daraya!" the page called out.

"That's me," the girl said. "Luck to you."

"And you," Keeree replied without thinking.

Daraya ascended the stairs and stopped before Issur.

The woman nodded.

Dancing shadows, Daraya had said. That would be a challenge in the bright sunlight, but it would be something to behold. Keeree held her breath.

Daraya frowned. Something was wrong. There was no fire. No shadows, dancing or otherwise. "I did it yesterday," she protested.

"Did what?" Issur asked. There was compassion in her expression, as if she felt bad for Daraya, and genuinely wished her to succeed. Keeree had not expected that. She thought the woman was a no-nonsense proctor with a heart of stone, yet here she was encouraging the girl.

"I raised fire," Daraya said. "It was brilliant."

Issur's voice was soft and musical. "Relax. Try again."

"It's not working." Daraya bounced up and down, biting her lip. She glanced around as if seeking the source of her troubles, settling down only when Issur reached out.

"Relax." Issur spoke in a quiet tone, as if her words were meant only for Daraya. She rose from her throne and placed a hand on Daraya's shoulder. Her eyes closed, revealing a dark color on her eyelids that almost matched the emerald fire coursing behind her. After a heartbeat, she whispered. "Try again."

Keeree strained to catch her words.

Daraya closed her eyes and furrowed her brow. She appeared just as the boy had, as if she were about to soil herself, then relaxed slightly and opened her eyes.

Keeree thought she saw tears.

"One moment." Issur turned to Charyl, the wizard seated in the center throne, and spoke. Charyl appeared shocked as he rose from his chair. His gait was deliberate, as if he struggled to make his way across the dais. He stopped before Daraya and carefully studied her face. He placed his hand on her head and closed his eyes. After a few moments, he lifted his hand, glanced at Issur, and shook his head.

They exchanged words.

Charyl shook his head, casting a furtive glance at Bannwor who was in the midst of examining his next charge.

Issur turned back to Daraya, gathered the girl in her arms, and leaned close. She whispered something into Daraya's ear that was not meant to be overheard, hugged her almost affectionately, and released her.

Daraya walked toward the narrow stairs, head hung low.

Keeree wanted to rush over and ask what had happened, but Issur had taken her seat and was consulting her scroll.

"Keeree?" she called out.

Keeree took a halting step toward the stairs. She paused, glancing back at her father who stood in the shadows where she'd left him. He nodded and mouthed words she could not make out.

"Keeree?" Issur called and looked around as if searching for her.

"I'm here." Keeree dashed for the stairs. Her foot slipped on the first one. She stumbled and scraped her knee. "Lizard dropping," she muttered, then recalled where she was. "Sorry."

Issur appeared to pay it no notice and patiently waited for Keeree to collect herself and step up for her examination. Issur held her hand out and nodded to her open palm. "Fire," she said.

This was it. The moment that would decide Keeree's future. "Fire," Keeree repeated the request.

She closed her eyes, imagined a candle floating in the air above Issur's hand. It was short, the stub of a well-used candle, not a new one. The wick was bent slightly with a blackened end. It was accustomed to the flame. It would welcome the fire once more.

Fixing the candle image firmly in her mind, Keeree added the visage of a fire burning in a hearth. Logs split into quarters rested on a rough iron grate, flames licking at the bark, brilliant orange tongues wavering in the air to the sound of popping and crackling.

She added the scent of burning pine to her mind's image. Tangy and just a bit sweet. When she had the image firmly in her mind, Keeree reached out an imaginary hand and plucked a flame from her imaginary fire, slowly bringing it in contact with her imaginary candle.

As she did, she felt the tingle rise up through her feet, swirl around her chest, and race from her fingertips. The memory of lighting not only a candle, but a raging inferno, rose up in her mind. The magic she needed was right there. As if it had arisen with the vision.

She held her breath.

Please work.

Her heart beat wildly.

Her insides tightened.

Please work.

The imaginary candle flared to life.

Keeree opened her eyes.

There before her, half a digit above the palm of the wizard, burned a small yellow flame. It sputtered and threw off a thread of smoke that wound its way into the tranquil midday air.

Keeree could barely contain her excitement. "I did it!"

Issur closed her hand, extinguishing the flame, then turned her gaze to Keeree. "Not a bad showing."

Across the dais, Bannwor grunted, as if voicing his disapproval. He'd just dismissed a failed candidate and looked displeased by the whole affair, but Keeree didn't care. She wanted to jump up and down and squeal with glee.

But something was amiss. Issur was peering at Bannwor, who was once again seated in the left-hand throne.

The wizard glanced at Keeree, then at the crowd lingering in the square. He turned his gaze back to Issur and shook his head ever so slightly. What did that mean?

The woman turned to Keeree. "I'm sorry. That was a decent showing, but you don't have the sort of control it takes to be a wizard. When did your power come awake?"

Keeree felt crushed. How could the woman say that? She had raised fire. Didn't that mean she was a wizard? "A moon ago."

"I thought as much," Issur said. "Perhaps, in time, you will grow into it." She turned Keeree toward the narrow stairs. "Next summer. After you've had some time."

"But, I made fire," Keeree protested. "I did magic."

"Everyone does magic," Issur said. "It's like walking. Almost everyone walks, but not everyone is a runner. We're not saying no, just not yet. Keep practicing. You're young. Not everyone acquires power at the same rate."

"But, I did magic," Keeree repeated.

"I know child, but that is not all of it." She cast a brief glance at Bannwor, then back to Keeree. "It's not enough. Not this time."

The hand on Keeree's shoulder was firm as it turned her toward the narrow stairs.

Toward failure.

5

FALLOUT

KEEREE

K eeree stepped carefully down the narrow stairs. The stairs of failure. She watched where she put her feet. The last thing she needed was to trip and further embarrass herself. She'd called fire. Wasn't that the requirement? To demonstrate control of her magic? Why had Issur looked at Bannwor like that? Was it somehow tied up with her father's shaded past? Why had she been rejected when others had not? This was nothing like the academy she'd been told about all her life. Fair and impartial. That was their motto, but not today. Today, they had rejected her when she brought fire.

And what about Daraya? If the girl was telling the truth, she had not only brought forth fire, but had a level of control that Keeree could only aspire to. Surely something was amiss.

She glanced back at Bannwor.

The senior wizard frowned at her when he noticed her glance and turned away.

She caught herself just before tripping and falling headfirst down the stairs.

"She's a damp-wick. What did I tell you?" Socha stood at the bottom of the stairs, blocking her path as if he'd been waiting for her, but she knew better. He'd positioned himself there to taunt and humiliate *everyone*. Not just her.

"Stuff yourself, Socha," Keeree said. "Are you blind?"

"I see just fine."

"Then you saw me raise fire. Or were you too busy playing games with yourself to notice?"

"I saw it." He raised his hand, his fingers spaced apart by half a digit. "It was a tiny little baby flame. So cute. So precious."

"It was fire!"

"So why are you coming down this way? Why not over there?" He jutted his chin at the wide stairs on the opposite side of the platform. The one that led to the academy. To success.

"They said to come back next summer," Keeree muttered. "When my powers have had time to grow."

"And next summer, you'll be walking down these same stairs. And the summer after that, and the summer after that. No matter how many times you try, you're not going to be accepted." Socha looked around as if checking to see who might be listening. "Do you think they'll *ever* let you in?"

She shoved him as she passed.

But he was ready for her. He pulled back just as her shoulder touched his.

She stumbled, snagged her foot, and fell to the ground.

"Learning magic is like learning to walk," Socha taunted her. "It looks like you're still having problems with that."

"I'll get even with you yet," Keeree said, but by the time she got to her feet, Socha was striding away.

"I'll get you," she muttered. Why did she never learn? She should have brushed past him and been on her way instead of making a fool of herself. So now what? Go home?

She searched the thinning crowd for her father, but the shadows where he'd been standing were empty. The square was almost deserted, with only a few families there, celebrating the success of their offspring or commiserating with those who had not been chosen. He'd been there when she took her place in line. He'd been there when she ascended the stairs, but now he was gone. Why hadn't he waited for her? Afraid she would pass and prove him wrong? Or afraid she would fail, and shame him? He'd been a powerful wizard and a star student in his day — until he wasn't. She never learned what he'd done to be stripped of his stars and expelled from the academy. Whenever she asked, he grew angry. Did his actions have something to do with *her* being passed over? Was that what Bannwor had seen? Her father? Had she been rejected because of something he'd done?

There could be no other explanation.

They would have words when she returned home. But that would be late. She didn't want to see his face right now.

She turned the corner intent on finding an inn or cafe to while away the afternoon before heading home, and almost tripped over a sobbing form curled up against the curb.

It was the girl who'd been in line in front of her. The white-haired girl. Daraya.

"Are you all right?" Keeree bent down and put her hand on the girl's back. Her knee landed in the dirt, the same knee she'd scraped on the steps. "Toad droppings."

"What droppings?" Daraya turned her head, her blue eyes filled with tears.

"Toad droppings," Keeree repeated. "I scraped my knee climbing the stairs, and now I bumped it again. What a day this has been."

"You've had a day? I just failed the examination. I was ready. I should have passed. But something happened. I couldn't even raise the smallest tongue of flame." She sniffed back tears. "Nothing. Not a spark. I was going to be accepted. I was meant to be on my way to the academy, celebrating with the other students. What am I to do now?"

"Don't feel bad," Keeree said. "I raised fire, and they still didn't take me. They said I could try again next summer. When my magic has had a chance to grow."

"Mine was *fully* awake. I was calling fire almost without thinking until someone stole my magic." Tears welled up in her eyes.

Keeree had never heard of someone stealing magic before. "Stole it?"

"Yesterday. I was hiding out in — never mind where — I was practicing my spells when a boy found me — from the academy — said he could heal me. I was such a fool to let him try."

"Heal you? What happened? Were you hurt?"

"Nothing happened. Never mind." Daraya pushed Keeree's hand away and stood. She wiped the tears from her eyes and turned to leave.

"They said your name is Daraya. Right? I'm Keeree."

Daraya ignored her, sniffed back a tear, and rushed off.

"Wait," Keeree called after her. Should she follow? She glanced at the road that led home. Let them wait. Daraya was headed in the opposite direction. Stolen magic. Keeree had to know more. How could that happen? Did that mean someone could steal *her* magic? Her curiosity got the better of her. She started out after Daraya, hurrying to catch up, but the girl was moving at a brisk walk, and Keeree's knee hurt. "Wait," she called.

Daraya continued quickly down the road as Keeree limped along behind her.

Before long, the road passed the outskirts of town and headed into the broad fields of hay.

Keeree had almost caught up to the girl when Daraya stopped and turned. "Do you see a path? There was a path here yesterday. I followed it to — to just over that hill there. I think it leads to the academy. Maybe they'll let us in if we prove we can find them on our own."

"Which hill?" Keeree asked. The hayfield was flat for a league and a half. No hill, no path, just greenery wavering in the slight afternoon breeze.

"There was a hill there. I swear it."

"I think you're seeing things," Keeree said. "I'm not familiar with this side of town, but there's no hill and no path."

"It was there yesterday," Daraya said. "The boy who took my magic said it was warded. He said I was on the academy grounds. That I was not supposed to be there. That no one without magic could even find it." Daraya pointed once more to the empty field. "It was right there."

Keeree looked where Daraya pointed. There was no hill, but there was something. The field of dark green hay dotted with lavender clover flowers waved in the breeze, the tips of green dancing in time with one another. The occasional wave raced across the field like ripples on a pond, only the ripples were rushing *against* the gentle breeze.

Keeree closed her eyes, letting the image fade. She counted ten heartbeats, then opened them. For just an instant, she saw a path leading up a hill, and then it was gone, replaced by the field of waving hay.

"There." Keeree pointed. "Close your eyes. Forget what they see, then open them."

Keeree watched the girl close her eyes. Daraya was not much older than she was, and only a digit or two taller. She was pale but tried to hide it with a hint of color on her eyelids and lips, something Keeree had never had the courage to try. Her long white hair had been twisted into a bundle and held in place with some sort of pins or clips that were not readily apparent. Still, something about the way the girl stood was a bit off. She hunched over just a touch, shoulders forward, as if she were accustomed to bearing a heavy load.

The girl's eyes opened, and she squinted at the field.

For a moment Keeree thought Daraya had seen what she herself had, but Daraya shook her head, her face falling into a scowl. "It's not there."

"It is," Keeree explained. "You just can't see it."

"Why not? I saw it yesterday. A path led over the hill, and there was a canyon and a..." she paused as if in thought, then continued. "It couldn't have moved since yesterday."

"Come on. Let's see what's really there. The path is only a little way from here." Keeree reached out to take Daraya's arm, but the girl shook her hand off.

"I'm not a lackwit," she said. "And I'm not a damp-wick."

"No one said you were."

"You thought it."

"I did not. Now come on." Keeree didn't wait for a response. She turned and headed off down the road until she came to where she'd seen the path. She closed her eyes once more, waited for the image to fade, then opened them. The path was just off to her right, behind a raspberry bush. "Here. This is where the path starts." Keeree stepped off the road and across the shallow ditch. When her foot came down, she felt not the hay her eyes told her was under her foot, but dirt.

She glanced down.

She saw her foot engulfed in hay. "The illusion is still there. But I can feel the path." Keeree held out her hand. "Come."

Daraya took a step toward Keeree and stopped.

"Feel the dirt?" Keeree looked down at Daraya's feet. "Maybe if you took off your shoes?"

"My shoes? You want me to walk in a field without shoes?"

"I do it all the time."

"Why ever would you do that? Aren't you afraid of stepping in something?"

"What's there to step in?" Keeree asked.

"Cow droppings?"

"Keep your eye out for them and you'll have no trouble."

"Where are your shoes, anyway?" Daraya asked. "Why aren't you wearing them?"

"I don't own any." Keeree concentrated on the path. One way or another, she was going to reach the academy.

6

TAMPERING
PHYR

Phyr was glad he wasn't the last student to face examination. If he had been, his mother surely would have rushed over to console him. That was the last thing he needed. He just wanted to be left alone, at least until he got over the idea that he was a damp-wick, unable to wield even the small magic, unable to light a fire or call up light in the dark of night when he needed to make water. These things would be beyond him. No one would ever choose him as a mate. No one would ever hire him. He was useless. He would raise no fire, much less perform the more complicated spells, the ones that truly mattered. He would have to accept that these would never be his. He would never raise a castle with his words alone, heal even the least infirm, or even find his way outside of his hometown without a guide. What sort of life was that?

He turned the corner to see a small crowd of students in their dark blue robes with a smattering of white stars on them. They were milling about outside of a public house, laughing and slapping one another on the back. One lad wore the dark blue of a student with no stars on it. A successful candidate. Just what Phyr had expected to be this afternoon.

If things had gone differently.

He turned and headed off down a side street, taking the long way home instead of the more direct route. The sounds of laughter faded into the distance. He'd never been down this particular street before. It was lined with craft shops. A chandlery, a cooperage, a winery, even a smithy, all closed, no doubt for the examination. Everyone wanted to get a look at the next batch of up-and-coming wizards. Everyone but him.

A sign announced an eatery.

He wasn't all that hungry, but the image of a magpie picking at what could only have been a magical talisman intrigued him. Beside the sign hung a pair of oil lanterns that could be lowered by means of a thin rope. A sure sign that the owner was a damp-wick and could neither light nor replenish the lanterns with magic. How odd. He'd thought damp-wicks were relegated to the most menial of jobs.

Perhaps he'd been wrong.

What better place to escape the wizarding world than an inn owned by a damp-wick? He needed to think before facing anyone he knew. Let his parents return home before he did. Maybe they would be so caught up in their own lives when he finally returned that they wouldn't notice his arrival. Their pity was something he didn't want.

He took a seat inside with his back to the window. The place was long and narrow with tables for four crammed against the wall. A few patrons sat at each table, enjoying the fare. The aroma of roasting pork came from the kitchen and set his stomach growling even though he wasn't truly hungry. He took in the dining room. Faded tapestries covered the walls depicting various magical acts. Between the tapestries hung an intricate carving of a snake encircling a globe. It was devouring its own tail. Beneath the image were inscribed the words 'The worldwyrm devours itself.' How strange. He would have thought that an establishment run by mundanes would avoid wizardry art.

A young girl appeared from the kitchen. Her white apron was lightly stained. "I'm Cheshi." She scooped a candle from the table before him, reached into her apron, and withdrew a fire-stick. She lit the candle with it and quickly shoved it back into the pocket from which it had emerged. He'd seen a device like that. The small silver tube created fire from physical effects Phyr barely understood. They were popular among those with little or no magic.

"Something to eat?" she asked. "Or are you drinking?"

"Just a bite," Phyr said. Despite his stomach rumbling, he wasn't truly hungry. He couldn't believe he'd ever be hungry again. Food held little attraction for him.

"I'm Cheshi," the girl repeated.

"Sorry. I'm Phyr," he muttered. "What've you got? I'm not that hungry."

"We have honey buns, sweet meat pies, and watered ale. Unless you're a student, then only water. We don't need any besotted wizards running loose in here."

"Do I look like a student?" Phyr grumbled. His gray robe marked him as the son of a wizard, and the lack of dark blue told everyone that he had not been accepted to the academy. Not yet. Not ever.

"I have to ask." Cheshi shrugged.

"I'll have the honey buns and dark tea," Phyr said. "No ale for me, watered or otherwise."

"Just the buns? We have roast fowl and boar. They're nearly done." She looked around. "Almost time for the midday rush. I may not have time to check in on you later. Best order now if you think you might be getting hungry."

"I'm fine. Thank you." He was in no mood for conversation.

Cheshi pulled out a chair and plopped herself into it. She was a few summers older than Phyr, with straw-colored hair cropped just below her ears. She would have been pretty save for the mark on her cheek that looked as if someone had poured red wine across her face leaving a stain behind that had soaked into her flesh. It was just the sort of thing a wizard could have fixed in his second or third summer at the academy. He wondered why she had never had it removed.

"You're sad. I can tell." Her smile made him forget the stain on her cheek.

Phyr looked the girl in the eye. Really looked, then flushed. Would she think he was looking at her birthmark?

"I'm a good listener." She seemed unflustered by his stare.

He didn't want pity, but he wanted someone to know that he had been treated unfairly.

"I was so confident, so sure of myself. I practiced. Daily. For a moon. My mother blocked my magic, and I was still able to raise fire. But today — when it counted the most — nothing. I'm a failure."

She looked him over as if studying him. "You don't look like a failure."

"I am. Both of my parents were distinguished students at the academy. My mother is the *head* of the academy. I was supposed to join them today, but instead, I'm here."

She reached out and patted his hand. "*Here* isn't so bad."

"You don't understand."

"No?" She touched her cheek, her fingers caressing the red stain. "I know a few things about failed magic."

"I'm sorry. That was thoughtless of me."

"I'm not offended. Being a damp-wick isn't all that bad. I do all right for myself." She stood and pushed back the chair. "I'll be right back with your order."

He watched for her to return, but she did not. Instead, another girl, looking much like Cheshi but a bit older, delivered a platter with the buns on it and a glass of tea with a small sweet-meat pie.

"Where's Cheshi?" Phyr asked.

"She's back in the kitchen. She only helps out front when I need a break." The girl nudged Phyr. "And I certainly needed a break just then. Would have spoiled your meal if I'd have had to wait any longer." She nodded at the plate. "Looks like someone's taken a shine to you."

He let his gaze wander over the plate. It was overloaded with food he hadn't ordered and was quite sure he could not eat. He blushed and reached for his purse. He would pay for it all. He didn't need any pity, not from a stranger, not from his parents, not from anyone.

The girl held up her hand. "It's on the house. A special treat for someone who needs cheering up."

"I don't need charity," Phyr said.

"It's not charity. It's a gift. From my sister."

"And where is your sister?"

"She's in the kitchen. Didn't you hear what I told you? She was just covering for me while I made my morning ritual."

"Will you at least send her my thanks?"

"That I will. And who shall I say is sending those thanks?"

"Phyr."

"Nice to meet you, Phyr. I'm Omosa." She smiled and turned to address a small group of patrons who had just arrived. After seating the new group, she turned back to Phyr and winked. "Enjoy your meal."

"That I will." He shook his head. Why were Cheshi and Omosa being so kind to him? Was it because he had just failed and they were both damp-wicks? Was there a hidden fraternity among those for whom magic was inaccessible? Was that why she'd added a sweet-meat pie and the other goodies to his order? Was he a part of that fraternity now?

He'd thought he wasn't hungry, but now that the plate sat before him, the aroma set his stomach growling. He lifted the golden-brown pie to his lips and took a small bite. Sweet. Raisins. Vegetables. Onion. And meat. Beef, or was that hart? He wasn't sure, but it wasn't pork, and it wasn't fowl. The gravy was thick and rich, with just a bit of bite. Black pepper. Who used black pepper for day-to-day cooking?

He let his thoughts roll over one another while he ate, trying to focus on the flavor and not his troubles. Soon enough, his plate was empty, and so was his cup. He glanced around the dining room to see that he was the only one seated at a table all alone. There were no empty tables, despite a line forming outside.

His face went red.

Here he was taking up a valuable table and eating food he hadn't paid for. What sort of heel was he? He stacked the utensils on the empty plate and shoved his chair back. He was tempted to try to see Cheshi and offer his thanks in person, but the place was busy and he felt certain he would only get in the way. Instead, he reached into his purse, pulled out a pair of silvers, and dropped them onto the plate.

They rang out clear and attracted the attention of Omosa.

He nodded to her on his way out, mouthing the words 'thank you' as he pushed through the crowd and out onto the street.

It looked like the day wasn't turning out all that bad after all.

He occupied himself on the walk home by trying to come up with a way to accidentally bump into Cheshi. He had concocted several possible scenarios by the time he reached his house.

The "demesne," as his father called their house, was large—too large for its place on the street. The curb side of the building rose two stories from the sidewalk, with windows on the top floor and a balcony that stretched around the sides. A short walkway led to a large double door that had been painted red and trimmed with brass. The fittings were meticulously polished by Phyr's hand once a moon to teach him the value of hard work, or so he was repeatedly told. But this was not the entrance family used. Only guests were received at this door. The family preferred a discrete side entrance that opened onto the kitchen. Phyr made his way to that door and quietly opened it. Perhaps he could sneak into his room without being noticed. It would be some time before his mother came to check on him, and when she did, he could pretend to be asleep.

He slipped into the kitchen, softly closing the door behind him. His parents were in the formal reception room, their voices clear.

"What happened out there?" Teil was asking.

"I did what you asked. I failed her," Issur said. "Despite her control of magic."

"Did you feel the power she carries?" Teil asked. "I certainly did. It made me so angry. I could kill Garyll. What is he thinking, raising a daughter like that? He just wants to spite us."

Phyr cupped his ear to better hear what they were talking about.

"And Phyr?" Teil demanded. "What happened there? Bannwor examined him. Why did he fail? He was ready. You said so yourself."

"I asked Bannwor not to pass him," Issur said. "He can raise fire, but he's not ready. The other candidates are much more adept. He needs another summer. Let him mature a bit. The academy is no place for my little boy."

Phyr's face went hot. *Asked Bannwor to fail him?* How could she do such a thing? So the examination had been rigged. The examinations were supposed to be the great equalizer. They were supposed to be blind to a candidate's circumstances. How then was it that he'd been singled out for failure regardless of his performance?

"I disagree," Teil said. "He's more mature than you believe him to be. He'll be crushed by this. He'll be home soon, and he's going to need us."

"What do we tell him?" Issur asked.

"Nothing. He mustn't know you subverted the examination. It would kill him."

"I don't like lying to our son," Issur said.

Phyr heard his mother's robes rustle. She was getting up to make a cup of tea, no doubt. Her voice was drawing close. In a heartbeat, she would know he was home.

He stepped back onto the sidewalk and quietly closed the door before his mother could see him.

She had told him that she would never lie to him.

That she would always be truthful.

But she wasn't. She'd lied. About the most important thing in his life.

7

BRAMBLES

KEEREE

*K*eeree let her feet guide her as she made her way over the unseen hill. The path was still not visible, not to her eyes. But, to her feet it was as real as real could get. Each step was met with the scratching of rough dirt and loose stones on her toughened bare soles. If she strayed from the path, she felt the dampness of the dew on the hay.

"How do you know where to step?" Daraya asked.

Keeree lifted a foot and wriggled her toes. "I can feel it. And if I concentrate, I can see it."

"I still don't see a thing." Daraya was puffing to keep up as the ground rose to crest the still-invisible hill.

"As long as we can feel our way, we can find the place," Keeree said. "Tell me about the boy who stole your magic. What exactly did he do?"

"He tricked me. He said he was going to heal me. He healed me all right, but then he did something else. I felt a wrenching in my chest, and I saw stars. I must have passed out. When I woke, he was gone. I thought at first he was just trying to distract me while he ran away. I didn't feel anything strange until I tried to access my magic during the examination. When I tried to raise fire — that's when I felt it.

There's a pressure in my chest, as if someone put a band around it and drew it tight. When I try to use magic, it becomes hard to breathe. I see stars before my eyes, just like I'm on the verge of passing out. I feel it even more now than earlier. Do you think that's because we're getting closer to the nexus?"

"What's a nexus?" Keeree knew so little of magic. Her parents had steadfastly forbidden her to learn anything despite their having been promising students in their day. They could not use magic themselves. Not any longer. Not a lick. They lit fire with a match. They found their way around by landmarks, but usually, they never left the farm. When they did, it was only for brief visits to town. It was as if they thought that the town would contaminate them. Keeree would have been fine with their occasional visits, but their aversion to the town extended to her as well. She had been schooled at home rather than attending one of the small one-room schools on the edge of town. Her mother had taught her numbers and cyphers and all manner of craft, but of magic? Not a word.

"I don't know what a nexus is," Daraya was saying. "The boy told me this place was a nexus, and I was lucky to have met him there. Lucky for him as it turns out, not for me."

"You never did say what he healed you from," Keeree said.

"No. I never did."

Keeree stopped and turned back to confront Daraya. The hint of color she wore on her eyes had faded and run leaving a faint blue line down one cheek.

"If we're going to be friends," Keeree said, "we should share things."

"Who said we were going to be friends?"

"I did. I decided. When I saw you crying."

"I wasn't crying."

"When I first saw you *crying*," Keeree said. "I told myself we were going to be friends. You looked like you needed one and I was the only one around. So, we're going to be friends — and friends share things — like why you needed healing — unless you'd rather not be my friend — then I'll just head back to town and leave you to find your way on your own."

"I don't need friends," Daraya said.

"Suit yourself." Keeree pushed past the girl and headed back down the invisible path. She cursed herself for getting drawn into someone else's problems. She should have left well enough alone. Why had she even bothered to try to make friends? Just because they both failed the examination didn't mean anything. Besides *that*, what did they have in common? Nothing. Daraya was from a merchant family in town by the looks of her, and Keeree had the stink of farm clinging to her. Was that why the girl didn't want to be her friend?

Keeree had only gone a few strides when she heard sobbing behind her.

She turned just in time to see Daraya sink to her knees and lower her head into her hands.

"I thought you didn't need any friends," Keeree called back.

"I don't, but I don't have anywhere to go."

"What do you mean, you don't have anywhere to go? Where do you live?"

"I ran away." The girl's voice was muffled by her hands.

"Why?"

Daraya turned her face to Keeree. Her eyes were red and puffy. "My father beat me for using magic. That's why I ran away. That's why I needed healing. He took a switch. He beat me until my back ran with blood. He said if I ever used magic again, he'd kill me. I was going to be selected and go live at the academy, but now I'm not. And I can't go home. And my aunt, Rodaso, she died. I can't go live with her. My father knows I entered the examination. He knows I want to be a wizard. He won't let me come back. And even if he did, how could I? You didn't see my back. You didn't see what he did to me."

Keeree felt shocked. Her own father was strict, and he'd occasionally taken a switch to her, but it was never enough to draw blood, and usually only a swat or two to get her attention when she'd done something supremely foolish. She couldn't even imagine anyone getting angry enough to draw blood from their own child. What could she say? What *did* one say to someone who suffered so?

"I — I'm sorry," Keeree said. "Sorry that happened to you."

Tears rolled down Daraya's face. She swallowed. "What am I going to do?"

Keeree rushed to the girl, dropped to her knees, and put her arm around her.

Daraya clung to her.

Keeree's words caught in her throat. "He won't hurt you again."

"He'll kill me."

"I won't let him."

"How are you going to stop him?"

"I have magic," Keeree said.

Daraya turned to face Keeree. "Then why weren't you selected?"

"I don't know. I raised fire. Just like everyone else did who got accepted. The woman who tested me, Issur. She glanced over at the tall one, Bannwor. He shook his head when he saw me. Then she told me I wasn't accepted. Said to come back in a summer when my magic had a chance to grow. I've heard of people being accepted who could barely raise fire, so that wasn't it."

"So, we're both wash outs." Daraya wiped the tears from her cheek.

"We're going to be friends then?"

"Does that mean you'll help me?" Daraya asked. "Maybe we can bring our complaint before the academy. They're sure to accept us when they find out we were both cheated."

"You seem pretty confident."

"Help me find the boy and get my magic back, and I'll help you get accepted. The boy said my presence triggered some sort of spell. That he felt it and came to investigate. I'm sure it will happen again. And with the two of us — well, he can't fight us both off."

"So you don't want to be friends, but you *do* want me to fight for you?" Keeree asked. "I've never seen anyone who needs a friend as much as you do. Someday you'll see that."

"But today is not that day," Daraya said. "Come on. It's ahead. Not much farther."

"What's ahead?" Keeree asked.

"The entrance to the academy. It's built on a floating island in the middle of the biggest canyon I've ever seen."

"Wait." Keeree grabbed Daraya's arm. There was something ahead, just out of the corner of her eye. It looked like brambles, thick vines with thorns on them that wove an impenetrable wall across their path. If she blinked quickly, she could see the afterimage of it.

Daraya shook off Keeree's hand and took a step along the unseen way.

She stopped short, as if something impeded her.

"What now?" Keeree asked.

"I think I did something foolish." Daraya turned to Keeree. Her face and hands were covered with tiny red dots that had just started to run with blood.

A bead of blood rolled across her eye.

She collapsed.

"Daraya!" Keeree knelt down beside her. It was as if Daraya were dead. Her arms were limp, and her eyes blank.

Keeree placed her hand beneath Daraya's nose.

She was breathing.

She was alive then.

She gently closed Daraya's eyes and draped the girl's arm around her shoulder. She stood and tried to drag Daraya with her, but the girl was too heavy.

"Moose droppings," Keeree spat. "What now?"

Tiny trickles of blood ran down the girl's face and hands. She was breathing deeply. What was Keeree to do? Leave the girl behind and fetch help? Was Daraya going to live long enough for help to arrive? But Keeree wasn't doing any good by being here. There was only one thing *to* do.

Go get help.

"Stay right here. I'll go get a healer or a wizard." Keeree rushed off down the path that was strangely no longer invisible to her eyes.

8

CRY FOR HELP

PHYR

*P*hyr raced down the back streets with little thought to where he was headed. All he knew was that he had to get away from home. How could his own parents lie to him like that? He was ready to begin his studies at the academy. He knew he was. Why did his mother think he wasn't? Was it because she'd seen how he touched the wild magic? And why had he not been able to raise fire at the examination? Had Bannwor done something to him? His parents had never been like that before. All he could think of was getting away from them.

Soon Phyr found himself back in the cafe where he'd met the girl with the wine-stained face. He secretly hoped she would be out front again but was only mildly disappointed when he took a seat and the older sister appeared.

"Back so soon? I know my sister's cooking is some of the tastiest there is, but you can't be hungry already." She favored him with a shy smile. "Or is there something else you hanker for?"

"I just needed a bit of fresh air," Phyr lied.

She looked around the emptying cafe. "Crowd's thinning. No need to rush off. I'll bring you a watered ale. Least I can do, seeing as how generous you were earlier."

"Thank you." Phyr *was* feeling a bit thirsty, and this was as good a place to sort out his thoughts as any. He had no idea what he was going to do next. He felt tempted to find a place to stay for the night just to let his parents know he was unhappy with them, but where would he go?

They would worry. They had no idea he knew what they'd done. No. He had to go home. Tell them what he'd overheard. Demand answers. That was it. He would demand an explanation. Wasn't he owed that much?

The watered ale arrived. Phyr drank deeply. He felt better now that he'd made up his mind. He would confront his parents. They wouldn't lie to his face.

He downed the last of his ale, thumped the mug on the table and pushed his chair back.

He felt ready.

He reached into his purse and drew out a single silver.

If he was going to continue eating here, he would have to be a bit more reasonable with his coin, but the girl and her sister had treated him well, and he found them both somewhat alluring, despite the seeming roughness of the older sister. He decided he'd be back, if only to see how the sisters were getting on.

As he turned to leave, Phyr ran headlong into a young woman dressed in well-worn homespun clothes. He tried to pull up short so he wouldn't knock her down, but instead he crashed into her and tumbled to the ground himself.

He brushed his robe off and stood, hoping the redness of his face wasn't obvious. He'd seen the girl before. At the examination. He'd heard whispers that she was the daughter of a disgraced wizard, one that his parents held up as a bad example. Why was she approaching him? She seemed upset about something. And she was out of breath.

She grabbed him by the arms and looked him straight in the eye. "Please. You must help me." Her words came out between gasps. "She's been enchanted. She's just lying there. She's dying. Please, help me." The girl didn't wait for an answer. She yanked on Phyr's arm. "Come on. She needs your help."

Phyr shook off her hand and studied her. The top of her head came up to his shoulder. She had short brown hair cut to just below her ears with a wave that said it would have been a mass of curls if permitted to grow much longer. She had a smudge of dirt on her face, and panic in her eyes.

"Who needs help?"

"Daraya. You're the son of a great wizard, aren't you? I saw you at the examination. You must know how to help. Daraya touched the wards. She's been enchanted. She's bleeding. I can't wake her up. You have to help. She's in the field. Back that way." She jutted her chin toward the road that led out of town. "Come on. She's dying."

"You don't expect me to just run off with you, do you?"

"You know about magic. Your family are wizards. Wizards help," the girl said. "Come on."

She reached for his hand, but he pulled it back.

"I'm not going anywhere until you tell me what happened. For all I know, this is a trick, or a game someone's playing on me, trying to make a fool of me. As if I wasn't already enough of a fool." He peered more closely at her. "Who sent you?"

"No one sent me. I found her crying, and she wanted me to take her to the academy. She couldn't see the path, but I could, and she ran into the wards, and she's bleeding, and now she's enchanted, or dying. I don't know which, but I can't wake her. I'm sure it's some sort of spell so she needs a wizard, and you're the first wizard I came across. You have to help." The girl balled her hands into fists and pressed them against her head. Her eyes misted over. "Please. She's dying."

Phyr watched as a single tear slid from one eye and etched a dark valley in the dirt on her face. Something about her was unusual. He'd felt it when she touched him. There was magic surrounding her. Strange and wild magic. The sort he had touched. The kind he kept hidden.

"What are you staring at?" she demanded. "Are you going to help her or not?"

"I'm sorry. You..." Phyr was about to tell her what he'd seen, but he stopped short. He'd never seen anything like it. If he told her, she'd want to know what it was, and he wasn't sure he could explain it.

The girl's face shifted from sorrow to anger. "I what?"

Phyr shook off her concern. "Who are you, anyway?"

"I'm Keeree. But that's not important. Daraya needs your help."

Keeree. He'd heard her name before. It was a name his parents had spoken when they thought he wasn't in the room. A name associated with a crime against the wizarding community. An ongoing crime. He tried to recall what they'd said about her, but it wouldn't come.

"Did you hear me?" Keeree interrupted.

"You need help," Phyr said.

"Not me. Daraya."

"Right. Daraya. Where did you say she was?"

"In the field. Outside of town."

"Can you show me?" Phyr asked.

"I'll take you." Keeree grabbed his hand.

He tried to pull away, but she was strong.

She gripped him firmly as she dragged him out the door and down the street.

"It's not far to the hidden path," Keeree was saying. "Just over there."

"I don't see anything." If the path was hidden, how would she find it? And how was a path hidden? He had imagined a wall, or a hedge, with a secret door, but they were trotting along an open road flanked by fields of hay. There were no woods, hedges, or walls for as far as he could see.

She pulled him up short. "Here. If you close your eyes and let the image you see fade, when you open them, you can see the truth. For just a heartbeat. The path. It's here. Keeree tugged on his hand, dragging him off the road behind her.

"Take off your shoes," she said. "You'll feel it."

Phyr had put up with her insanity for this long. Taking off his shoes and subjecting his tender feet to the ravages of an open field was too much to ask. "I'm not taking off my shoes."

"Then close your eyes." Keeree reached up and covered his eyes. When she took her hand away, for the briefest of moments, he saw it. A path worn into the hay by traffic, whether man or beast, he wasn't certain, but it was there. And then it wasn't.

"I saw it," Phyr said.

"I told you." She tugged at his hand. "Come on. Just ahead."

Phyr let Keeree drag him along the path and up a slight hill. At the crest of the hill, lay the girl Keeree had been talking about. Phyr glanced down at her. She was dressed more in line with the rest of the town folk than those who worked the land. For some reason, he expected her to be dressed much as Keeree was.

"Tell me again what happened?" Phyr knelt beside the girl in the hay. But as he did, a wave of nausea washed over him. He struggled to keep his balance.

His guts twisted inside.

He was awash in magic.

It felt as if the well from his imagination had overflowed and was washing him away in a river of silver.

He reached out a hand to steady himself.

He felt a prick.

He pulled his hand back.

A tiny drop of blood appeared on his palm.

He looked up at Keeree.

Her face was distorted, as if he were seeing her through a fog.

"Frog poop. Not you too," she said. But her words were muffled.

Her face faded and then everything went black.

9

DISTANCE

KEEREE

"Wake up!" Keeree shouted, but Daraya and Phyr lay unmoving. The rippling waves of hay surrounded them, wavering under the gentle hand of the afternoon breeze that carried the slight scent of clover with the sweet tint of kine droppings. Overhead, a raven called to its flock, its shrill cry echoing off the distant hills.

"They're not dead," Keeree screamed at it. At least she hoped they weren't.

She glanced back at the two still forms. As she did, her vision wavered. She'd been here before, not just this morning, but summers past. Memories flooded into her mind. Three young people. One young man, two young women. They'd stood on a hill much like this, frightened, expectant. In her mind's eye, another triad approached, their faces were cloaked in darkness, but she knew they were not friends.

The visions strengthened. The sky darkened. Thunder rolled off distant hills. As the sun vanished, a fiery gryphon materialized high overhead. It folded its wings and plummeted toward her. Beak wide, it screeched out its anger. Claws the size of Keeree's forearm tore at the protective shield she held. Was it she who held the shield? The memory seemed as if it were hers, but she had never done such a thing.

As the gryphon struck, she felt the impact. The shield might have staved off the worst of the attack, but she knew it couldn't hold out much longer. "Hold on, I will need all your power for this." The memory of uttering those words seemed both strange and familiar. It was not her speaking, but the young woman in her vision.

At her words, brilliant flashes of light shot from her companions. Not only those in her vision, but from the two asleep on the hay. The light intertwined to strengthen the protective shield. Power coursed through them all as her defenses strengthened.

With the next strike, the gryphon exploded in a shower of sparks. The protective shield vanished along with it.

The world wavered, and Keeree's vision faded. Once more she was sitting on the hay beside two still forms. What had she just witnessed? Where had those memories come from? They were not hers, but she felt as if she had actually been there. The spells that she used in the vision remained with her, as did the sense of power. Was that what it was like to wield the wild magic?

She knelt beside Daraya. "You're not dead, are you?" She stretched out her hand toward the invisible barrier that Daraya and Phyr had both run afoul of. As her hand neared it, she sensed the sharp thorns, as if a bramble had grown across the path.

She blinked rapidly.

There.

The thick ropy vines intertwined with one another until they formed an impenetrable wall filled with needle-sharp thorns. Each tiny sword dripped with venom.

How was it she could perceive this while the others had not? Daraya said she possessed magic, powerful magic, if she was to be believed. The boy, Phyr, came from a long line of wizards. How was it that neither of them could see what she, the daughter of a disgraced and powerless failure, could?

Keeree drew her hand back from the bramble. It faded from view.

Hand out.

Brambles.

Hand in.

Clear sunny afternoon, breeze wafting across an empty field.

Hand out.

Brambles. Sharp thorns dripping poison.

Hand in.

Clear afternoon meadow.

She was getting nowhere.

Keeree touched a thorn. Not on the point, but gently stroking the side of the wood-like bristle. The rough bark of it scratched at the flesh of her fingertip. It was real. No doubt about that.

She let her finger slide to the tip of one spine, carefully collecting the droplet of poison. At least she thought it was poison. What else would have paralyzed her friends?

She brought her finger close to her face. The substance was clear, almost. Deep within the droplet, a bright ochre fleck swam like a tiny fish in an even tinier pond.

She sniffed the liquid. Bitter. Rancid.

For a moment, she imagined what it would taste like, but stopped herself, hand halfway to her mouth. Best not. No telling what it would do to her if she ate it. For a moment, she imagined what it would be like if her tongue were paralyzed. She shuddered. Best not to find out.

Her fingers tingled as if she'd slept wrong on her arm.

Then they went numb.

She wiped her hand on her pants.

Her leg went numb.

She toppled over.

"Rat snot." She massaged her leg. Was the poison that strong?

She rolled onto her side. The side that wasn't paralyzed.

What a fool.

Her father had often told her that silent contemplation solved more problems than ill-considered words and actions. That her words and actions had consequences that she would one day come to regret.

She'd paid him little heed.

Of course, her words had consequences, as did her actions.

She glanced down at her leg.

"Ill-considered," she muttered.

Perhaps she *had* been a bit hasty.

She sat down and tried to collect her thoughts.

"I could sure use some help," she called out to no one in particular.

The world around her wavered as if seen through the heat rising from a freshly plowed field. She was becoming familiar with the visions. Had she summoned this one with her words?

When the shimmering settled, an image appeared before her. It was as if she were seeing a dream play itself out while she was awake. In the dream, she saw a young woman not much older than she was now. The woman was slight and mousey, bent over a book filled with the wizards' script. She ran a hand along the script and it shimmered, changing to the cypher language Keeree's own mother had taught her.

Keeree peered at the cyphers. The words they formed were strange, yet somehow familiar. She read them over and over again, committing them to memory. She was not sure why, but it just felt right. As if she would need them.

The vision faded to be replaced by a trio of young wizards. Two young men and a young woman. The woman reminded Keeree of Issur. She had the same black hair and striking features, yet it was one of the men whose eyes glowed red, not hers. Why was she seeing this? Why now?

The trio approached her along the path. The young man wielded a sword that glowed with an internal fire as if it had just been pulled from a forge. Foe Hammer. That was the sword's name. How could she even know that?

A chill ran up her spine. What was she witnessing? Keeree's mother had told her the magic would soon awaken in her, but it wasn't the magic that had awakened. It was the visions. Just like this one. Visions of strangers doing strange things. Things that filled her with a sense of foreboding.

A scream split the air as the young man wielded the sword.

She felt a hand slip into hers, then another. A voice spoke in her ear. "Ave praepotentem heroes," it said.

Was that the spell she needed? She struggled to see who had spoken, but as if to thwart her efforts, the vision faded. She was alone in the field with her two friends once more.

She crawled over to Phyr and Daraya. She took Daraya's hand and placed it in Phyr's. Then she took Daraya's free hand in one of hers and struggled to place her paralyzed hand in Phyr's.

"*Ave praepotentem heroes.*" This time the words came to her in her father's voice. Strange. She had never heard him utter a single word in the wizards' tongue. She felt certain the words were in the wizards' tongue, and they held power.

"*Ave praepotentem heroes.*" She let each syllable roll off her tongue as if savoring a strange new flavor.

Even before she finished uttering those strange words, she felt it. It was as if she were sitting above a blast from a blacksmith's forge. The air shimmered, growing hotter and hotter by the moment.

She broke out in a sweat, drenching her clothes in half a heartbeat.

And then the earth shook.

The fields around her rippled as if a great stone had been thrown into a pond, and she and her friends were that stone. Ripples rose to half a man-height, rushing away from her with the speed of a hart fleeing a wolf.

The noise of it was deafening.

When the rumbling stopped.

Keeree sat there stunned.

She let go of the hands she was holding, wondering if they had felt it too.

A high-pitched ringing filled her ears, making it hard to hear.

Daraya sat up, her eyes wide. "What happened?"

Daraya's words came to Keeree's ears as if from far away.

Keeree shook her head to clear it.

She glanced over at Phyr. His eyes fluttered beneath closed lids, then sprang open. He levered himself into a sitting position and turned a fierce gaze on her. "Just what did you do to me?" he demanded.

10

DISTURBANCE

ISSUR

*I*ssur paced the kitchen. It was late afternoon, and Phyr still had not returned from the examination. He'd been disappointed. She saw that. Surely he would have come straight home to the comfort of his family, but he hadn't. Usually, she knew where he was. She always felt his presence, but not now. He'd vanished, and try as she might, she could not discern where he was.

"Where's Phyr?" Issur turned to her husband Teil. Her heart pounded in her chest like a prisoner trying to escape its cell.

"He's probably still in town with friends," Teil said. "He'll need a bit of time to adjust after that fiasco this afternoon."

"No, not where is he located. Where is his essence? I've always had a connection to him. Ever since he quickened inside me." Issur let a hand drop to her belly. "Always. I've always felt him. Knew his heart was beating. Knew he was breathing. Knew he was all right, or that he was hurt, or lonely, or sad. It's always been there and now it's gone."

Teil stood and set down the tome he'd been studying. He towered over her, his slightly graying and neatly trimmed beard tickled her forehead as he took her in his arms.

His strong arms usually gave her a sense of protection and comfort.

Not this time.

Issur used her magic to seek out her son. "Something's wrong. I know it."

She always kept the slightest spell of protection about Phyr. But that spell had dissipated.

"I felt a ripple. A twist in my magic, then Phyr was gone." Issur said. "Something's happened to him."

"Do you think it's related to what transpired this afternoon?"

"I doubt it. If it were, I would have sensed it earlier."

Teil's eyes bored into her. "There's something you're not telling me."

Issur drew a breath. She'd done something unforgivable. She'd done it with the best of intentions, but Teil wouldn't see it that way. How much to reveal? He would get the truth out of her. Best to give him something to chew on. It might keep him from digging deeper. "I felt Phyr draw power from the earth beneath his feet when I dampened his magic," she said.

"What?" Teil gasped. "When did this happen? Why didn't you mention it to me?"

"It was late last night. I wasn't certain what I'd witnessed. I didn't want to believe it, so I guess I just put it out of my mind."

She glanced over at him for any indication to what he was thinking. He stood there, still. His unadorned black robes falling straight to the floor, not a wrinkle on them. His neatly trimmed beard framed a small mouth, lips pressed tightly together. His eyes were cold and hard as granite.

Teil guided her to the table. He pulled out a chair and gently ushered her into it. He stepped to the stove and twitched a finger. The fire beneath the kettle sprang to life.

He reached for a tin of bitterleaf, filled a pair of silver tea infusers, and set them beside a pair of mugs. He reached for a jar of honey and gently pried the top from it, plunging the dipper into the honey and letting the amber fluid flow into each cup. He poured boiling water on top of the honey and dipped an infuser into it, gently stirring it to release the flavor. All this he did without uttering a word. The only sounds were the crackling of fire.

Issur prepared herself. When Teil got like this, it was never good. He was holding himself under tight control to keep from saying or doing anything he'd regret. She'd seen him do this on a few occasions, and when he did finally speak, it had been ugly. His words had been cutting and indisputably accusing.

She swallowed.

"Are you telling me our son is a focus?" When he finally spoke, his words were soft, quiet, and enunciated to perfection. There could be no mistaking what he asked.

Tears filled her eyes, and her throat grew tight.

Teil slid the mug of tea toward her.

She took a sip, letting it warm and open her constricted throat.

Teil reached out and gently touched her chin, raising her face. "Issur?"

"I was preparing him for the examination. We were practicing lighting the candle. He was doing fine. Just as you'd expect. I trickled magic into him the first time to get things rolling, but quickly enough, he was drawing it from the fount without my help."

"And?"

"Then I put the talisman on him. I was trying to make him struggle. Let him know what it might be like. I intended to allow just the smallest bit of power through, just like it would be for the examination." She shook her head, her vision going blurry with tears.

"Issur. Tell me," Teil said softly. "I need to know."

"He drew power through the talisman as if it wasn't even there. And not just a tiny bit of magic. He drew so much power from the earth, it was all I could do to keep him from roasting himself. I was so scared. I just walked away. Went in my room and hid beneath the bedcovers."

She glanced over at Teil. His eyes focused on her, but his face remained at rest as if he bore no emotion. He did. She knew that. This was a mask he wore when he was truly upset. Not a trace of what he was thinking or feeling showed through that mask. How could he be so calm when her insides were churning? How could he sit there as if he were reading the end-days' news and finding it a bit boring? How could none of this show on his face?

Teil closed his eyes. He was composing himself. She felt certain of it. A tiny twitch flickered in one eyelid. He was reaching for something. His magic was questing deep within the earth. He was checking up on her story. Did he not believe her? He'd never doubted her before.

She swallowed.

Best get the argument started.

Phyr was still missing, and this wasn't helping one bit. She rehearsed her words, playing out one argument after another, testing to see which one her imaginary bond-mate would most likely be receptive to. It was something she'd learned. Something she did while Teil was quietly composing his thoughts. It was what had kept them together for so long. A lesser woman would have waited for him, or worse, jumped in with a half-baked argument that he would refute in less than a heartbeat. She fabricated and tested half a dozen opening lines and rejected them, finally settling on one that would most likely be met with a favorable response.

Perhaps.

There was no guarantee.

Issur wet her lips, her tongue lingering for a moment on a particularly dry spot.

She bit her lip.

Drew a breath.

Held it for five heartbeats.

Ready.

"Teil," she said.

Her bond-mate's eyes flew open. His hands grasped the edge of the table, his knuckles white.

"Hold on," he shouted.

Issur glanced around the room. The tea in her cup rippled, gently at first, but with growing intensity. The painting of her family fell from the wall to land on the floor with a crash, followed a moment later by the polished tile floor buckling as the earth beneath her began to shake. The noise was deafening. Dust rose up, choking her. She felt the firm grip of Teil's hand on her arm.

Before Issur could think, she was under the table with Teil. All thoughts of magic and Phyr pushed aside. Something was wrong with the world. The fabric of magic itself was twisting, as if someone had wrung a wet cloth out and squeezed all the water from it. How strange? Who would have such power?

The earth bucked beneath her. The floor shook. Up and down at first, then swaying from side to side as if great waves passed beneath them.

Pots and pans swayed above the stove, banging themselves together as if some mad shivery was taking place. Then came the noise. It was as if a great wind had grabbed hold of the house. Whistles erupted from every door and window in the place. The walls shook. Paintings and decorations crashed to the floor. Glass shattered noisily as a statue Issur had purchased on one of her excursions hopped from its shelf and crashed to the tile floor.

And then it was gone.

The wind was gone.

The earth fell still.

Nothing remained of the great disturbance but a few particles of dust floating in the air, wild motes of sparkling gold chasing one another through the sunbeams that streamed in the now-quiet windows.

"What was that?" Issur asked.

"It's not over." Teil's voice quavered.

Issur braced herself for more violent shaking, but what happened next, she was ill-prepared for. It was as if a giant hand took hold of her heart and squeezed. It was hard to breathe. The air held no taste, no substance. Her lungs expanded and contracted, air whistling in and out.

Stars formed before her eyes.

Tingling erupted in her feet and spread quickly to her fingers.

Pain flared in her arm, and her vision dimmed.

"Issur!" Teil cradled her face in his hands.

Funny. His face was no longer stony and cold. His eyes held concern for her as they had not done in a long time. It comforted her to know that he did love her even when he was angry with her. Sometimes it was hard to believe that. He was such a good bond-mate. Strong and noble. Wise and powerful, and such a great father. She hoped he would continue to be one even after she was gone.

"Issur. Hold on," Teil was saying, but his words were fading.

Darkness crowded around her, but it was all right. Everything was all right. Phyr was back.

11

DISCOVERED

DARAYA

*D*araya glared at Phyr. She'd seen him around town. She avoided people like him. Her father said wizards were not to be trusted. And anyone who ran around in gray robes just to show who their kin was, was even less to be trusted. The boy stood taller than she'd thought, seeing him from afar. His dark hair had bits of hay in it and was in desperate need of a brushing.

"Why did you bring him?" Daraya demanded.

"When you fainted, I couldn't wake you. I ran for help. Phyr was the first person who agreed to come."

"And did he help?" Daraya felt certain she already knew the answer. She'd seen the boy on the platform during the examination. He was no more able to raise fire than she had. How could he have helped?

"I tried," Phyr said.

"You tried, wizard boy." Daraya spat. "But you failed. You with your fancy robe and influential family who look down your noses at the likes of me. Yet, you were unable to help. As usual." She glanced at his bloodstained hand even as he tried to hide it in the sleeve of his robe. "Admit it. You touched the wards, and Keeree had to save the both of us."

"It doesn't matter who saved who," Keeree said.

"It does to me." Daraya stood and brushed the hay from her clothes. She was still a bit fuzzy about just what had happened, but she recalled Keeree guiding her along the hidden path. The path that had been obscured by an illusion. And then they had run into the wards.

She glanced down.

There was the path.

She was standing on it.

"The path," she said.

"What about the path?" Keeree asked.

"It was hidden and now it's not." Daraya turned toward the barrier that had stretched across the path. She'd been unable to see it before. She wasn't certain what she would see now. The way was clear, just as it had been the day before.

"This way. The caretaker's cabin is just over that hill." Daraya didn't wait for Phyr and Keeree to answer. She started off along the path with a widening stride. Soon enough, she found herself standing at the edge of that great chasm. The stone island floated in the middle, vines dangling into the open air.

"That's the academy?" Keeree asked.

"I presume so." Daraya turned to Phyr. "Is it, wizard boy?"

"I've never been there, but from what my parents describe, I'd say, yes. It is."

"So we've made it," Daraya said. "We found the academy. Does that mean they'll accept us?"

"I wouldn't think so," Phyr said. "Why would finding the academy qualify one for entrance? We were tested. We fell short. Why would they accept us simply because we found them?"

"We didn't just find them. We passed the wards. We proved we have magic."

"I don't think it's that simple," Phyr said.

"You said the caretaker's cabin was nearby. Can you take us there?" Keeree asked.

Daraya swept her hand toward the cabin. "After you."

Keeree paused as if she were uncertain whether to follow Daraya's direction, but Phyr headed off in a rush.

"It's safe," Daraya said.

"You had your magic stolen away there. It doesn't sound so safe."

"Perhaps we'll find a way to get my magic back. What's to lose?"

"Plenty." Keeree shuddered.

"Suit yourself. Stay here. Go home. It matters not to me. I'm going to get answers. Don't you want to know why they rejected you when you showed mastery of your magic?"

Keeree shrugged but turned to follow Daraya.

They found Phyr standing beside the caretaker's cabin. He was staring at the floating rock suspended in the middle of the great chasm. As they watched, stones leaped from the walls and assembled themselves into an arching bridge that stretched out from the academy toward the cabin. So there *had* been a bridge. Daraya wondered what Phyr had done to trigger it that she missed.

"I knew it." Daraya stood beside Phyr as the bridge assembled itself block by block. It appeared sturdy. It would have to be, to span such a great gap. "See, they're welcoming us," she said.

"Not necessarily," Phyr said. "Maybe they're sending someone to investigate."

"The last time I was here, someone showed up in short order. I don't know where they came from."

Phyr nodded to the bridge. The span was almost complete. "I presume it was from there."

"Are we going to cross that?" Keeree stepped close to Phyr, as if he could keep her safe. It bothered Daraya, but she couldn't say why.

"We're being invited to the academy," Daraya said. "Why wouldn't we?"

"I can think of a number of reasons," Keeree said.

"Well. You two can stand there. I'm taking my place in the academy." She stepped onto the now-completed bridge. For half a heartbeat, she wondered if it was a trap, but her foot on the stone told her it was completely solid. She turned back to Keeree and Phyr. "Coming?"

Phyr shrugged. He reached out and took Keeree's hand. Together they stepped onto the bridge behind Daraya. She didn't wait for them to catch up. She was on a mission to enter the academy and no one was going to slow her down.

She hadn't gone more than half a dozen steps before the wind picked up. The bridge was solid, but the gust drove her sideways, threatening to cast her off. The low wall appeared to be more to keep wagons from running off the edge than to catch pedestrians. To make matters worse, the wind was cold and Daraya wasn't dressed for cold.

"Careful, it's windy," Daraya called out to Phyr and Keeree. The pair was only a few paces behind her. They were both holding their arms close to their bodies, as if to ward off the wind. She wished they would hurry. She felt a strange foreboding of being watched. Was this a test? Was that it? Were they to face a series of tests to prove themselves worthy? If so, she would show them.

"Daraya. Come back," Keeree said.

Daraya turned to see Keeree frozen in place.

"It's fine. Just a bit windy." Daraya paused. Was she going to have to go back and take Keeree's hand? Guide her across like a skittish horse?

"Daraya. Please come back."

"Why? They extended the bridge. They know we're here. Why stop now?"

The bridge beneath Daraya's feet shook as if something massive had landed on it. She turned back toward the academy. Sitting in the middle of the bridge was a gryphon. Its eagle head plucked at the stones that made up the bridge, dislodging them and casting them into the great void.

As it tore stones from the bridge, the gryphon's beak flared. It was as if stars had been torn from the night sky to shower down upon the bridge sliding off the tortured stone and falling into the great chasm beneath to vanish in the still air. The glowing embers that made up the body and wings of the beast flared as if the fire that spawned them had been subject to the breath of an unseen bellows, pumped by the hand of a hidden giant.

Daraya took a step back.

A huge stone went hurtling into the depths, only to return and slam into the bridge, taking up its place as if irritated by the actions of the great fiery beast.

The gryphon ripped a stone from the bridge and hurled it into the depths.

Again, the stone shot through the air and returned to its rightful place. Why was the gryphon trying to stop them? Had they not passed this test? And why was the bridge repairing itself? If the gryphon guarded it, certainly its actions were acceptable to whoever controlled it.

"Daraya," Keeree called. "Please come back."

"It's not destroying the bridge. If we can figure out a way around it, we can still cross. The bridge is sound."

"Yes, but *they* might have other ideas." Keeree was pointing to the opposite end of the bridge. A sea of dark blue robes swarmed from the gate, blocking their way.

12

HEALER
ISSUR

Issur blinked back the darkness, her vision fuzzy as if someone had smeared something over her eyes. She was lying flat on her back. Blurry white figures approached her and walked away. The sound of voices told her someone was attending her, but she couldn't make out who it was. The last thing she recalled was being beneath the table when the house shook.

She blinked.

Her vision improved, but things were still hard to make out. She tried to turn over, but she was restrained. Had she been injured? Why had they restrained her? What about Teil? Had he been injured as well?

She struggled to breathe. It felt as if the air had lost its sustenance and no matter how hard she drew a breath; it mattered little.

"Why is it so hard to breathe?" Issur asked.

"Shush. Don't try to talk," the voice said. "You've been through a lot. Lucky for you, I was passing by when things went awry. If I hadn't, well, you know what would've happened."

Issur blinked again. This time she could make out the healer. The girl had been in one of her classes not that long ago. She was a competent healer, but not one of the great ones, yet she did have a knack for matters pertaining to the heart. Was that why she was attending?

"What *did* happen?" Issur asked. "All I recall was the earth shaking, then I woke up here." She glanced around. Things were becoming clearer. The room, what she could see of it, was white. Stark white. Floors of white marble cut into tiles were laid so closely together that the seams barely showed. The floor butted against walls covered with the same marble tile. The walls reached to a height of a dozen spans. Windows high on the wall stood open just a crack to let the afternoon breeze in. The air carried with it a hint of clover and fresh rain.

The sound of footsteps drew near and fell silent.

Issur turned her head, but she was unable to make her muscles cooperate.

"She's awake?" a man's voice asked.

"Yes. We've been having a chat."

"You didn't give her any false hope, I trust," the man said.

"Certainly not. She's been trying to talk, but all I can make out are a few words. Nothing intelligible."

Nothing intelligible? Was the girl daft? Issur had been talking as clearly as she always had. What a silly girl to say such a thing. Or was she? Thinking back, Issur realized she had said only a few words since she woke, and the girl had acted as if she'd remained silent.

"Watch over her as best you can," the man said. "I have other patients to attend to."

"Yes, sire. I'll take good care of her."

"What's happening?" Issur asked.

The healer placed her hand on Issur's forehead. "Don't try to move or speak until we can get the spells back in place. Until then, you just rest."

"What's happened?" Issur heard her own words. They sounded like an infant's gibberish. "Why did you bring me to the sanitarium?"

The healer brushed her hair back. "Don't try to speak — you can't — just rest — for now. Perhaps in a few days, you'll be able to make the words come out right."

"Where's Teil?" Issur managed to make the name sound almost right.

"Your bond-mate's name is Teil. I think you're asking about him," the healer said.

"Teil, yes, Teil. Where's Teil?" Issur's words came out as nothing more than noises poorly stung together. Her tongue had turned traitor and her lips fought every effort to make them cooperate.

"Teil. I understand. I'll send someone to ask about him." The healer stood. "There were a lot of people injured. But let's keep our spirits up and hope that he's all right. There's nothing you can do about it, anyway."

"Phyr?" Issur demanded.

"Are you cold?" the healer asked. "Are you asking me to start a fire?"

"P - P - P - Phyr," Issur struggled to get the name out.

"Phyr. That's your son," the healer said.

"Yes. Phyr," Issur mumbled.

"He wasn't in the house. I'm not sure where he is. I can send someone to look for him once things calm down a bit. You shouldn't worry about anyone but yourself for now."

Issur tried to nod but couldn't.

She closed her eyes slowly and opened them again, hoping that signaled her gratitude.

"I bet you're wondering how you survived, aren't you?" The healer sat on the bed beside her. "Lucky for you, I was close by. I've been studying the healing magic, and how to power spells when the magical field is sparse. I recall how you told us you wore that crystal to focus the magic around you and maintain the spell that keeps your heart beating properly. You told us about the day you were almost killed. When that spell went so wrong and your friends *were* killed. And your heart was damaged. You probably thought I wasn't listening, but I was.

"I made my own crystal to store magic just like you taught us. I charge it up when I'm around powerful magic and draw on it little by little when I'm not. I'd just charged it up when everything went awry.

I have no idea how, but the nexus shifted, and your house was left on an anti-node. No magic at all. Not a lick. Not a single line of magical force was left where your house used to stand. And your crystal failed. Don't ask me how that happened, but it did, and so did your heart. You were dead when I got to you. No heartbeat. No breathing. I almost left you there for the undertakers, but then I remembered how you used that spell to keep your heart beating.

"I still remember that day you told us that. That spell and that class. I was smitten with a boy." The healer waved her hand as if dismissing the idea. "Don't even recall who it was, but I was smitten. Still, I paid attention to your lecture. I remember everything. That's how my mind works. I can recall exactly what you wore, how you stood at the blackboard, who was around you, what the weather was like. Every word you said. Stuck in my head." She tapped her forehead.

"So, I remembered the spell you told us about. I figured all it needed was a bit of magic, so I drew on my freshly charged crystal, and I re-cast that spell for you.

"You had turned all blue, but once I cast the spell, you started to breathe again. In no time at all, you were pink as a newborn and gasping for breath, so I brought you here where your crystal can work again. I transferred the spell back to it. You should be safe here unless something else happens. Not that I know what happened. I never saw such a thing. One heartbeat the magic was there — strong as ever — then the ground shook and nothing. The magic was gone. Let me tell you, that frightened the wits out of me, but I heard screaming and I just sort of unfroze, and there you were in need of help. Everything faded away until all that was left was you and me.

"I carried you here by myself. All the way. On my back."

Issur kept her gaze firmly on the girl's lips. Perhaps she could figure out how to make her own lips work like that.

"Anyway. Someone is here to see you." She stepped back almost reverently.

"She doesn't speak so well." The healer addressed the newcomer in a lowered voice that was still clear to Issur's ears.

"I hear we have you to thank for saving her," a deep voice said.

Issur tried to turn her head. She would have recognized the voice anywhere. Bannwor had one of those voices that was immediately recognizable. Deep and bassy with a smooth quality to it that made it a joy to listen to, no matter what words came from his lips. He was a busy man. If he had taken time out of his day to see her, things must certainly be dire.

"It was nothing," the healer was saying.

"You have my gratitude at the very least. Now, do you mind if we have a bit of privacy?" Bannwor asked.

"Just don't tire her out."

"I'll be gentle. And thank you again. You have done us all a great service."

"You're too kind." The sound of light footsteps receded into the distance.

Bannwor's face came into view. "You were fortunate beyond belief."

"I don't feel so lucky," Issur said.

"Sorry. I can't make out a word you're saying. Do you mind?" Bannwor extended a hand and placed it on her forehead without waiting for her answer.

Mist rose up and surrounded her, a cold clammy mist that soaked into her flesh and sent a shiver up her spine. A shiver she had not been able to make only moments before. The mist grew thicker until she could no longer see. Eyes open or eyes closed. Either way was the same.

Her insides twisted, and the mist vanished.

Issur found herself standing in a delightful cabin nestled on the shore of a crystal blue lake. Off in the distance, mountains rose to challenge the sky. Peaks covered in snow threw storms into the air as the wind swept over them. Great conifers surrounded the cabin, their branches protecting the thatch roof from the sun and rain. A pair of harts grazed in the woods, a doe and newborn, a tiny replica of its mother, except for the white spots on its fur. It stood unsteady on its legs.

Off in the distance, a pair of doves called to one another.

The sun shone warmly on her face, but not too warm, just the right amount to take the chill out of the wind.

Before her stood a young man of a score of years. He bore a sheepish grin and wore a blue robe with a smattering of white stars on it.

"I don't know why you insist on that appearance," she said. "It's not like I've forgotten you're an ancient and doddering old fool and have been since the day I met you." It gave her great joy that her words came out as clear as they usually did.

"It's the form I had when I learned this spell." It was strange to hear the sonorous voice of the old wizard coming from that young face.

"What happened?" demanded Issur. "Where's Phyr? I felt him disappear, then he was back. Is Teil all right? The healer said the nexus shifted. Is that what happened?"

"Slow down. First, let's talk about you. You're in very bad shape. Your heart stopped for longer than we would've liked, and there was considerable damage. They tell me you may recover in time, but it's going to be a long road."

"You sound like you're about to relieve me of my duties," Issur said.

"Unless you can convince me otherwise." The young wizard glanced down at his feet, then back to her face. His piercing grey eyes had not changed in all the summers she had known him. "You know this spell — the one that maintains this place — is very taxing. It's my spell, so it can accommodate me. You and I have known each other almost all your life, so it will accommodate you, but if anyone else should wander into it, their mere presence will drain the magic. If the magic is gone, you'll find yourself back in that bed, and I won't be able to restore the spell. Even so, we don't have all day. I'll keep things under control as much as I can — and we'll meet like this whenever we can — but for now — don't you agree that stepping down is for the best?" Bannwor waved his hand at the imaginary scenery. "I don't want your job. I want you back."

Issur placed a hand on the young man's shoulder. "Before you go. How about Teil and Phyr? Do you know if they're all right?"

"Teil is in the sanitarium in the bed next to yours. I'm afraid he's not in much better shape than you are. Not physically. He has broken bones — several — but otherwise he is healing and should recover fully in time."

"And Phyr? Is he all right?"

"As far as I know." The sheepish grin on the boy's face faltered. He glanced around as if looking for an avenue of escape. "I must take my leave."

"So what aren't you saying?" Issur demanded.

"It looks as if Phyr might have had more than a passing role in all this. At least in some measure."

"My Phyr?"

"Your Phyr." The boy paused. "I hope you're not going to tell me you hadn't already discovered it for yourself?"

Issur held her breath. Did Bannwor know what she'd discovered? What she'd done?

"He's a focus," Bannwor said. "And he's not the only one. There are three of them. They've formed a triad. And, they moved the nexus. I needn't tell you what that means."

13

ESCAPE

KEEREE

*K*eeree studied Daraya with disbelief. The girl had no fear. She stood in the middle of a magic bridge, battered by icy winds, facing down a fiery gryphon even as a swarm of students raced toward her. Did nothing scare her? The cluster of dark-blue robes was almost upon her. At the head of the procession came the thin dark-haired man who had been sitting in the left-hand throne at the examination. Bannwor.

Daraya backed away from them, eyes fixed on the gryphon.

The great beast spread its wings and leaped from the bridge. It caught the wind and soared into the sky until it was no longer visible.

Keeree felt Phyr's hand slip into her own. "We better go."

Daraya raced past them. Keeree turned to follow her but stopped.

The sky rippled like a pond on a windy day. Not another vision. That was the last thing she needed.

But it was not a vision.

An ear-piercing screech split the air.

A raptor's cry from a bird a thousand times larger than a hawk threatened to deafen her.

A huge rust-colored cloud formed before the three of them, blocking their retreat.

Growing darker and darker, the cloud coalesced into the gryphon. The lion's body of the creature was easily as tall as a man. Its powerful legs ripped at the bridge once more. Its eagle head towered above Keeree.

A long, forked tongue reached out as the mighty creature drew back its head. Its eyes swirled with sparks that fell from them like tears of fire. It reared back its head, beak wide open, towering over Daraya as if ready to consume her.

"Watch out," Keeree shouted.

Daraya turned toward the gryphon and froze. She stood transfix as the great beak stabbed at her.

"Daraya! Move," Keeree shouted.

Daraya dove to the side, but the gryphon shifted position to block her path.

"Daraya. Back this way." Keeree started toward Daraya but stopped short.

The air before her shimmered as if heat were rising from the stones at her feet. Through the distortion, a tall wooden door appeared. It was easily twice Keeree's height, mirror-smooth and brilliant crimson.

The door opened and a short, balding man with close-cropped gray beard and a balding pate stepped out. He shoved his spectacles up his nose and squinted at Keeree. It was Charyl.

"Well, well. I didn't expect you this soon." Charyl closed the door, and it vanished.

Keeree noticed the gryphon was urging Daraya in her direction. Its great beak closed tight, still dripping cinders and ash.

"You were expecting me?" she asked.

"Not yet. You need to go," Charyl said. "It's too soon."

"Go where?" Keeree asked.

"Anywhere but here, isn't that obvious?"

"But your gryphon is blocking the way. Where can we go?"

"Anywhere you'd like. The choice is yours. Always has been."

Keeree glanced back. The crowd of blue robes was drawing closer. How were they to escape?

"I see you've begun it," Charyl said. "What's begun must be ended, but that's not a discussion for today."

"What are you talking about? Let us by," Keeree insisted.

"Let you buy what?" Charyl appeared confused. "Oh, wait. Let you pass. Why didn't you say that?"

He reached behind him and yanked.

The door that he'd emerged from reappeared.

Keeree took a step toward it, but he held out his hand.

"Not you, all of you." He gestured to Daraya and Phyr. "Join hands. We don't want you separated. Not yet."

Keeree took Phyr and Daraya's hands. As they touched, she felt a spark and almost let go.

"Together now." Charyl waved a hand at the open door. "Before the others arrive."

Keeree stepped across the threshold. The magic beneath her feet erupted as if she stood in the throat of a volcano. Hot. Swirling. Filled with odors both pleasant and painful. The red of molten rock rose up around them. The bridge fell from beneath their feet. They were falling. Three failed wizards, hands joined, rushing toward the abyss. The air grew thick and hot, then dark.

When the light returned, Keeree found herself standing in a long corridor filled with doors. Polished marble tile stretched out to eternity. Stone walls stood perfectly straight, set with towering identical doors every yard or so.

"Where are we?" she asked.

"The void." Phyr tugged on her hand, dragging Keeree and a befuddled Daraya behind him. "Follow me."

"Do you know where you're going?" Keeree demanded.

"I hope so. I've only been here once before."

"Where's here?"

"This?" Phyr gestured to the corridor. "This is everywhere. You want to go home? Pick a door. Want to go to the market square? Pick a door. Want to visit far-off lands? Pick a door."

"But where will we go? Where will we be safe?" Keeree asked. This was all well and good, but just where could they go?

Phyr touched a door, then shook his head. He touched another one and shook his head once more.

"Are we lost?" Keeree asked.

"No. I'll know it when I feel it." Phyr touched another door, his face twisting up as if he had caught a whiff of something foul.

"What if we're stuck here, or we come out so far from home we're never going to get back?"

"I thought you trusted me," Phyr said.

"Why should I trust you?" she asked. But she *was* starting to trust him. He was the last person she would have ever thought to make friends with. A city boy with influential parents. Wizards, no less. He couldn't be more different from her. Still, he had shown he could be relied on when things were desperate. She did trust him.

"It's all about knowing where you want to go. If you truly know your destination, picture it, and open a door." His palm rested on a door that looked just like every other door. "This is it."

Phyr yanked the door open and pulled Keeree after him.

Once again, the darkness rose up around them.

They were falling.

For an eternity.

And then they weren't.

The earth became solid once more.

They stood in a house that had been shaken and damaged. The walls bore great cracks. Some had tumbled down. The floor was warped and cracked. Fresh dirt showed between mirror-like slabs of marble.

Phyr kicked up a broken tile. He reached out and straightened a painting of an elderly couple that hung crooked on the wall. He paused for a moment, then kicked the broken fragment of some figurine that had crashed to the floor. It skidded into the corner and broke into a thousand pieces.

"What's the matter?" Keeree felt strange, as if she were immersed in water that was just a bit chilly. The air seemed to suck the energy out of her. It made her dizzy.

Phyr bent down and picked up a broken cup. His eyes filled with tears. "This is my house."

Keeree shivered. She glanced around, taking in the carnage. Dust covered broken furniture. Decorations had been thrown from the walls to shatter on the floor. Everything was out of place. Little had escaped unscathed.

She turned to Daraya, hoping she had words of comfort for Phyr, but she was not there.

"Phyr?" Keeree asked. "Where's Daraya?"

14

CABIN
DARAYA

*D*araya felt a pull.

One of the doors was begging her to enter it.

She let go of Keeree's hand.

She stepped up to a door that looked like every other door. Twice her height, the door was cut from deep-grained hardwood. The brightly polished silver overlay accentuated the grain. Deep-set panels reflected back a distorted vision of a slight white-haired girl. Daraya winced at her reflection but pushed away the dissatisfaction she usually experienced when confronted with her own image.

Now was not the time.

Something was calling to her.

Just on the other side of the door.

She grasped the ornately wrought handle and twisted.

The door swung open as if it were on hinges of air.

The door led to a path in the woods.

How strange.

Daraya drew a breath and held it. What was she thinking, separating from Keeree and Phyr? Where did this door lead? Phyr had said the doors led everywhere. She could be stepping out onto the top of some distant mountain for all she knew.

Mountains. Woods. Lake. A cabin.

She was definitely leagues from home.

Daraya glanced down the path.

Perhaps someone was here. Someone who could help her return home. She should not have left Keeree and Phyr. Surely they'd already found the door Phyr sought. Why had she pulled away? What was wrong with her?

Now she was alone.

And something was still calling to her.

Stronger now.

She exhaled, drew a fresh breath, and started down the path.

"Hello?" Daraya shouted.

Her voice faded into the woods.

"Is anyone around?"

She was alone. Her throat grew tight. "I'm not going to cry." She spoke aloud as if her words would banish the anguish that threatened her.

What had Keeree said? That she could feel the magic beneath her feet? What an odd girl. Keeree carried the faint smell of cow droppings and cut hay. She was clearly uneducated, or educated in an unconventional manner, yet she spoke with an authority that Daraya herself lacked. And the girl had clearly accessed some powerful magic. Perhaps there was something to her claim that she could feel the magic because she possessed no shoes.

Daraya knelt and unfastened her left shoe. She reached up, rolled her stocking down, and slid it off her foot, tucking it into the shoe. She repeated the process with her right shoe. Once both feet were free, she tied the laces together and slung her shoes over her shoulder.

She stood and let her feet feel the path.

It was scratchy.

A small stone beneath her right foot jabbed into her tender flesh.

How had the girl tolerated this? Was it something to which one might become accustomed?

What about the magic? Daraya tried to relax and feel the magic. It should be there beneath her feet. If the girl was right.

She let her senses expand.

Hard-packed dirt.

A small, sharp stone.

The warm sun.

Insects buzzing.

The breeze whispering as it swept the deep foliage growing amongst the trees.

Daraya wriggled her feet.

Hard-packed ground.

Damp.

It must have rained recently.

Toes.

Scraping against hard ground.

The sudden release of an earthy smell.

Magic?

No.

Where was that magic?

Daraya thought back. Back to the time in the caretaker's cottage where she had raised fire. Fire that obeyed her will. Fire that danced above her palm. Before the boy had sealed away her magic. What had *that* felt like?

She reached for that feeling, letting her memory come alive. It had been an exhilarating thing to do magic like that. She'd never been able to do anything even approaching that before. It had been so dramatic, she would never forget that feeling.

She held out her hand and tried to recall the feeling.

"Fire," Daraya shouted.

Nothing.

The boy who had stolen her magic had said that the cottage was on a nexus.

What was a *nexus*?

It sounded vaguely familiar.

She's heard the term before.

Something to do with the concentrations of magic.

A place where the lines of magical force converged.

Was this place a nexus?

Was that why she'd been drawn here?

If she could connect with the magic, she could call it up from the earth, just like Keeree did. Her shoes were off. Why shouldn't she be able to do it? If a farm-girl reeking of dung could draw magic from the earth, certainly she could.

But how?

Daraya let her senses expand even further. It was a chore, but she managed to feel her surroundings, and even into the earth beneath her feet.

But the earth beneath her feet was an illusion.

It wasn't solid.

It was a creation, an artifact.

She pushed her senses further.

Beneath the soil, no more than a half a span, was what?

Nothingness.

There was no magic.

There was no earth.

What sort of place was this?

"How did you get here? You're not my son." A voice startled Daraya.

She spun to see a woman standing behind her. The woman wore her black hair down to her shoulders. A gold band on her forehead was set with a gleaming jewel. Her eyes glowed red.

Issur. Phyr's mother. The one who'd cast Daraya out, destroyed her chances at becoming a wizard. Stolen the safety of the academy from her.

"I asked you a question," Issur restated.

"You ruined my life."

Issur drew a breath as if to scold her, then paused. She studied Daraya. "You're the girl," she said.

Daraya stepped back. "The one you rejected? The one whose life you ruined? You're from the academy. How do you not know they sent a boy to steal my powers the day before the examination? How could you do something like that to me?"

Issur's chin rose. Her nostrils flared.

Daraya flinched. This is when the whippings usually began. She steeled herself for a beating but held her ground. Cowering before her father had never lessened his anger. Rather it seemed to inflame it. Daraya wasn't about to back down. Let the woman rant. She would have answers. Even if she had to suffer for them.

After half a hand of heartbeats, Issur's brows lowered. She sucked her cheeks in and shook her head as if conversing with herself. Finally, she raised an eyebrow, and spoke in a calm and quiet voice, "Let me get a look at you."

Daraya held back. No beating? The only one who had treated her with kindness and compassion was Rodaso, and she was long in the ground. Maybe she was wrong about this woman. She felt angry, of that there was no doubt, but still she showed compassion.

Daraya relaxed, but held herself in readiness.

"Come, child. I won't hurt you." Issur reassured her. "Your magic is sealed away, but it is still a part of you. It will always be a part of you."

Daraya's heart pounded, and her stomach fluttered. Would she be able to do magic again? Like before? "Can you fix me?"

"Not unless you come closer so I can see what's been done."

Daraya stepped closer.

Issur stretched out her hand and held it over Daraya's head. A warmth emanated from her flesh followed by a tingling sensation that lasted only half a heartbeat. Issur then held it in front of Daraya's chest. The same tingling sensation arose once more to die away just as quickly.

"It's no use. I don't have access to my full power here," Issur said.

"So, you can't fix me?" Daraya demanded.

"No. Not in this place."

"Just where is here?" Daraya asked.

"A place of magic. A place of healing. A place built just for me. A place I'm curious that you were able to find, much less enter."

"I don't understand."

"I was injured. When the nexus shifted. I'm in the sanitarium resting. I can't speak. I can't move. This place was constructed for me by a ..." she hesitated for a moment, then continued, "... a friend. So I don't go mad while the healers figure out how to restore me."

"So you can't help me?"

"I'm afraid not. Not in this place." She folded her arms and looked down her nose at Daraya. "So, tell me. How did you enter this place? Bannwor said it would be difficult even for him, but here you are, a slip of a girl with her magic sealed away from her." Issur pursed her lips. "So how did you do it?"

Daraya hesitated.

Could she use Issur's curiosity as a bargaining point to secure a promise to heal her? Did she even trust the woman? What use was a promise to heal her if Issur herself was in no shape to do anything?

"We were at the caretaker's cottage. There was this gryphon attacking me. The wizard told us to hold on and opened a door from nothing. He told us to enter and then we were in this corridor filled with doors. I let go of Keeree's hand because I felt a pull. I opened a door and stepped through it, and here I am," Daraya blurted everything without taking a single breath. Why had she done that?

The woman bit her lip. "I tried to summon Phyr, but I got you instead. Who are you? You know Phyr?"

"He's my friend." Let Issur wonder how Daraya knew who she was and how one such as she had come to know Phyr. Perhaps she wouldn't be so reluctant to help out.

"How is he?" Issur asked.

"He was fine when I last saw him."

"In the void?" she asked. "You must find him. Bring him here."

"How do I do that? I don't know where here is, and I don't know how to get back home." Daraya shuddered at her own words. Home was not somewhere she could return to, even if she found her way out of this place.

Issur reached into the air and grasped at something unseen.

A door appeared. Looking exactly like the one Daraya had entered that led her to this place.

"You must go." Issur gestured to the door. "Find my son. Bring him here."

Through the door was the cleanest room Daraya had ever seen. Beds covered in white linen were set against walls of alabaster marble. Attendants in white floated between beds filled with all manner of ill and infirm. In the nearest bed was the still form of a woman. Hair draped on the pillow, reaching to her shoulders, eyes closed, a calm and quiet expression on a face that seemed somehow misshapen, as if half of it had been paralyzed.

"Go. Find Phyr." Issur placed her hand on Daraya's back and guided her to the door. "Bring him here."

"Why?" Daraya asked.

"Because his magic has been sealed away, just as yours has. You are all in great danger." With that, she pushed Daraya through the door.

15

SANITARIUM
PHYR

hyr took in the shambles of what had once been his home. The only place he felt truly safe. The cracked and tumbled walls lay scattered across the uprooted floor. Beneath it all, a sense of power that was no longer present. It was as if an echo of the magic that used to permeate this place remained. Just the faintest shadow of its former self. He paused. He'd felt this before. In the square. Where the prospective students had been examined. Had the square once contained power as this place had, and if it had, where had that power gone?

And where was Daraya?

The girl had been holding Keeree's hand as they made their way through the void, and then she was gone. Just like that. He hadn't noticed at first, and by the time he had, he was already opening the door he and Keeree stepped through. And where were his parents? "Issur? Teil?" he shouted, his words echoing off the empty walls. "Where are you?"

"Maybe they weren't here when this happened," Keeree said.

"They were here. I came home from the examination and over-heard them talking. They were waiting for me."

"Where would they have gone?"

Phyr knelt beside a table. It was covered in dust and debris. "See that?" He pointed to a disturbance in the dust beneath the table. "And these?" He pointed to several faint sets of footprints that led from the table to the door. They were a woman's, from the size of them. Beside the footprints were long wandering marks, heavy, as if someone had been dragged. His parents had been here, and they'd been injured. "Something's happened to them."

"How can you be certain?" Keeree asked.

"Shh." He held his breath for several heartbeats and then pursed his lips. "Someone took them."

"Who?"

"I don't know. But both of them were hurt. Look at the drag marks. Two sets."

"Where would they take them?" Keeree asked.

"To a place of healing." Phyr reached out and took her hand. "Come on."

"Are we going back to that place with the doors?"

"No. We're going to the sanitarium."

"What's a *sanitarium*?"

"A place of healing. Have you never heard of a sanitarium? It's where the injured and infirm are taken."

"Why would you put all the infirm in one place?" Keeree asked. "Doesn't that concentrate the bad aether? We try to stay as far from someone who is ill as possible. Don't want the bad aether spreading."

"That's a myth," Phyr said. "There is no such thing as bad aether. Infirmity is passed by breath. Cover your face and you're fine. Mostly. And besides, they keep the sick in a separate wing from the injured. Don't you know anything?"

"I know lots, just not that," Keeree said.

He felt her finger relax as if she were preparing to release his hand, but her grip returned.

"Is it far?" she asked.

"A few streets."

Phyr led Keeree along the deserted city avenue. Every so often a broken cobblestone or some other form of debris lay in their path, testament that his house had not been the only structure damaged. But none of the other homes had anything like the kind of damage his did. What could have happened? Did it have anything to do with the quake they'd felt in the field beside the academy? Had he somehow contributed to the damage that injured or killed his parents?

When they reached the sanitarium, he paused at the door. The sanitarium was a large, stark building that occupied the entire block. It rose from the street four floors. Marble walls with small windows dotted each floor. Above the door was a large cross painted blood red.

As they ascended the stairs, Keeree released his hand and stopped. She looked as if she were about to lose the contents of her stomach onto her bare feet.

"Are you all right?" he asked.

"Give me a moment." Keeree paused, hands on her knees. She took a few breaths and stood. "I'm fine."

Phyr opened the towering doors and pulled her along a stark and sterile hallway until they reached a branch where the hallways formed a cross. The center of the cross was occupied by a large marble desk. Behind the desk sat a woman dressed all in white. She wore a white hat with a red cross on it.

"I'm Phyr. Are my parents here?"

The woman tilted her head and raised an eyebrow. "Do they have names?"

"Issur and Teil," Phyr said.

"When would they have been brought here?" she asked.

"Today. Not long ago. They were fine just a few glasses ago when I last saw them."

"Then what makes you think they're here?"

"Our house collapsed. They would have been in it. They were injured. They must be here. Can you please check?"

"Hmm. Let me see." The woman consulted a large book, flipping the pages back and forth. "I see. Yes. Issur was brought in not long ago. Room at the end. It's where they put the new patients. Next to Teil."

"Come on." Phyr placed his hand on Keeree's back and turned her toward the hallway.

She skipped a step to match his pace without releasing his hand. "It'll be all right," she said.

Phyr paused. He knew Keeree was just trying to reassure him, but how could she know? His parents were here, so they were alive, or had been when they were brought in. But they could be near death at this very moment. "You can't know that," he said.

"They're here. That means they're not dead. That's always a good place to start."

Phyr halted before a set of double doors. They barred the hallway with a window in each one. Beside the door stood a laver with a large bowl and a ewer of steaming water. "A lot comes between all right and dead," he said.

He guided Keeree to the laver. He picked up the ewer and held it above the bowl. "Wash your hands. Clean towels are beneath."

Keeree extended her hands over the basin.

Phyr doused them with scorching hot water.

She pulled her hands back. "That's hot."

"It's supposed to be hot. Now soap." He raised his chin to indicate a bar of yellow soap that sat in a dish beside the bowl. "All the way to your elbows."

Keeree picked up the soap and slid it across her wet skin.

"To the elbows," Phyr said.

She scrubbed as instructed and extended her hands over the bowl once more.

Phyr poured more steaming water over her arms and hands.

Keeree reached for the basket full of white cloths beside the laver.

"Clean towels beneath the bowl," Phyr said. "Those are dirty."

Keeree took a clean towel and dried her face and hands. She tossed it into the basket with an expression of contempt, then turned for the doors.

"Not yet." Phyr reached into another basket beside the towels and came away with a pair of white cloth squares with long strings attached. "Put this on." He lifted the cloth to cover his mouth and nose and tied it neatly behind his head. "Turn around." He took the cloth, placed it over Keeree's mouth and nose, and deftly tied them behind her head.

Gooseflesh rose on her arms at his touch. Was she afraid of him, or was she excited by his touch? Phyr had no experience with girls. He felt uncertain which it was. Neither seemed like the reaction he would have expected. He shoved the thought aside. "Now we can go in."

He used his foot to push one of the doors open. "Don't touch anything."

"If you say so." Keeree followed him through the door and into a large open area filled with beds.

Beside the bed they had been told contained Phyr's mother was another bed. That one was curtained off to hide the patient from view. The woman had said his father was in the bed beside his mother. Was that him? How hideous were his injuries that they needed to be hidden from casual observation?

He shuddered. Issur first, then. He turned to her bed where a young woman was bent over. She wore an ill fitting white gown like those who cared for the infirm that clearly was not hers. A mask covered her face, and her hair was tucked under a cap bearing the same red cross as the rest of the healers.

As they approached the bed, the young woman turned to them. "Took you long enough to get here."

"Excuse me," Phyr said.

"I knew you'd come here once you found out what happened. I only just arrived myself, but I decided to see to Issur while I waited for you."

The girl removed her mask.

It was Daraya.

16

BALANCE

PHYR

*P*hyr pushed past Daraya to the bed where his mother lay. He'd never been in this wing of the sanitarium before. The bed was made of metal painted a light green. It had rails to keep her from rolling onto the floor, but they were currently lowered. She was restrained by straps that encircled her arms and legs and bound her tightly to the bed. Why? What had happened to her?

He stepped close.

His mother looked to be asleep.

He leaned in closer. She seemed to have suffered no physical harm. She wore no bandages he could see. She had no bruises.

Phyr whispered. "Mother?"

A sound came from her lips that was not quite his name.

Phyr noticed that her face was no longer as he recalled it. Part of it was slack, as if she had no control over it. Her mouth drooped, and drool slipped from one side to roll down her cheek.

Phyr spun to face Daraya. "What happened to her?"

"Hold on, wizard boy." Daraya dabbed away the spittle from Issur's cheek. "I don't have all the answers."

Phyr grabbed Daraya by the arms and shook her. How had she gotten here? He had last seen her in the void. "Tell me," he demanded.

"Calm down," Daraya said. "Let me explain."

"How did you come to be here?" Keeree asked. "You frightened us half to death when you just up and vanished."

"It's a good thing I wasn't with you," Daraya answered. "Or else I would never have had a chance to speak with Issur."

"You spoke to her?" Phyr glanced at his mother once again. Her slack face bothered him more than it should have. She was still his mother, but what if she never recovered? Would she be like this for the rest of her life? He suppressed a shudder. "Why can't she talk?"

"When we were in the void," Daraya explained. "I took a different door. It called to me — the door. When I stepped through it, I came out in the woods — somewhere — and there was Issur."

"Where?" Phyr asked.

"She said it was a construct, something someone had made for her, so she didn't have to lie still and silent in bed all day. She said it was very difficult to enter, and that she was surprised that I was there. I had no problem getting in. I just opened the door and stepped through."

"That still doesn't explain how you got here," Phyr said.

"I'm getting to that. Issur and I spoke for a while. Your mother was very courteous. She's worried about *you*. She asked me to get you and bring you to her."

"Worried about me? There's nothing wrong with me," Phyr said. How could she be worried about him at a time like this? She was the one in the bed.

"There *is* something wrong with you," Daraya explained. "Just as there is with me. She told me that your magic had been sealed away. Just like mine."

Phyr was shocked. He knew that his failure at the examination had not been his own fault, but his magic sealed away? How could someone have done that to him? *Why* would someone have done that to him?

"Don't look so surprised," Daraya said. "You failed the exam just like me. Wasn't that a bit suspicious?"

"She told you all that?" Phyr asked. "In some magical land that'd been created just for her? You? A complete stranger?"

Before he could get any answers from Daraya, Phyr was interrupted by a young woman dressed in white.

She glanced at Keeree, her gaze lingering as if she recognized the girl. She frowned, then blinked, and turned her attention back to Phyr. "I take it you're Phyr?" she asked.

"I am."

"A wizard was here. He asked me to give you this." She handed him a folded piece of parchment with a large C stamped in the wax that sealed it shut. "He also told me to let you know your father will be fine in time. That you are not to worry."

"Is that my father?" Phyr nodded to the dazzlingly white curtain shrouding the bed beside his mother.

The healer nodded. "He's sleeping just now. He has a few broken bones, but they're mending. He will be here for half a moon or more, but he's expected to make a complete recovery."

"I want to see him."

"You may not. There's a spell surrounding him that speeds the healing. Should you disturb that spell, his healing will take much longer than we would like. He's going to be fine. He's in good hands here."

Daraya nodded to the parchment in Phyr's hand. "What's it say?"

Phyr slid a finger beneath the flap and broke the wax seal. The wax vanished as if it had never existed.

"Well?"

"I'm getting to it." Phyr read the note. The script was heavy-handed, but the message clear.

Phyr. Your magic has been sealed away. You and your friends are in grave danger so long as at least one of you retains their magic, but the whole of the wizarding world is in danger should all three of you become sealed. Your mother has prepared a talisman that will dampen any magic used against it. It is scant hope against the forces gathered against you, but all we can offer. Find it. Protect it. Whatever you do, do not let them seal the last of your triad.

The note was signed with a bold block letter, C.

"What sort of talisman?" Daraya asked. "How can something like that protect you?"

"It blocks magic." Phyr said. "Didn't you get that part?"

Daraya balled up a fist and struck Phyr in the arm. It hurt like fire. "You're an arrogant one for a damp-wick wizard boy," she said.

Phyr rubbed his arm where her knuckle had struck, then dropped his hand. He didn't want to admit how much it hurt, and he certainly wasn't going to remark on her clearly missing the term the wizard had used to describe the talisman. *Earumque oppress*, it had said. To dampen magic. It was the talisman his mother had used when she tested his ability to call up fire. He shuddered. To be in that world. The one without magic. The one where colors and tastes were lacking. The place where magic could not enter.

"Wizard boy?" Daraya asked. "You all right?"

"I'm fine," Phyr lied. "Come on. We have to go back to my house."

"Where's your betrothed?" Daraya asked.

"Betrothed?"

"The farm girl," Daraya explained.

"She's not my betrothed." Phyr glanced around the room. Keeree was nowhere to be seen.

"Excuse me," Phyr called to the woman in white who attended his mother. "Did you see where Keeree went?"

"The one with the curly hair and dirty clothes?" The healer wrinkled her nose.

"Yes. That's the one."

"She left."

"When?"

"Not long ago. She looked a bit green in the gills. Maybe all this clean was making her stomach upset."

Daraya snickered. "Come on. Let's go. We don't have all day."

"Don't you think we should wait?" Keeree wasn't the sort of person he would have chosen as a friend, but Phyr realized he was coming to care for her. When they'd entered the sanitarium, she'd been uncomfortable. He'd ignored it at the time, but now it gnawed at him. What sort of friend was he? He certainly wasn't going to abandon her. Perhaps she'd stepped outside for fresh air. If she wasn't outside, they could always come back and search for her.

"She probably had to go back to the farm," Daraya said. "The kine need milking, or the eggs need gathering. You know how those folks are. They're strange, and to be honest, she has an odor clinging to her that I find a bit off-putting." She gave him a look of disgust. "You going to wait for an errant farm girl or take the advice on your note?"

"I don't like the way you talk about her," Phyr said.

"Was anything I said untrue?"

"No, but that doesn't matter. It was cruel. I don't know what makes you so mean."

"Life made me the way I am," Daraya said. "And if you have half a wit, it will do the same to you."

"That's just sad."

"That's just life," Daraya turned to go. "Day's a wasting."

Phyr rushed to keep up with Daraya. Why was she so bitter? She'd had nothing good to say about anyone. Keeree might have the aroma of the farm about her, but at least she was honest and kind.

Daraya stood at the large double doors, hand poised ready to push them open. "Come on, wizard boy."

"I'm not *wizard boy*. My name's Phyr."

"Sure it is." Daraya shoved the door. It swung halfway open, then hit something. She shoved again, but it didn't move. A whimper came from the other side of the door.

Daraya pushed again.

"Stop that," Phyr grabbed her arm and pulled her back. He stepped through the other door to see what was barring their path. It was Keeree. She knelt beside the ewer of water where they had washed their hands.

Phyr crouched down beside her. "What's wrong?"

"This place. It's so unsettling," Keeree said.

"Too clean for you?" Daraya asked.

Phyr shot her a menacing glance. He turned back to Keeree. "How so?"

"I feel unbalanced. As if I were about to fall over."

"We're leaving. Going back to my house," Phyr said. "Let me help you."

He reached out to Keeree and took her hand. He'd never had much of a relationship with a girl before. Not done the hand holding he'd seen in other students. Her grip was strong, not affectionate, yet she made him feel wanted. It was reassuring.

"What did you learn?" Keeree asked.

"My father is also here. He was injured."

"Is he going to be all right?"

"The healer said he would recover," Phyr muttered, "but it will take time." He glanced around the room. "I'm not sure this was an accident. Someone wanted my parents dead or out of the way."

"Who would do such a thing?" Keeree asked.

Phyr shrugged. "I only wish I knew."

17

HOMELESS

DARAYA

araya followed Phyr back to his home. She had expected a palatial residence with high walls and gilt windows. Powerful wizards were wealthy, were they not? Why else did one seek power? What she saw made her heart sink. She had hoped Phyr would take pity on her and put her up for the night, but it appeared he was in much the same predicament as she.

"What happened here?" Daraya asked as Phyr led them into the tumbled-down marble that had once been his home.

"I don't know. You spoke to Issur. Did she tell you anything?" Phyr asked.

Daraya thought back. The woman had mentioned the nexus shifting. Had that caused this? "The nexus moved?"

"What?" Phyr asked.

"The nexus moved," Daraya said. "She mentioned something about the nexus shifting."

"What's a nexus?" Keeree interrupted.

"It's a convergence of lines of magical force," Phyr explained. "A place where the magic is concentrated at the surface of the earth rather than deep beneath it. It's why we live — lived — here."

Keeree doubled over.

"What's wrong with her?" Daraya asked. Was there something wrong, or was Keeree just seeking attention? Daraya wasn't certain if she believed the girl was truly ill. Keeree seemed like someone who wanted to be the center of attention and would go out of her way to make sure she was noticed.

Phyr knelt beside her. "Keeree?"

"She's at it again," Daraya said.

"Keeree," Phyr asked. "What's wrong?"

"I feel..." Keeree's voice was weak. "It's overwhelming. Too much."

"Maybe she *is* ill," Daraya said. "Should we take her back to the healers?"

"No." Phyr said. "Go look for the talisman. It's in that room." He pointed towards his parents' library, the room that held their magical tomes and textbooks. "In a book on the shelf. Top left. The thick one. Titled 'Magical Systems'."

"Fine." Let the girl have all the attention. She didn't need anyone worrying over her.

Daraya ducked beneath a collapsed lintel and into a large room containing shelves of books. Most of them were still in place, if covered in dust. But several had been thrown to the floor. A pair of overstuffed chairs flanked a low table that faced a fireplace. Resting on the table was a book, opened and face down.

Daraya picked it up. *To harness and store power from a nexus or even a single line of magical force, one must be able to access the lines of equal magical potential and discern where the points of conjunction create nodes of power as well as where the conjunctions create anti-nodes of relative safety so one may access them without fear of coming into contact with too much power.*

She had never seen a book about magic before, much less one that spoke of how to locate and harness the powers all around them. Just what was Phyr's family involved with?

Nodes and anti-nodes are stable, shifting only marginally over centuries. The only thing that can cause a rapid shift in a nexus is the combined strength of a focused triad. While one might think that shifting a nexus might be beneficial, it rarely is. The nexus is tightly coupled to the lines of magical flux around it. Disturbing the secondary lines of flux almost always results in disaster.

"Did you find it?" Phyr's voice came from the doorway.

Daraya closed the book and placed it back on the table. "Not yet. Still looking."

She had to climb over an upended couch to reach the shelves he'd indicated would contain the book. There it sat, just out of her grasp. She needed something to let her reach the book. But what?

She dumped all the books from the lower shelf and stacked them on the floor before the shelf she needed to reach, careful to arrange them in an overlapping pattern so that each layer covered the one below and lent it strength. When she was certain she had enough of a pile, she climbed her mountain of books and stretched. Her fingers just touched the lower edge of the large tome on the top shelf.

She meant to grasp it, but it slid forward, tumbled out of the bookcase, and struck her on the head.

"Drat," Daraya shouted.

"You find it?" Phyr called.

"Yes. I have it."

The book rested on the floor. It bore a leather strap and a lock. No key. What was she going to do now?

The lock looked simple.

Perhaps she could force it.

She grabbed the leather strap and yanked. The lock was small, but it wasn't about to budge.

She searched the room for something to pry the lock open with.

Nothing.

Perhaps finesse?

She reached into her hair and withdrew a small pin. She used them to keep her hair up, but she'd come to learn there were other uses for them, like opening locks. Simple locks.

She plunged the hairpin into the lock and twisted.

It popped open.

She was so surprised she dropped the book. It landed on the floor, splayed open. It had been hollowed out and something placed inside, and that something was lying on the floor in the dust. The talisman Phyr had described. It was a short lace ribbon made of brilliant crimson. At one end, an intricate figure made of of brass had been sewn bearing a small purple gemstone. Around the gemstone were several smooth and highly polished river stones. This had to be it. It didn't look all that impressive.

Phyr had said it was supposed to suppress magic.

She wondered if it worked.

She placed the ribbon over her head, letting the cold brass come to rest against her flesh.

Nothing.

She fingered the gemstone.

It was cold and lifeless.

"It doesn't work," she said.

When she emerged from the library, Keeree was retching violently.

"What's wrong with her?" she asked.

"She's sensitive to the magic," Phyr said. "This place may not have as much as it once did, but there is still a lot here. We have to get her out of here."

Daraya removed the talisman from around her neck and handed it to Phyr. "Didn't you say this suppressed magic?"

"Good thinking. Maybe it'll help." Phyr dropped the ribbon around Keeree's neck, brushing her hair out of the way as it settled against her flesh.

Keeree immediately stopped retching.

"I think it's working," Phyr said.

"Let's hope so." Daraya turned her nose up at the bitter odor rising from a small puddle of yellow liquid slowly spreading before Keeree. "She's made a mess of the place."

"Come on." Phyr helped Keeree to her feet. "We need to get you out of here."

The color was starting to come back to her cheeks already.

"Can you walk?" he asked her.

"I'm fine. You don't have to help me." Keeree straightened up and shook off Phyr's hand.

Daraya noted the tenseness between them. Were these two going to be more than friends? The last thing she would have expected was for Phyr to have a soft spot for the farm-girl. They had almost nothing in common. Yet, the closeness they seemed to share excluded her. Not that she wanted any part of it, but being excluded hurt. "Are you two done?"

"Where will we go?" Phyr asked. "Your house?"

Just the thought of returning home set Daraya's stomach twisting. Home was not an option. "No. No going home for me."

"Then where?" Phyr asked.

"My house," Keeree said. "You can both stay with us as long as needed. We have room. Plenty to eat. Clean water. Warm fire."

"On the farm?" Daraya asked. "Do you think I want to smell like you?"

"Suit yourself," Keeree said, "But where will you stay? I recall you saying you could not go home. Do you really want to take your chances on the streets?"

"Fine. But I'm not sleeping with any animals."

"We don't sleep with the animals," Keeree said. "But if you don't start showing a little more gratitude, I may put you in with the hogs. They could teach you a thing or two."

"No thanks. I don't want to let that smell get on me. But as you say. I have nowhere else to go, now do I?"

Keeree turned to look her in the eye. "No. You don't."

18

FOSTER HOME

KEEREE

*K*eeree led her friends along the road to the home she shared with her father, mother, and her younger sister. It was small but comfortable. It kept the weather out and the warmth in, even on the coldest of winter nights. It had been built from the very trees felled to clear the space for the main building. Keeree's parents purchased the farm before she'd been born, and she'd known no other home.

The house might have been old, but the barn, that was another thing. The barn had been constructed in recent memory — within the last decade — and stood straight and tall. The beams that Garyll and his friends had hauled from the woods and hewn smooth, stood like soldiers at attention, and supported a roof of shake that rarely needed the attention that thatch did. The barn was where a dozen kine, half a dozen hogs, and a flock of hens lived.

She peered inside to check on the beasts. A water trough stood at one end of the row with a pump to bring the water straight from the ground. The trough was half full. No attention required. Hogs rooted in the earthen floor of their pen, seeking out every last bit of feed that had been thrown to them. They appeared happy. Garyll must have already completed his chores. Some days Keeree thought her father cared more about the kine and hogs than his own family, but she knew that wasn't fair. The kine fed the family — supplied them with milk and meat, and coin when they sold the milk or occasionally an aged milker.

Keeree rolled the barn door shut and turned to the house, satisfied that the animals were safe and fed. She drew a deep breath. "Home sweet home."

"There's nothing sweet about it," Daraya quipped.

"Hogs," Keeree said. "You'll be sleeping with the hogs if you keep that up."

"Sorry, but how can you stand the stench?"

"You get used to it," Keeree said. "In the morning, you won't even notice it, only the smell of biscuits and pork gravy." She inhaled deeply. Her mother had been cooking and from the aroma, the evening meal was not far off. "Evening meal is almost ready. Smells like roast boar and root vegetables. Plenty for everyone and even fresh bread if my nose is correct."

"I don't smell any bread," Daraya said.

"You will. And we make our own butter. Sweetest you ever tasted." Keeree had pulled open the gate leading to the courtyard. She stood back and held it, waiting for Daraya and Phyr to pass through, then fastened it behind them. No point in letting the animals escape just because she had company.

"Sama? I brought guests!" Keeree called out.

"Boy, girl or goat?" A voice came from within the house.

"One of each."

Sama appeared in the doorway, a towel over her shoulder. Ersa, Keeree's sister, five summers old and small for her age, clung to Sama's skirt.

"A girl *and* a goat?" Sama asked.

"A girl and a *boy*." Keeree gestured to her mother, then her friends. "Sama—Daraya and Phyr." She crouched down before Ersa and made the hand sign for friends. Ersa clung tightly to her mother.

Keeree stood. She made the sign for *friends* once more, and pointed to Phyr, then to Daraya.

Ersa waved her hand before her face, then extended it, palm forward, fingers spread.

"Yes, she's pretty," Keeree mouthed the words silently and nodded. She brushed her clothes straight.

"She's deaf?" Daraya asked.

"Fever when she was small. The healers say there's nothing they can do."

"What about magic?"

"Magic can't restore something that's gone," Keeree said. "She gets by. If you like, I can teach you a few signs."

"Maybe later."

Keeree got the impression that Ersa's inability to hear bothered Daraya more than she let on. It was a shame, and all the worse since the healers could do nothing about it, but she had grown accustomed to signing with her sister and barely gave it a second thought.

Sama guided the child to a chair and seated her. She turned to Phyr and said, "I trust you're hungry? The rule in my house is, if you're here when feeding time rolls around, you eat. Family, friend, stranger, or foe. Everyone eats."

"Thank you, ma'am," Phyr said.

"No need to thank me. The land provides. Everyone eats. Sit. Take a rest while I finish up." With that, Sama disappeared back into the kitchen.

"Come." Keeree motioned Daraya and Phyr to the table.

"This place is sort of small," Daraya muttered.

Keeree reached out and pinched Daraya's arm. "Hogs," she whispered. "Be nice."

"You have a lovely home, Sama," Daraya said loudly. "Very quaint."

"It's not much, but it's ours. Pull out a chair. Have a seat." Sama turned to Keeree. "Dear, you want to set the table?"

"With pleasure." Keeree wended her way to the cupboards and removed six plates.

Sama reached into her apron and drew out a match. She extended it toward the stove to light a fire beneath the kettle. For an instant, Keeree thought the match burst into flames without being struck. But that could not be. Sama had no magic.

Before she could pursue the thought further, Phyr stood and asked, "Are you sure you don't want any help?"

Keeree pulled Phyr back to his seat. "There's not much room to navigate. You sit. I'll take care of everything." She fished the wooden spoons from the drawer and deposited one beside each plate. "I carved some of these myself."

Phyr picked one up and examined it. "Nice work." He placed the spoon beside the plate and folded his hands.

Keeree noticed that his knuckles were white. She knew he was having a hard time with the loss of his home and worrying about his parents in the sanitarium. Best let Sama know. She had a way of comforting anyone who needed it. More than Keeree ever had. Sama mothered everyone. Kin or stranger.

"Sama," Keeree said. "Phyr's parents are both in the sanitarium. And his house collapsed. No one knows why, but it's a shamble. Can he stay with us for a while?" She didn't feel the need to ask if Daraya could stay. She'd work that into the conversation once Phyr's worries had been allayed.

"That's horrible," Sama said. "You must be worried to death." She wiped her hands on her skirt and placed one on Phyr's shoulder.

She began massaging slowly.

"You have kin looking after you?" Sama asked.

"No, ma'am," Phyr blurted. "I'm all alone."

"You're not alone. You're right here with us. And you're welcome to remain here or return as often as you need until your folks are back up to snuff, and even after they're fit. We can always feed one or two more."

Sama rubbed Phyr's back for several heartbeats longer, then slapped it lightly and said, "You understand?"

"Yes, ma'am." Phyr's voice was thick, his eyes welling with tears.

"I'm nobody's ma'am. Call me Sama, or just ma."

"Yes, ma," Phyr said.

"Good." Sama turned back to her cooking. "Keeree, why don't you take your friends out to wash up before we eat?"

"Yes, ma." Keeree said. Sama was a gentle and giving mother, but Keeree always felt like Sama was holding something back. On more than occasion, she'd overheard Sama and Garyll arguing. Usually about something Sama felt was important to teach Keeree that Garyll disagreed with. Whenever she asked Sama about it, she dismissed it and changed the subject, almost as if embarrassed by the whole thing.

Keeree turned to her sister and signed. *Be right back. Must wash.* Ersa nodded but did not reply. Ersa was not comfortable with strangers. *New friends,* Keeree signed, then led the way to the pump behind the house. She grabbed the handle and pumped. "Go ahead. It's cold, but clear."

"You want us to wash our hands in that?" Daraya asked.

"Of course, what else?"

"You're not going to warm it first?"

"You afraid of a little cold water? Your city hands can't take it?" Keeree asked. "Or maybe you don't get dirty in the first place."

"I get dirty," Daraya said. "But I just washed at the sanitarium."

"And you're going to wash again. You come back inside without wet hands and Sama will not be so kind." Keeree nodded to the gushing water as she worked the pump. "In you go."

Daraya placed her hands into the water and rubbed for a few heartbeats. She withdrew them, shaking the water off.

"Phyr?" Keeree asked.

"Oh, yes. I supposed I need to wash too." Phyr stuck his own hands into the water and scrubbed.

When he was done, Keeree glanced over at Daraya. "Mind pumping for me?"

Daraya threw her a look and grasped the handle. She yanked hard on it, and it seized.

"Slow and steady," Keeree said.

"Like this?" Daraya slowly stroked the handle up and down and was rewarded with a steady gush of water.

Keeree washed her own hands and shook them dry. "Food should be ready by now."

"Why is your mother so generous?" Phyr asked.

"Generous?" Was Phyr not used to common courtesy? What sort of household did he come from where guests were not welcomed with open arms? Keeree had never even imagined *not* feeding a guest. It simply wasn't done. Everyone needed to eat, and the land provided.

"She doesn't even know us," Phyr said. "And she's treating us like the closest of kin."

"How else would she treat you?"

"But, we're strangers."

"I don't see how that matters."

"But food costs silvers, or at least coppers."

"No, it doesn't. It grows from the ground. Rain falls from the sky, the sun shines on everything. Crops grow, kine eat the crops, we eat the kine, and the crops. Nothing cost a copper. Just a bit of work."

"Doesn't your work have value?" Phyr asked.

Keeree shrugged. "If we didn't work the land, what else would we do?"

Phyr shrugged.

"Doesn't it rankle you to work like a serf?" Daraya asked.

"We're not serfs. My family owns this land. It's ours, and it not only feeds our family, but many more. Do you think we could drink all the milk these kine produce, or eat all the eggs the hens lay?"

"I don't suppose so," Daraya said.

"Without people like us," Keeree said, "people like you would starve."

Daraya nodded toward a figure rushing down the dusty road toward them. "Is that your da?"

Before Keeree could react, her father scooped her up in his arms, twirled her around and set her back on her feet. He examined her, letting his gaze travel from head to toe, then let out a sigh. "Thank the land," he said. "I thought you were dead, or worse."

"What's worse than dead?" Keeree asked.

"You'd be surprised," he said. "Didn't you feel it?"

"Feel what?" Keeree had a suspicion that Garyll already knew what they'd done. He was that sort of person. He noticed things others missed, but often kept his observations to himself.

"The ground shook," he said. "The sky rang with the sound of it. There was some pretty big magic going on this afternoon." He gestured toward the hills where the academy lie. He must have felt it, when they joined their hands, something had happened, but things had been so frantic that Keeree had little time to think about the implications of what they'd done.

Keeree glanced at Phyr who was looking at his shoes, then at Daraya. Neither seemed inclined to admit anything. "I didn't feel anything," Keeree lied.

Garyll shrugged, then examined each of Keeree's friends in turn. After a moment, he sucked air through his teeth and frowned. "I'm surprised you found one another so quickly. Not surprised you found one another. Surprised it happened so fast."

"What do you mean found one another?" Keeree asked.

"The three of you. You were destined to find each other," Garyll said. "Sooner or later." He jabbed a finger at Phyr. "Of course you're one. Knowing your mother. How could you be anything less?"

Phyr's gasped. "You know my mother?"

Garyll nodded. "When we were young, not much older than you." He turned to Daraya, leaned closer, and squinted. "*You*, I should have expected, but I didn't." He paused a moment. "Your father must be turning inside out over this."

Daraya went red.

Her mouth opened as if she were about to speak, but nothing came out.

"Garyll, what are you talking about?" Keeree asked.

"You three," Garyll said. "You're all focuses. And if my guess is right, you've already formed a triad."

19

TRIAD
KEEREE

Garyll settled into his chair at the head of the table, letting his gaze wander over the three young people seated around him. The day Sama had continually warned him about had finally come. Keeree's power had awakened, and she'd formed her triad, just as her mother predicted.

"There is something you should know," he finally said. "Something about your parents." He turned his gaze on Daraya. "All of your parents. And their magic."

"My father hates magic," Daraya interrupted.

"But that was not always the case. He was once a very promising student."

Daraya humphed.

"He was, but he was also careless and selfish, and he caused a lot of pain."

"Now, that I can believe." Daraya folded her arms across her chest. "He *does* enjoy causing pain."

"I could tell you what happened," Garyll said. "But it's better that you see for yourself. You've already formed your triad. This should be no problem for you."

The three of them looked at him as if he was daft.

"Join hands," he said.

He leaned in to Keeree and whispered in her ear. "You have the memories. All of them. It's just a matter of calling them up. The spell is simple. *Imponam super memorias.*"

Keeree intoned the words, "Imponam super memorias."

The world around her faded to be replaced by a waking dream. In the dream, she saw her parents and a strange girl as youngsters, not much older than she.

They stood on the hill that overlooked the farm where Keeree had grown up. It looked old and abandoned, not alive and productive as she knew it was. Yet, she saw it with fresh eyes.

She turned her gaze upon the folk standing at the foot of the gentle hill.

Her father and Sama were both familiar and strange to her eyes at the same time. They were so young. It was almost impossible to imagine that her own parents had once been the age she was now, but it was the third girl that caught her eye.

Endwa was slight and short, with dark brown hair that fell to her shoulders. She was startlingly beautiful, and from the way Garyll looked at her, he was completely smitten.

Keeree paused for a moment? She had always imagined Garyll and Sama being together since they were children. It had never crossed her mind that this might not have been the case, but here they were, and her father was definitely taken with this stranger.

Garyll grabbed Sama's hand and reached out to Endwa. "Take it!"

"No." Endwa tucked her hands in her armpits as if that could protect her from Garyll's touch. "Bannwor won't allow it."

"Bannwor may seal away our magic," Garyll said. "But Adrylt is going to kill us."

"Not me," Endwa said.

"You know what Adrylt wants. It's not you. It's your magic. He cares little for anyone. You know that. He is prepared to kill one of his own triad to make room for you. If you let him kill one of us and he re-forms his triad with you, Bannwor won't just seal away your magic — he'll execute you — all three of you. There's only one way." He shook his hand at her.

"How do you know the spell will work?" Endwa demanded.

"If Sama says it will work — it will work." Garyll glanced over at the shy young woman who was the talk of the wizarding world. He'd only met her the past summer, when she'd joined the academy. She was plain and quiet, and most of the students thought her somewhat of a mouse, but he saw beyond that.

For one so young, she had command of magic on a scale he'd never even imagined. In her first summer at the academy, she devised her own brand of magic based on a language she created. She called it her 'cypher language'. She had even devised a spell that translated the wizards' script into this new language, revealing the intricate details of any spell.

While doing this research she'd discovered the spell that she said would save them.

If fate smiled upon them.

So far it hadn't.

Adrylt had formed a triad with Kalswor and Issur. They escaped detection by the academy for two summers, growing constantly stronger, but when Endwa arrived, Adrylt had become smitten. All he could think of was possessing her. Even though Garyll and Sama had sworn never to use the wild magic, Adrylt considered them a threat, and had pursued them mercilessly.

As if to emphasize his thoughts, lightning crackled over his head. "There's no time to waste," Garyll hissed. "Take my hand."

"No," Endwa wailed.

"Endwa! Stop that." Sama's words held a force that Garyll found compelling, even though they were not meant for him.

Sama was already taking defensive action. She stood tall, heedless of the danger. She raised her hand into the air, grasped the lightning, and wrestled it back toward its source.

As she did, Garyll felt her draw power from the earth itself. This was a skill that normally was only available to a triad, but Sama had something others did not, an innate feel for all magic, not just the small magic or the wild magic, but sources Garyll had a hard time believing even existed.

Sama had explained that magic came in many forms, just as light, when split by a prism, contained an array of colors. Magic was everywhere, she said, and it came in an infinite variety. It was one of these unseen forms of magic that she wielded now. Her lips pressed into a tight, thin line, her eyes hard and dark. Her nostrils flared and her teeth were bared. It frightened him just a bit to see her this way. This was not the mousey young girl he knew.

Sama screamed, "Proin mihi molestus amplius." The lightning flared and rushed back toward Adrylt. It struck him with a mighty flash and the sound of thunder.

For a moment, silence descended, but Garyll knew that was not the end.

"See," Endwa said. "There's no reason to join our magic. Sama can handle it."

As if to put a lie to those words, great black clouds burst into being above them. The sun faded. Darkness descended. Thunder rolled. The earth shook.

This time it was Sama who spoke, admonishing Endwa. "Take our hands. We cannot let him succeed. Magic is for everyone. This must end now, and you know what that means. Someone is going to die today. There is no other way." She stretched out her hand and slapped the younger girl on the shoulder. "He's shifting the nexus. He means to steal the power for himself. He will kill us if we don't stop him. I know it's not what you hoped for yourself, but we have been forced into this. There truly is no other choice." She paused, drawing a deep breath before continuing. "I don't need your cooperation, no more than Adrylt does, but I'd prefer not to force this union."

"I'm frightened," Endwa said. "I don't want to die."

"There are few paths that end in anything other than our deaths. This is one of them." Sama wagged her fingers at Endwa. "Don't fight me."

Timidly, Endwa took first Sama's hand, then Garyll's.

As their fingers clenched, lightning flashed through Garyll's arms and flooded into his chest. It accumulated there, burning with flame as if it were about to sear through his flesh and bone and leave a gaping hole in his chest. It grew hard to breathe. As if the very air had abandoned him. Then the colors vanished, and the world took on a sepia tone.

This was not what Sama had told him to expect. What she'd described was a flood of power, colors, tastes, smells. This was not that. Everything was muted. Colors faded to monotone, the taste of the very air gone.

Then it hit him.

A sound, so loud it rattled the very earth, struck Garyll, a cacophony of immense proportions. The sound of a thousand wizards chanting in a chorus of half a hundred spells. The magic burst forth. Colors he'd never seen before, or even imagined, jetted around and through him. His eyes were blinded by the afterimage of the immense power.

He turned to Sama. "Why didn't we do this sooner?"

"This is the second worst outcome." Her words seethed with rage. "We do this because we're forced to. Because all other paths lead to our deaths."

"What now?" Endwa asked.

"We wait," Sama said.

Garyll took a breath to try and calm himself. Was there no other way? They had to stop Adrylt, but already he was more powerful than anyone else at the academy. Sama assured him that this was the only way. Form their own triad and wrest the power from Adrylt. Only then could they defeat him. All other paths led to their own deaths at his hand.

As Adrylt and his cohort crested the hill, Garyll's heart raced. The moment Sama had predicted had finally come. They were committed. No backing down.

Garyll stretched out his senses to discern what they were up against, but Adrylt had constructed a shield that blocked his probing.

"Can you tell what he's planning?" Garyll asked.

"He's performing a sending." Sama held up a hand to silence him.

"Custodire ab infra sursum." Sama's voice was barely discernible over the sound of rushing wind.

Sparks arose above the newly formed triad. Great shafts of brilliant vermillion burst forth to arc over and form a dome that enclosed them. As the shafts of vermillion solidified, a canopy of sparks flashed into being, as if a great umbrella of fire had been opened above them. The spell settled into place not a moment too soon.

The roiling black clouds overhead parted, and a great smoldering gryphon descended. A black shadow against the single shaft of sunlight, the gryphon burst into flames as it fell, growing brighter and brighter, as if the sunlight infused it with its energy.

The clouds closed, pinching off the sunlight, leaving only the light from the gryphon that plummeted steadily toward them.

The canopy Sama had constructed flickered as if in anticipation.

"Hold on. I'll need all your power for this," Sama shouted.

Garyll had no time to react. Power coursed through him, scorching the earth beneath his feet. It shot up his legs, merged, and continued upward, until it struck his chest. The magic twisted at his insides, threatening to sear its way out. For a moment, Garyll panicked, but the magic raced from his heart to his fingertips and leaped from his hands. Brilliant cobalt fire shot from him surrounding the shaft of light Sama had constructed. Half a heartbeat later, a crimson shaft of magic joined his, intertwining itself with those of the original vermilion Sama had cast. As they merged, the magic flared white.

The canopy overhead shone with the light of the sun as the flaming gryphon careened into it. Claws the size of Garyll's forearm ripped uselessly at the sparkling motes that wove a protective pattern above their heads.

The beast screeched out its rage as it tore ineffectively at the canopy, its beak striking repeatedly, each impact sending shivers up Garyll's arms.

The spell was weakening. If the gryphon broke through, they were finished. Its head was the size of Garyll's whole body. Massive and filled with fire, there would be no defense against it. How had Adrylt managed this spell? Garyll let his senses probe the gryphon. It was filled with the wild magic. Could Sama harness that magic for their use? She had said as much, but Garyll was skeptical. He glanced over at her.

She had her eyes shut. Her face was twisted in concentration.

Endwa, too, shut her eyes, but not in concentration. Tears pinched from between her eyelids to roll down her cheeks.

Garyll peered up to see the opposing triad approach. Adrylt, Kalswor and Issur, the three most powerful students at the academy. Power coursed around them as they drew it from the earth and fed it into the raging, impotent gryphon.

As they drew near, a flaming sword appeared in Adrylt's hand. The jewel in the headband he wore flashed as he drew power from it.

Rumor had it that he'd found a spell to summon Hostis Malleo. The foe hammer.

Adrylt flicked the sword from side to side, a trail of ochre sparks streaming behind it like an afterimage.

"Give her to me," he shouted. His words echoed off the distant hills as if amplified by the magic, and with his words, his visage twisted with anger. His eyes flared a brilliant red, the color that Garyll had come to associate with the wild magic.

Endwa's grip on Garyll's hand tightened. "Don't let him have me."

"He's not getting anyone." Sama stretched out her hand and the foe hammer shot from Adrylt's grasp.

"You didn't think it would be that easy, did you?" Adrylt took a step forward. He raised his arm, and the sword appeared once more.

"Garyll. It's time." Sama sounded tired, on the verge of collapse.

"Is there no other way?"

"I'm afraid not."

Garyll summoned his courage and stood. Sama had worked with him endlessly, committing the words of this spell to memory. It was a last resort, and one Garyll hated, but he saw no other course of action. Adrylt was prevailing. He'd made it clear he would reform his triad with Endwa, but he hadn't said which of his existing triad would have to die to make room for her. What was certain, was that he and Sama would have to die to release Endwa from the bond they had just created. There truly was no other choice. "Ave praepotentem heroes," he shouted.

At first, nothing happened, then a tingle erupted in Garyll's toes. It was as if he'd stepped into an anthill and was suffering the bites of untold tiny creatures.

His hair stood on end.

The wild magic rose up from beneath him. A single stream of molten magic, like lava from the fire mountains. It launched itself upwards, splitting into three separate streams. One stream leaped from Garyll, one from Sama, and one from Endwa. Three mighty snakes of fire writhed and wrapped themselves around one another as they rushed toward their prey.

Adrylt swung the sword and sliced the head from one of the snakes. As sword met apparition, Endwa screamed in agony and collapsed.

Adrylt hesitated.

The two remaining serpents struck. One pierced Kalswor through the heart.

He exploded in a shower of sparks and vanished.

The remaining serpent rushed for Issur.

She raised her arms to fend it off, but she was too slow. Fangs the length of her arm pierced her chest, but before the serpent had a chance to rip her heart from her, it burst into sparks that fell to the ground and vanished.

Issur clutched at her chest and tumbled to the ground.

The shield Sama held vanished with a pop, sparks flashing.

Garyll turned to Endwa. She had collapsed on the ground, a lightning scar extended from her fingertips to her face where it had burned her flesh away. She lay still, moaning in pain.

Adrylt, impotent without his triad, rushed to Endwa. He dropped to his knees and took her in his arms. "Endwa."

Her eyes fluttered open, then closed. "You arrogant fool."

Her breath caught in her throat.

"Endwa!" Adrylt shook her, but it was no use. She was gone.

Garyll groaned. This was all his fault. He'd urged Sama to find the spell. He'd convinced Endwa that they could keep her safe. He deserved to be dead, not Endwa.

Sama knelt beside Issur. She held her hand on the woman's heart. "Garyll, come here." Her voice wavered.

Garyll rushed to her side. Issur lay on the ground gasping for breath. Her face was ashen, as if she were already dead. The holes in her chest where the magical serpent had sunk its fangs in glowed with an angry red light.

"She's dying," Sama said.

Garyll wasn't eager to help her, but he never intended that anyone die. She was part of Adrylt's triad, after all, or had she been coerced into participating just as Endwa would have? He knew so little, but did anyone deserve to die? Not by his hand, they didn't. She deserved to live, if only to face the judgement of the academy.

He examined the burn on her flesh. "What can we do? I'm no healer."

"Go to Adrylt," Sama said. "Get his headband. I can keep her alive for a few moments, but my magic is failing. She needs power or she'll die."

Garyll was momentarily paralyzed with fear. Would Adrylt cooperate? Issur was part of Adrylt's triad, but what if he refused? Garyll was already guilty of the death of two students, he didn't need Issur's death on his hands. He would swallow his pride. The worst Adrylt could do was to say no.

He rushed to Adrylt, still kneeling beside the burned Endwa. "Your headband," he said. "Sama needs it to save Issur."

Adrylt turned his gaze on Garyll. "Why were you keeping her from me?"

"Issur lives still, but not for long. Do you want to lose her as well?"

"I've lost everything else. Why not her?"

"Because you're not a murderer."

"I am." He gestured to Endwa. "I killed her. I was foolish."

Garyll spoke softly. "You can still save Issur."

Adrylt reached up and lifted the headband from his forehead almost as an afterthought. The brilliant garnet flared, then fell dark. The fire in his eyes, his most prominent feature, fell dark with it. "Take it," he said. "I'll have nothing more to do with magic."

Garyll grabbed the headband from Adrylt and rushed to Sama. He handed it to her.

Sama slipped the headband onto Issur's forehead.

The fallen woman's eyes flared red as the magic infused her.

"Numerus aeternam." Sama waved her hand over Issur's heart and a brilliant yellow light flared.

Garyll could feel the spell take hold.

Perhaps they were not too late. He held his breath.

Issur gasped.

She drew a breath.

Color returned to her face.

"What happened?" she asked.

"Kalswor is dead, and so is Endwa."

Issur shook her head. "That fool, Adrylt. I told him to leave it alone." She reached up and touched the band Sama had placed on her forehead. "What is this?"

"A gift from Adrylt," Sama said. "I used it to cast a spell to keep your heart beating. I'm afraid, without it, you'll die."

20

WHISPERS

DARAYA

*A*fter the vision faded, No one spoke for the longest time. The table was cleared with formal efficiency and the evening fire set. Before long, it was time to settle in. Keeree escorted Daraya and Phyr to the barn, explaining that she would sleep with them as it would be impolite for her to enjoy the comfort of her bed while her friends slept in the hay. Daraya felt worried that they were going to sleep with the beasts, but, there was a loft above the animals.

The loft was accessible by means of a ladder that poked through a small opening. The upstairs was for hay storage. That much was clear. Keeree spread blankets on the hay and lay down to sleep. The hay gave off an odor that was slightly off. The dust tickled Daraya's nose threatening her with a sneeze that never came.

Despite the strange surroundings, she lay down on the blanket and soon enough found herself drifting off. She woke in the dark more than once, the hay beneath her scratchy. The blanket she had did little to protect her from the chill of the evening. Mercifully, the smell had diminished, and the animals had finally fallen silent. If only Keeree were silent. Snores erupted from the sleeping girl at irregular intervals. She sounded almost as bad as the hogs had before they finally fell silent. To make matters worse, Daraya was thirsty and felt the need to make water, but neither urge was strong enough to drive her from the hay and out into the yard. She could wait.

"Can't sleep?" Phyr's face was partially lit by a slice of moonlight that worked its way between the loose boards on the barn wall.

"You can?" she asked.

"I was sleeping, but all your moaning and jostling woke me. What's wrong?"

"Do you believe that vision?"

"It explains a lot."

"My father? A focus?"

"Stranger things have happened." Phyr brushed the hair from his eyes and sat up. The moonlight cut across his face as if he had a scar, but it was enough to see that he was also ill at ease. "I'd heard bits and pieces of the story. My parents said Garyll and Sama broke some rule, that Keeree is an abomination. That she should never have been allowed to be born."

Daraya cast a quick glance at the sleeping Keeree and whispered. "Can it be possible? That she has the memories of her mother and father within her? That she could be the most powerful wizard of our time? She sure doesn't look all that powerful."

Phyr watched Keeree for a moment before speaking, perhaps reassuring himself the girl was asleep. When he spoke, his voice was soft, so soft Daraya had to lean in to hear him. "I'm afraid. Truly afraid. For the first time in my life."

"What could they do to you? Your magic is already sealed away."

"I wish Garyll was more forthcoming about what that meant. I asked him when we were alone, but he said it was better that he not influence my decisions. Said I would know what to do when the time came."

"You say you're afraid. Think of what it's like for me. I was going to be accepted. I was going to move into the academy, get away from my family, but look at me. I'm sleeping in a barn."

"It's only for a while."

"Not for me, it's not. I can't go home."

"I'm sure you can. Your family will miss you. They must be worried about you right now."

"You have no idea what it's like. You with your fancy home built on the lines of power. You with your gray robes announcing to the world that you harken from a family of powerful wizards. You who are untouchable. You who are rich. You who have a family that loves and supports you. Remember, I spoke to your mother. I know her. She was genuinely worried for you."

"And your family won't worry about you?"

Daraya spat, "My father will celebrate the day I left."

"You can't say that."

Daraya moved into the moonlight and turned her back to Phyr. She lifted her shirt, exposing the scars. "Do you have these? These are the welts from the switch my father used on me."

Daraya wasn't sure why she felt comfortable exposing her shame to Phyr, but she did. He had seen into her heart. What harm could come from seeing her scars? Would it put him off? Would that be a bad thing? Let him shy away from her. She wasn't certain she wanted anyone this close. Revealing this to him felt like putting an end to the pain and suffering Adrylt had dealt her. A burden shared was a burden lightened, unless the wizardling couldn't accept her the way she was. She needed to know.

She reached out and grasped Phyr's hand, drawing it toward her back where the worst of the scars lay. "Feel them."

His fingers touched her flesh, tentatively at first, but then with more confidence. The light pressure of his fingertip lingered on the largest scar, tracing the path of it from her shoulder blade to her rib. Gooseflesh rose on her arms at his touch. She remembered that scar. It was from the first time Adrylt had caught her using magic. She'd been so proud of herself. So excited that the magic had finally come awake in her. She could hardly contain herself. She'd brought a tiny flame to life and extinguished it. Over and over again the flame appeared in her hand, only to be snuffed out by her will. Her life had changed that day. She had magic. She would be a wizard. She would be a healer. She would be respected. But Adrylt hadn't seen it that way. He yelled that she was a devil and had brought shame on his house. He took her by the arm and hauled her into the kitchen. He grabbed the leather strap he used to hone his knives, beating her with it until she thought she was going to die. Each stroke cut her flesh with a pain that could not have been worse had he taken a red-hot poker to her. When he finished, he shoved her back on her bed and locked the door.

"Daraya. I never knew." Phyr's words were barely more than a whisper. "We won't let him touch you again."

Phyr's hand still rested on her back, gently touching her exposed flesh. Why did his touch bring tears to her eyes? He couldn't truly care about what happened to her. Could he?

A tear rolled down her cheek.

Was this the way things were to be for her?

The only ones who cared for her were strangers.

She sobbed, letting the pain flow out of her. It was as if her anguish were seeping from her flesh, beads of bitterness oozing from her pores to be wiped away by Phyr's gentle hand. It hurt her deeply, but somehow it was what she needed. To get it all out. All the pain. The fear. The uncertainty. The loss.

Suddenly it was all too much. She began to move away.

Phyr pulled her back and held her tight against him.

"Let it out," he whispered. "Let the bad out of you. Don't hold it in. It's poison."

His words broke the dam that held back her emotions. It was as if a mighty river had been held back behind the dam of her worries and was now flowing with raging force. The power of the rushing water swept away everything in its path. The debris of her life was being washed out to sea by a raging torrent.

At first, she held on to it, as if afraid to lose any of the hurt she'd endured, but, the hurt was only harming her. It *was* poison. It would kill her. Let Adrylt and his switch go. Let his hateful words go. Each horrid memory was swept away by the current of her emotion, carried away by the great heaving sobs until she was completely drained.

Emptied.

Physically.

Emotionally.

Until her throat hurt from crying.

Finally, the torrent subsided. The violent waters had carved a new channel. One with a new family. A family that she herself had chosen. One that had chosen her. They were here. Reassuring her. Caring for her. Supporting her. Loving her.

Her breathing returned to normal.

She would be all right. Somehow, she would get her magic back. She would be a wizard. She knew she would.

She dried the tears from her eyes, for the first time realizing that Keeree had awakened and now sat beside her. Their legs pressed against each other. Keeree's arm wrapped around her shoulder.

Daraya felt shame. Shame for letting her darkness out on her new friends. Shame for exposing them to the hurt that was her life. She shook off Keeree's arm, then reached back and gently removed Phyr's hand from her back where it rested. She guided it to rest on his own leg, patted it gently and said, "Hands to yourself wizard boy."

21

CHORES

PHYR

*P*hyr found himself lying on a blanket in the hay. Light filtering in through the gaps in the wall of the barn signaled the sunrise. Golden motes of dust floated through thin blades of deep orange light. He glanced over at the empty blanket. Keeree was already gone. Working hard, no doubt, but Daraya lay fast asleep.

Had that really happened last night, or had he just imagined it?

What was it like for Daraya to have a family that despised her because of something she had no control over? He couldn't imagine it, but now that he'd seen the pain she carried, he knew why she pushed everyone away. He wouldn't let her push *him* away.

Her eyes opened. "What are you looking at, wizard boy?"

Phyr grinned. After all that happened during the night, Daraya was still herself. "Just checking to see if you were still alive."

"I am." She grabbed the blanket and turned her back to him. "I want to sleep some more."

"I think we should help with the animals." It was only fair that they repay the hospitality they'd been shown, and a little manual labor never hurt anyone.

"Those stinking beasts?"

"It's only fair that we try to repay the kindness we've been shown. At least in some measure."

"Can I make water first?"

Phyr laughed. "I suppose that would be wise."

Daraya cast off the blanket and headed down the ladder. "Good, because I really have to go."

As Daraya descended, Keeree passed her scampering up. She made her way into the hay even before Daraya reached the ground.

"Glad to see you're finally awake," Keeree said.

"Rough night, wasn't it?"

"Much needed, I think." She nodded toward the privy, where no doubt Daraya was pursuing her morning ritual.

"To be honest, I wasn't much liking her," he said.

"Porcupines have the sweetest meat if you can get past the quills," Keeree said. "Looks to me like you got past the quills last night."

"I could have used the sleep."

"Sleep is for city folk. Here on the farm, you get up before the sun or you waste precious daylight. You know how to use a fork? Not the kind you eat with, but the kind you work with."

"I'm sure I can figure it out."

"Good. That hay over there needs to go in the trough for the kine. Just shake it a bit with the fork before you dump it into the trough to fluff it up. They like that." Keeree raised her chin toward a pile of hay at the far end of the barn. "And be quick about it. Take too long and they'll all bunch up and complain, and you don't want to have to listen to that."

Phyr clambered down the ladder, fetched the fork, and jabbed it into the pile of hay. He lifted a bit and carried it to the trough. Much of the hay fell off the fork and scattered about the walkway, but some ended up in the trough. The kine headed straight for it, huge heads poking through the stanchions, long tongues licking the hay into their mouths. One particularly insistent beast jostled and shoved the others out of her way, then proceeded to finish off all the hay Phyr had deposited.

"Hurry up, wizard boy," Keeree said.

Phyr noticed a smirk on her face. Was she making light of his efforts or mocking him using the name Daraya called him? He would show her. He stabbed the fork deep into the pile and lifted. It was heavy. He wrestled the overloaded fork to the trough and shook it. Hay fluffed off the fork to land in the trough as he worked it along.

Kine rushed to stick their heads through the stanchions and began feeding.

"Now you're getting it," Keeree said. "Keep that up and you'll grow some muscle on those skinny arms of yours."

"I like my arms just the way they are." Phyr worked at the hay pile until he had it all spread along the stanchions. The kine munched noisily. The jostling and bellowing fell silent as each of them found a place to eat. Phyr returned the fork to its resting place and sat heavily on a bench that flanked the door. The sun was up now, the first rays of day streaming in. The physical work was grueling, not what he was used to, but the accomplishments of the morning gave him a touch of pride.

"Where's Daraya?" he asked.

"In there." Keeree nodded toward an interior wall. "Collecting eggs."

"Willingly?" Phyr asked.

"I offered her the choice of collecting eggs or feeding the hogs. She chose the fowl."

"It was a fowl choice," Phyr said. "That will lead to fowler deeds."

Keeree glanced at the door without smiling. "I better go check up on her."

"Do you think she'll ever get her magic back?" Phyr called as she disappeared into the fowl room.

Before Keeree could answer, Garyll entered through the large rolling door. He wore ragged garments that had been patched so often the original fabric was hard to spot, yet they were clean and well cared for. He bore a serious look on his face that made Phyr nervous.

Garyll took a seat on the bench beside Phyr.

Phyr wanted to ask what the man had on his mind, but decided it would be better to wait. Whatever it was, Garyll would either reveal it, or not. Phyr's questions would do little to elicit information from him.

After a few breaths, Garyll fixed Phyr with a stare. "If Sama is correct," he said, "and she usually is, there may be a way, if you can all survive this."

"What do you mean?" Phyr asked.

"Why do you think we live here? Not on the land, but here?" Garyll asked. "It's because this is an anti-node. There is no magic here. None. Keeree possesses no magic of her own. No reserves. Not a lick. Without her own magic, the spell used on you and Daraya can't work on her. That's why you're in such danger."

Phyr turned to gaze at the man. Losing his magic had cost Garyll everything. Phyr tried to imagine his own mother or father in the same situation. They probably would have ended their own lives if they lost their magic. Yet Garyll had not. He had moved his family to the land and taken up the life of a mundane. And he seemed happy. Truly happy. Was that what the future held? Would he have to accept the loss of his magic? Could he?

But Garyll was saying there was a chance. It gave him hope. "I wondered about that," Phyr asked. "But what does that mean?"

Garyll glanced around. "I wanted to have a talk with you. Man to man. You understand? While Keeree is occupied."

"Not sure that I do, sir."

"Don't go all formal on me," Garyll said. "I need to ask you to do something for me. A favor — a favor I have no right to ask — but I'm going to ask, anyway."

"What sort of favor?" Phyr felt nervous. What sort of thing would this man ask of him? Why the preface? Man to man. Phyr was no man. He was barely more than a boy. He should be just beginning his studies and learning what it was like to be a man in the wizarding community. But, instead, he was here, hauling hay for the beasts just as if he had no magic and never would.

"You are in a unique position to help me out."

"What do you need me to do?" he asked.

"Watch over Keeree," Garyll said. "She's an impulsive young girl. She's naïve. That's my fault, but it was the only way I could think of to keep her safe. I feared this day would come, but I thought if I kept her here on the land, she might not come to the attention of those who would seek to do her harm. And so far it's worked. The two of you were discovered and dealt with. Ruthlessly dealt with if you ask me, but so far, she remains unharmed. The only thing that has kept her safe is their ignorance. They can't think of a way to stop her, so they bide their time. But it won't last forever. Soon they'll act, and when they do. I need you to be there for Keeree. Only with the three of you working together can you prevail."

Garyll shifted as if preparing to stand.

Phyr shrugged. "I'm not sure I understand."

"They can't seal away her magic because of the way she is. But if she spends too much time away from here, she'll accumulate her own magic, and then they'll be able to harm her." Garyll's shoulders slumped. His eyes went dull. "Help me keep her safe," he whispered.

"I don't know why you think I can do anything to keep her here. You may have noticed she has a mind of her own and a will to match."

"I know, but when the time comes, explain it to her, but not until it does."

22

SWEET MEAT PIES
KEEREE

Keeree glanced around at the buildings on the outskirts of town. The thatched roofs still dripped with the evening's rain, the scent of ozone strong in the air. It was chilly, but not so chilly as to warrant a coat. The racket of a town alive surrounded her in all directions, indistinct conversation overlaid with the sound of uncounted folk toiling to make their daily bread. It was unnerving to her. Was it never quiet?

She reached into her pocket and touched the silver coins she squirreled away for just such an occasion. She insisted that she be allowed to repay the kindness of her friends with a meal in town. Garyll had been stubborn, but finally relented. Chores more than filled every waking moment, especially when the days were long this time of the season. To be excused from work, even for a day, was a privilege she had not often requested. So why was he so resistant?

When the three of them reached the outskirts of town, Phyr pulled the talisman from his pocket. "Are you sure you don't want to wear this? It may keep you safe."

"Safe from what? We're not going back to your house, are we?" Keeree asked.

"No. I have another place in mind."

Despite her initial enthusiasm, Keeree was growing anxious about treating. She was unfamiliar with the eating establishments in town and feared she might embarrass herself. Where would they go? Did she have enough silver to pay for the three of them? What if she didn't? What did people like Phyr and Daraya eat, anyway?

She decided to bide her time, bite her lip, and see what transpired. Let Phyr take the lead. He seemed to know his way around. Maybe things would work out for the best. But after they passed up several likely looking places to eat, Keeree started to wonder if she'd made the right choice. "Where shall we eat?" she asked.

"What do you like?" Phyr bore a sly smile that told her he truly *did* have a destination in mind.

"Anything I don't have to cook myself," she said.

"Sweet meat pies?"

"Sweet meat pies sound good."

"The place I'm thinking of makes the best sweet meat pies. It's not far from here. I've been there twice and both times the fare was excellent."

The expression on Phyr's face told Keeree he was interested in more than just a meal. She'd play along to see what had him so excited. "How could I pass that up?"

"Here," Phyr said when they reached a small cafe on a side street.

The place was not the grand eating establishment Keeree feared, but rather modest. It was adorned with tapestries and carvings that caught her eye. The most predominant one was of a snake encircling a globe and devouring its own tail, as if that were even remotely possible. Something was engraved beneath it in the wizards' tongue. "What does that say?" Keeree jutted her chin at the carving.

"The worldwyrm devours itself," Phyr said almost absentmindedly, glancing toward the kitchen.

The odor of wood smoke permeated the place, overlaid with the unmistakable aroma of roast pork and baking bread. The floor had a hint of stickiness that most ale drinking establishments tended to acquire not long after opening. From the kitchen, the clinking of pots told Keeree someone was hard at work preparing for a rush of patrons that no doubt was just about to arrive. "Looks like we beat the rush," she said.

"Good. That means we'll receive excellent service." Phyr guided them to an inside table where he took a seat facing the kitchen. It was an odd choice from what Keeree could see. There were plenty of seats farther from the kitchen where the constant rush of the server would not interfere with their meal. Keeree decided once again to see what Phyr had in mind, but as she scanned the seats, she grew nervous. Something said danger. Something was not right. She chose a seat where she could watch the entrance. The thought of sitting with her back to the street set the hairs on her neck standing. She couldn't say what was bothering her, just that it made her feel safer to be able to see the door.

Despite her revelation of the night before, Daraya had resumed her combative manner. Was she ashamed? Angry? When Daraya noticed Keeree peering at the door, she asked in a rather sarcastic tone, "Expecting company?"

"I'm just nervous," Keeree explained.

"Not me. No one's trying to hurt me. Not anymore," she quipped.

"It's not that. I just don't like all that noise going on behind me. Makes me jumpy."

"Doesn't bother me," Daraya said.

Daraya nodded at Phyr, who was straining to catch a glimpse of something going on in the kitchen. "What's he so interested in?"

Keeree turned to get a better look. Whenever the kitchen door opened, steam poured out obscuring much of what lay inside, but occasionally, she managed to catch a clear view. A pair of stoves were attended by two women. One was dressed in white, the other dressed much as anyone on the street, save that she wore an apron that came to her knees. It was the woman in the apron who eventually came to take their orders.

Phyr looked disappointed.

"Well, if it isn't my old friend," the serving girl said as she approached the table. "Back again so soon? You must really love our sweet meat pies."

Phyr blushed. "I brought friends."

The girl cast a lingering glance at Keeree and Daraya. Her gaze settled for a moment on each of them, as if taking in all that they were. Keeree felt the weight of that gaze, judging her, deciding if Keeree was fit to eat at her table. She'd seen it before.

The woman folded her arms across her chest and pursed her lips. "I see my efforts to seduce you with free food have been for naught."

Phyr's face turned an even brighter red, if that were possible. He turned his gaze down and stammered, "They're just friends."

"And do just friends like sweet meat pies?" the woman asked. "By the way, my name's Omosa, since Phyr neglected to introduce me."

She glanced at Keeree. "How about you, dearie? A sweet meat pie?"

Keeree laughed. "He speaks so highly of them. How could I resist?"

Omosa addressed Daraya. "And you?"

"If I must. But, do you have anything less filling? I'm still feeling my morning meal."

"Sticky buns. Or cross buns?"

"Cross buns," Daraya said. "No meat for me."

"Watered ale all around?"

"Fine," Phyr and Daraya spoke in unison.

"Be right back." Omosa turned and disappeared into the kitchen where Keeree caught sight of the young woman standing by the stove. Had she been watching the whole thing?

Phyr's gaze remained firmly fixed on the kitchen doors. Could he be captivated by the woman at the stove?

"You're smitten," she told Phyr.

"Pardon me?"

"Smitten," Daraya chimed in. "You're smitten. Besotted with that woman."

"Am not," Phyr's face would have caught on fire if it were any hotter. His hands moved nervously around the table as if in search of a safe place to land.

"You — are — so — smitten," Daraya said in a singsong voice, emphasizing each word.

"Am not," Phyr repeated.

Keeree glanced around the cafe. An elderly couple pushed back their chairs and departed in a rush, leaving behind half of their meal. A young mother, who had just been seated, cradled her infant in her arms and stood, making her way out the back door.

Something about their actions set Keeree's nerves on end.

She turned to the door to see two people enter the cafe and head straight for their table. She was grateful she'd chosen the spot she had. The two heading their way could be nothing but trouble. They were *the* students that Keeree would rather have avoided — Socha and a young woman, Skeli. Skeli was one of those who had accompanied Socha when he spied on Keeree's efforts to raise fire. Whatever their purpose, the determined expression on Socha's face said they were not seeking a pleasant midday meal.

Socha approached the table and glared at each of them in turn. His gaze settled on Keeree. "Would you look at that? Three damp-wicks all at one table."

"Go stuff yourself, Socha." Keeree was in no mood for it.

"Damp wicks don't belong in our cafe," he said. "Go find your own place. Somewhere you won't spoil my appetite with your ugly face."

Keeree leaned forward to push back her chair, but Daraya's hand on her arm stopped her.

Garyll's oft admonishment to pause and consider the possible consequences of her actions loomed before her as if her father were standing there speaking. It was a lesson Keeree struggled with, but one that Daraya seemed to have mastered. Probably better not to make a scene in public, anyway. It gave her pause to think that Daraya was the reasonable one. Did she see something Keeree did not?

Keeree settled back in her chair, drew a breath, counted to ten, and *then* spoke. "This is a public cafe. We're free to eat here if we wish."

Keeree glanced around the cafe. The patrons had paused in their meals and were staring at the two of them. Probably wondering if an altercation was about to begin, and assessing their avenue of escape should one break out.

Not today. Keeree prided herself on her restraint. She reached out to pat Daraya's hand to reassure her that she had her anger in check, but Daraya's hand was no longer on her arm. Instead, the girl was scooting over beside Phyr, leaving Keeree sitting all alone. Was she trying to distance herself in case Keeree lost her temper—or getting a better seat to view the impending fight? Why move now? And why was she leaning in to Phyr like that? Was something going on between them?

A chair toppled as a young man dressed in the robes of a student wizard rushed past the pair menacing Keeree. Was he afraid, or gone to summon someone in authority?

No matter. Socha knew better than to threaten her with magic, and she felt confident that she could take him in a fight. Perhaps it was time to teach Socha some manners.

Keeree pushed her chair back and stood.

As she came to her feet, a hand clamped onto the back of her neck and another seized her arm.

Keeree twisted to see who was behind her, but she was held fast. What was happening? Had Socha simply been distracting her to give the girl an opportunity to sneak up behind her? How could she have been so foolish? She knew she was in danger just as Phyr and Daraya had been, but it never occurred to her that she would be attacked in a place like this.

She twisted again, to no avail.

A woman's voice began whispering in her ear. "Inde tollere atmet."

Keeree's insides knotted. It was as if someone had torn her chest open and reached inside. Was this what it felt like to have your magic sealed inside you? Was this how Daraya had felt?

"Keeree!" Daraya shouted.

She had her hand in Phyr's pocket.

"Catch!" Daraya drew out the talisman they'd retrieved from the ruins of Phyr's house and tossed it to her.

Keeree reached to catch it, relieved that Daraya had been better prepared to meet the danger than she, but as her fingers closed around the ribbon, the talisman slipped through them and landed on the floor.

Keeree dove for the floor, letting her knees buckle beneath her. That should have broken the grip of anyone trying to hold on to her, unless Skeli was a lot stronger than Keeree.

The hand closed tighter on Keeree's neck, holding her up.

Keeree glanced at the kitchen door. Now would be a good time for the server to appear, but maybe the woman was no more interested in interfering in whatever was going on than the patrons had been.

Keeree tried to twist out of Skeli's grip but failed. No one had a grip like that, not even her father.

Was she using magic? In public? That was forbidden. Had Skeli gone rogue, or had the academy decided that Keeree was so dangerous as to warrant a public show of power? No matter the reason, she was in danger. She reached for the talisman, twisting to gain the extra digit she needed to reach it. She stretched for it, dragging Skeli down along with her. Almost there. But the pain was growing worse. She wasn't sure how much more she could stand. Stretch. Reach. Her fingers brushed the talisman. Only half a digit more.

"No, you don't." A foot kicked the talisman from her outstretched fingers.

Socha's foot.

"Swine snot," Keeree muttered. Things were getting bad. The pain was intense. Her vision was receding, closing in on her. Soon she would be blind. There had to be a way to get free. What did she know of fighting? Roll. That was it. Roll and her attacker would be tossed to the ground. If she was lucky. Roll. Keeree bucked and rolled to her side.

It only made the pain worse, but Skeli lost ground. The hand gripping Keeree's neck loosened a bit, and the pain diminished. Her thoughts came back to her. All she needed to do was get her hands on the talisman and stop the magic, but where was it?

Keeree wished she knew magic.

If she did, maybe she could summon the talisman. If only she knew a spell. If only she could call up one of her visions on demand, but alas, they only came when she was not expecting them. So many *if only's* passed through her head. None of them did the least bit to help her.

She was lost.

She'd failed.

As the darkness closed in, she heard a new voice speak. "Not in my place, you don't."

The pressure on her neck relented.

The pain diminished.

Her vision returned.

Keeree sat for a moment while she regained her senses.

She rolled, shoved the dead weight off her back, and sat up.

Beside her, Skeli writhed in pain.

Hunched over her was the younger woman Keeree had seen in the kitchen. Her whites were stained from the various dishes she'd no doubt been preparing before coming to Keeree's rescue. Now that she was close by, Keeree noticed that she had a stain on one cheek as if she'd spilled wine on her face, only it wasn't a stain. It was her flesh. Discolored. A birthmark.

The girl had her hand on Phyr's talisman.

It was draped around Skeli's neck.

She glanced at Keeree. "When I say 'now', you lower your head. This works better if the talisman is on you. But all I could think of was to put it on her, to stop her magic. When I take it off, her magic will be free again. You won't have much time."

She looked Keeree in the eye. "This is probably going to hurt a bit."

Keeree glanced up. Socha stood, facing down Daraya, who waved a knife in his face. Phyr stood beside her with an expression of horror that told Keeree he had never been in a fight in his life. The older serving girl stood in the kitchen door holding a butcher knife with a scowl.

"Are you ready?" the girl with the wine stain asked.

Keeree nodded.

As the ribbon came free of Skeli's head, pain returned worse than before. Keeree's guts twisted. Her head throbbed. Someone shoved needles up her eyes and into her brain. Her bowels erupted in fire. Everything hurt. Through the fog of pain, she felt the ribbon slip into her outstretched fingers. A firm but gentle hand guided it toward her head.

She let the ribbon drape around her neck.

The talisman settled against her flesh.

No more pain.

No more pressure.

No more throbbing.

No more twisting of her guts.

And no more colors.

The world had gone lifeless, everything painted with brushes of sepia and grey.

"Come on. We have to get out of here." Phyr's voice intruded on Keeree's new solitude.

She stood, letting him take her hand and lead her from the cafe. But where was he taking her? Where could they be safe?

23

FORBIDDEN

PHYR

Phyr led Keeree from the café. Glancing back over his shoulder. A wave of guilt washed over him. He'd been the one to recommend the cafe. He'd been the one to choose the table. He'd put Keeree in danger, and it had almost cost her her magic. Garyll asked him to watch over her, and he'd failed miserably on their very first outing. He felt responsible. He had to find a place where she could be safe, if only for a while.

Who was behind this?

He felt the pressure of Keeree's arm around his shoulder as he helped her along. She had worn the talisman before. It had dampened out the magic of his house even though it made her uneasy. This time it seemed to have a greater effect. Was that because she was absorbing magic from her surroundings and now the talisman had more to work on? "I'm truly sorry," he said. "I thought you would be safe. At least for a while. I'm such a fool."

"It's not your fault," Keeree answered.

She was unsteady on her feet and seemed to have difficulty seeing what was in the street just ahead.

Phyr wrapped her arm in his and gently guided her along. He wasn't turning out to be a very good friend. He was a wizard, or should be, but he'd frozen when magic erupted, and a mundane had stepped in where he had not. There was more to Cheshi than he'd first thought. How was it that a mundane, a damp wick was unafraid of magic? He wished there was time to find out, but they were not out of danger. They needed to find a safe place to regroup.

"Where are we going?" Keeree asked.

"To my home, or what's left of it." It was the first thing he could think of. Even though it was in shambles.

"That's the first place they'll look," Daraya interrupted. "We can't go there."

"I don't know where else to go," Phyr said. "Do you? A place they can't follow us? I'm all ears."

"I think I do," Daraya said.

"And where would that be?" Phyr asked.

"Where I met your mother. You recall how you took us to that place with all the doors and I got separated from you?"

"That's not how I recall it." She hadn't become separated from them. She'd bolted off on her own, but she did have a point. If they could enter the place where his mother's spirit resided, he could see her, get her advice. It was worth the risk, wasn't it?

"Do you think you can guide us there?" Daraya asked.

Phyr glanced at Keeree. It was her magic that they had drawn on to take them into the void the first time. With the talisman in place, her magic was sealed no less than if she'd fallen under Skeli's spell. What could she do?

"Who's going to provide the magic?" Phyr asked.

"She is. Take the talisman off. Just long enough to enter the void. Then put it back on."

"And she becomes vulnerable to whatever they have in mind." Phyr wasn't about to take that sort of chance with Keeree. She was the only one of them who had access to her powers. If she lost them, the three of them would be powerless. And Garyll had asked him to watch out for her. He wasn't taking any more chances.

Phyr blinked. He had just entertained a thought so strange that he simply *had* to stop and examine it. Was that how things were now?

The three of them? Together? He would never have chosen to associate with the likes of these two, but it seemed they were somehow meant to be friends, or at least their fates were tied together. What affected the two girls also affected him. He saw that now. Accepted it.

"We can't risk Keeree. She needs to keep the talisman on. There's no knowing if that witch needs to be in contact with her to work the spell."

"I think she does," Daraya said. "Why else do you think she snuck up behind Keeree in the cafe?"

Phyr shrugged.

"Think it through, wizard boy. I'll wait." Daraya folded her arms across her chest and tapped her foot. When Phyr didn't answer immediately, she raised an eyebrow at him. "Well?"

"Just a moment. I'm thinking." Phyr said. Was he willing to risk it? Was it a risk? How would he feel if it was his fault that Keeree lost her magic? "No. It's too much of a risk."

"Phyr, we can't stay here." Daraya nodded at Keeree. "She can't stay here. Look at her. That talisman may be protecting her, but it's not doing her any good. She can barely see. She can't live like this. We have to get her somewhere safe."

"I'm willing to give it a try," Keeree whispered.

"Are you sure?" Phyr asked.

"No other choice," Keeree whispered.

"All right. I want to remove the talisman. Get ready." Phyr gestured to Daraya to take Keeree's left arm as he wrapped the girl's right arm over his shoulder.

"Ready," Daraya said.

"Ready," Keeree whispered.

"Now."

He lifted the talisman from around her neck.

Her magic coursed through Phyr like molten lava. For a moment, he thought how strange it was, but he pushed the thought aside. No time for that. He grasped her magic and called up the void. He visualized the straight hallway, the expansive marble floor, the rows of doors uncounted — each one identical to the next — stretching out forever, or at least as far as the eye could see. He let his vision expand to take in Keeree and Daraya, visualized the three of them standing there, safe and secure.

His guts twisted.

Keeree's magic encompassed him like his mother's warm embrace.

With a slight wrenching, Phyr was in the void. And so were Keeree and Daraya.

"That was horrid. Is that what's it's like for the two of you?" Keeree asked.

"Is what like?" Phyr asked.

"To have your magic sealed away?" Keeree asked. "It was awful. All the colors were gone. Everything smelled bland. Even the air tasted weak, as if it had lost its ability to sustain me."

"Not me," Daraya said. "I don't feel anything different, I just can't do magic any longer."

"What about you, wizard boy?" Daraya asked.

"I don't know. I don't feel any different. I was never that good with magic. I'd just started to call up fire. When my mother was training me, she used the talisman to dampen the surrounding magic. The same thing happened to me then. The colors were gone, the air seemed somehow thinner. It was very unsettling."

"And you were completely unable to do magic then?" Daraya asked.

"No, that's the strange thing. I *was* able to do magic. I reached for the magic in the ground beneath the house and found a source of power I had no idea existed. I drew from it and was able to light a candle." Phyr explained. "A little too much power, as it turns out. I lit the candle but melted the whole thing in an instant. It shook my mother so bad, she left without comment."

Keeree said, "You were able to draw magic from the earth while your mother had your magic shielded?"

"Quiet," Daraya interrupted. "They're here! The two from the cafe. That witch and her accomplice. I felt them arrive."

"How did they get here? How did they know where we were? Is no place safe?" Phyr moaned. Just when he thought they'd escaped, they were once again being pursued. "So where's the door?" he asked. They had to get Keeree out of there and find his mother. How had Daraya found the door? Luck? He had no choice but to rely on her.

"Daraya," he said. "You're in charge. Find us that door."

Daraya headed down the hallway, her stride long and confident. "This way. I think."

It was all Phyr could do to keep up, pulling Keeree behind him.

"Be ready to put the talisman back on her if they catch us," Phyr said.

"In here?" Keeree asked. "Won't that trap us here? Or will it send us someplace we don't wish to go?"

"I don't know, but we can't let them seal your magic," Daraya said. "We need it."

"Glad you need me," Keeree said.

"It's not like that," Daraya said. "We need your magic, at least until we can restore our own."

Phyr turned to see Daraya standing in the middle of the hall facing a door, or what used to be a door. It was no more than a blackened lintel and posts. The door was gone.

"This was the one. I'm certain of it," she said.

"What happened?" Phyr felt his knees go weak. His mother! Had someone attacked her? What if she had been in that place when the door was burned? Had she been injured? Killed? Was she even now lying dead at the sanitarium?

"The sanitarium," Phyr said. "How did you find it?"

"Your mother showed me the way," Daraya said.

"Take us there," Phyr said.

"Not from here. She showed me the way from that place. I don't know how to get there from here."

Before Phyr could react, a chill came over him.

He glanced back down the hallway.

Socha and Skeli stood side by side, blocking their retreat. Skeli moved her hands in an intricate pattern, and fog poured out of them.

The frigid air drifted to the floor and settled up around his knees. It filled the hallway with an eerie light that crept slowly toward Phyr and his friends.

When the fog touched Phyr's waist, it set off a deep-seated fear in him that he didn't even know existed. He let out a scream. He was drowning, gasping for air as his water-laden clothes dragged him beneath the surface of an icy winter lake. He'd crept out onto the ice, following an errant ball that he'd been kicking around. The ice looked solid. It felt solid.

It hadn't been.

Just as he reached the ball, the ice beneath his feet made an awful cracking sound that echoed off the naked trees. He tried to run, but he wasn't fast enough. One huge crack chased him down and swallowed him whole. The icy water sucked him under in half a heartbeat.

The fog was like that. Icy. Threatening. Cloying. He gasped for air but was unable to breathe. He stretched a hand up, just barely able to reach the air above the cracked ice.

"Please. Someone. Help!"

His hand sank beneath the water.

He kicked his legs until his hand touched the ice.

Ice.

He was trapped beneath the ice.

He was dead.

No one was coming to help him.

Just when he thought he'd breathed his last, icy fingers closed around his and pulled.

He glanced up to see the lintel of a doorway just as blackness took him.

24

PUZZLE

DARAYA

*D*araya pulled Phyr through the doorway even though he still screamed and thrashed as drowning. The fog had choked her, but not so much that she feared for her life.

She rolled Phyr onto his back and put an ear to his mouth. He was breathing, but sounded labored, as if he had swallowed water.

"Phyr." She pushed on his chest with all her might.

He spat water and coughed.

Slowly, the color came back to his face.

"You scared me half to death," she said. "What happened?"

"I was drowning. Fell through the ice." He panted as if struggling to get his breath.

"Well, you're safe now." Had the magic affected him more than her? Was it because he carried a memory of a similar event and she did not? She wondered. Was that the way magic worked? She had never stopped to think about it, but whatever it was, Phyr was safe. There was no danger here.

She glanced at him to reassure him, but he had not calmed down.

His eyes were wide.

He pulled her close. "Stay down so it doesn't see you."

"What?" Daraya turned to see what had caught his eye. They had emerged beside the caretaker's cottage. Sitting beside the structure was the gryphon that had menaced them on their last visit. Its head was bowed as if examining something on the ground before it. "What's he doing?" she asked. "Why is Theored here? Is Charyl around?"

She searched the area, but there was no sign of the wizard. Only his gryphon, who studied the engraved tiles as if attempting to solve the puzzle they represented. She got the impression it was waiting for them to do something. The fire that had been so active the last time she'd seen the gryphon were still, barely shedding any sparks as the great lion's body rested comfortably on its paws. What did it expect them to do? Solve the puzzle? She stood up, ready to duck back down. The gryphon raised its head and looked at her, then returned its gaze to the tiles. "I think he wants our help," she said.

"He's guarding something," Phyr said. "That's the only reason Charyl would have left him here."

"What would he be guarding in an abandoned cottage?" Daraya asked.

"I don't think it was all that abandoned. Why do you think they sent Socha after you? Wasn't it *here* that he attacked you, sealed your magic?"

"Yes." Daraya admitted. Just the memory of what he had done to her set her back itching.

"So maybe there is something about this place," Phyr said. "Something they don't want people like us finding."

"There's something on the floor," she said. "He's looking at it like he's trying to figure it out. The last time I was here, I noticed it. The tiles are all marked with gold engraving."

Daraya scooted over to get a closer look. The fiery head of the gryphon was fixated on the tiles. The eagle's eyes strained, sparks of fire falling to the floor to die out as soon as they contacted it.

"The tiles bear marks of some sort," Daraya carefully made her way to the floor where the gryphon sat. As she approached, he raised his head, eyes the size of dinner plates lifting to focus on her. He seemed puzzled. He glanced back at the tiles on the floor, then at Daraya, then sat back, as if making room for her to approach.

"I've never seen characters like this before," she said.

Phyr crawled beside her.

She glanced up at Theored the gryphon. Charyl's familiar would not have gone far from the wizard. Did that mean he was here? Waiting for them, perhaps. Surely the wizard would not let his familiar injure anyone, least of all a prospective student.

Theored pointed to the tile with his beak and made a motion as if he wished her to move one.

She slid one over.

The tile moved easily into the vacant spot.

"They're meant to be moved," Daraya said. "But, moved to form what?"

"What do you think?" Daraya glanced at Keeree, who seemed intent on ignoring the whole matter.

"I can't read the wizard's script. My father was dead-set against it. Said it would interfere with my education."

"Well, these aren't the wizards' script," Daraya explained.

Keeree peered at the tiles. "That's cyphering."

"These? They're meaningless." Daraya jabbed a finger at the strange symbols.

"They're cypher symbols," Keeree replied.

"Cypher? Like something used to do numbers?" Phyr chimed in.

"No. Cypher," Keeree said. "Those are sound symbols. Each one represents a sound. You cypher them in order and they tell you what to say." Keeree pointed to the square. "This one means *oh*, when you see this one you say *oh*." She pointed to another one. "This one makes the sound *sm*. So when you put them in order like this." She scratched in the dirt. "See. Now they say smoke."

"*Sss*." Keeree pointed to the first figure. "*Mmmm*." She pointed to the second scratching. "*Oh*." The third. "*K*." The final one. "Smoke," she repeated.

"How bizarre," Daraya blurted.

"They're meant to tell you how to say a word." Keeree recalled one particular vision where she'd scribbled down a host of symbols, searching for precisely the ones she wished to convey each sound. She had finally settled on symbols that represented the shape her mouth made when she uttered each sound. Only it was not her in the vision. It had been Sama. Her mother had invented the cypher language. Why then was it here on the threshold of the academy?

"That makes a lot of sense," Phyr was saying. "You wouldn't have to memorize the words. I can see how this might be useful."

"You planning to teach magic sometime soon?" Daraya asked.

"You know how hard first summer students have to work to stay in the Academy." Phyr jabbed a finger at the symbols. "But this would be easier. If you can show how a spell is said, you can learn any spell in moments, not days or moons. This would really help new students."

"Calm down, wizard boy. If it's that simple, why doesn't the academy use it now? Do you think they're *trying* to make it hard to learn magic?"

"Maybe," Phyr said, sounding reasonable.

"Well," Daraya said, "We can argue about that later. What do you think he wants us to do?"

Keeree elbowed Daraya out of the way, casting a wary eye at the gryphon. "Those symbols can form a word if you arrange them properly."

"The tiles slide." Daraya grasped one of the tiles and moved it. It made space for another tile to move.

The gryphon screeched and placed a massive paw over the tiles. It shook its head.

"I don't think he wants us to move them," Phyr said.

"He doesn't want us to just shove them around," Daraya corrected. "They need to say something, to mean something."

"Here. Let me try," Keeree said. "This one. It's *S*." She slid it over. "This one is *M*." She slid that one over, but the tiles didn't line up. She shifted them again. "This isn't working."

The gryphon began to glow brighter and shift around as if it were agitated. It was as if the coals that made up its body had been subjected to a strong breeze. Fire flared within it, throwing off a heat that Daraya could barely stand. She backed away and took a deep breath. "I think it's angry because we're not getting it. The tiles have to *mean* something."

"Keeree. Where do you want this one?" Phyr asked.

"This one." She touched the *S*. "Here. This one." She touched the *M*. "Here."

"Slide this one over here, then this one, then here." As Phyr slid the tiles around, Keeree saw his strategy for arranging them, how he moved one tile to what appeared to be the wrong spot just to make room for another one that he needed to move. It was complex, and she was not certain she could have done it herself. He had a knack for the puzzle it appeared. With his last move, the tiles lined up as Keeree indicated marking out the word. "*Smoke*," she said.

The gryphon roared, throwing back its head. It released a stream of fire that stretched half a dozen spans into the still air. It stepped back, revealing another set of squares.

These symbols were different.

She looked over at Keeree expectantly.

"That one goes here." Keeree pointed to one of the tiles. "That one there and the other one over here." The first cypher took the form of an inverted Y with a hatch across it, the second one a square with sharp edges. Keeree pointed to each tile as she indicated which was which. Phyr deftly shifted them and quickly had them in the order she specified. As he slid the last one in place, the gryphon once more screeched and took a step back.

"What do they say this time?" Daraya asked.

"Earth," Keeree replied.

The next set of symbols went much quicker.

The last one even faster.

When all the tiles were in place, the gryphon let out a mighty screech. Its breath reeked of brimstone. It turned its head sideways, as if waiting for them to say something.

Some password? Daraya wondered.

"Smoke, fire, air, earth," Keeree interrupted Daraya's thought. "It's not magic. It's a password."

Daraya shook her head. Had Keeree read her mind, or was it that obvious?

"Here. Take my hand," Keeree said. "Stand here." She positioned them before the gryphon. "Read the words." Keeree pointed to the symbols they had arranged.

Phyr haltingly read each word, pronouncing the sound discretely, as if struggling to recall what Keeree had taught him.

"Now, you say it." Keeree squeezed Daraya's hand. "You can do it."

Daraya stared at the strange symbols, wishing she'd paid more attention when Keeree had explained what each one meant. "S-eM-Oh-ka." she struggled to get the sounds to come out right. "Ef-eye-air. Eye-air-tha."

"You're doing great." Keeree's optimism seemed unfounded.

This was not as simple as she made it out to be.

When Daraya completed the last sound, the gryphon let out a roar and stepped back once more. It stretched out a flaming paw, hooked one fiery claw into the vacant space where the tiles had rested, and lifted.

The whole floor rose free, shedding dust as it tilted back on hidden hinges to reveal a set of stairs descending into the darkness.

"What's that?" Daraya asked. "A secret passage? I wish I had known about that the last time I was here. Should we enter?"

"I think that's what Theored wants," Phyr said.

"Do you think it's safe?" Keeree asked.

Daraya peered down the darkened stairs. "As safe as any place. Maybe Socha doesn't know about this place. Do you think the students can read Keeree's cypher language?"

"Let's hope not." Phyr took Daraya's hand. "Come on. Let's go."

"If we only had some light," Daraya said.

"I can take care of that." Keeree stretched out her hand and said. "Incendio igneous."

Nothing happened.

"Something wrong, farm girl?" Daraya asked. Keeree's magical abilities seemed spotty. When they truly needed them, they were mysteriously absent. Focus or not, Keeree was not one to be depended upon.

Keeree reached into her pocket and drew a match. She scraped it along the stone and tossed it into a small trough of oil that flanked the stairway. The oil burst into flames, illuminating wide marble steps that descended into the bowels of the earth.

Daraya took one tentative step and glanced back at the gryphon.

It nodded.

As soon as they had descended far enough, the mighty beast slammed the floor down above them, sealing them in with a resounding thud.

25

CHAMBER

KEEREE

The dust settled around Keeree as the great door slammed overhead with an echoing thud. She glanced down the stairs. Daraya and Phyr were already racing far ahead. By the time she reached the final step, she was breathing hard. It was a long way down.

She lifted her gaze to take in her surroundings. She was standing at the foot of the great stairs, her bare feet, resting on cold marble tile that stretched out for an acre if it was a digit. How had someone created such a huge structure so far beneath the ground? It had to be magical.

Pillars reached from the glistening marble floor to the ceiling high overhead. Each pillar was topped with a set of arches that spanned the space between it and its neighbors. The arches bore intricate gilt engravings that threw back the flickering flames that lit the room. To Keeree's eyes, those arches were small and insubstantial, but she had the distinct impression that they were massive and distant.

"Wow," Keeree let the words escape her lips without even trying to contain them.

"Wow is right, but look at this. Can you see anything here?" Phyr was pointing to a small grouping of pillars that rose from the floor not far from where he stood. The pillars were spaced half a dozen spans from each other. They formed an octagon that supported a dome of pure gold. Graven around the perimeter of the dome were characters that Keeree could not read, but somehow seemed familiar. She touched one of the pillars wondering what such a structure was for. She'd seen similar things in gardens to shelter the occupants from the afternoon rain, but deep under the earth, such a thing would surely not be needed. "What are you expecting to see?" she asked.

"Magic?" Phyr asked. "This is a concentrator. It's used to focus the lines of magical flux. It tempers the natural magic. Cools it. The dome reflects the magic back down to a buried collection of crystals that store it until it's needed. It looks like it was used until recently. Now it's dead. As if the magic is only recently gone."

"How do you know so much about this, wizard boy? You've never been here before, have you?" Daraya asked.

"No," Phyr said. "We had one of these in our house."

"You had a magical collector in your house?" Daraya placed a hand on the dome. "This is made of pure gold. It must be worth a fortune." She said as if in thought. "Several fortunes."

"It wasn't ours." Phyr sounded defensive. "It belonged to the academy. My mother used it to aid in her studies."

Keeree touched the dome as Daraya had. She felt nothing, simply cold metal. "Well, whatever it is, it doesn't seem to be working."

"Come on. Let's explore," Phyr said.

"Aren't you worried about being followed?" Keeree tried not to fret. But what if Skeli and Socha found their way down here? She'd barely escaped them last time, and only by luck. She couldn't count on luck to hold.

"You worry too much," Phyr said. "We found this place by accident. Do you suppose they will, too?"

Keeree glanced back at the giant stairway. They had moved deeper into the room by dozens of spans, yet the stairs were clearly visible, lit from above by the troughs of burning oil. She wondered, if the place were deserted, who replenished the oil? That gave her pause. Perhaps this place was not as deserted as she had at first thought. "We should keep an eye out for anyone," she said.

"You worry too much," Phyr said.

"Maybe you worry too little," Keeree said.

"*You* can stand there all day," Phyr said. "*I* want to explore. Who knows what we'll discover down here." He rushed off without another word.

Daraya told Keeree, "It will be fine."

Her reassurance did little to calm Keeree's fears. The knot in her stomach was just as tight, her breath just as shallow, her knees just as weak as they had been only moments before. "I hope you're right." She took a deep breath and tried to shake off the feeling. "What do you expect to find here?"

"Not sure," Daraya said, "but with something so grand, this place must be full of secrets. I wonder why they abandoned it?"

"You think it's abandoned?" Keeree asked.

Daraya said, "See the dust on everything? The students at the academy dust and clean everything as part of their duties. This place hasn't been touched in ages."

"And yet the floor is clean," Keeree remarked.

"Strange, isn't it? I wonder why that is," Daraya quipped.

They reached a hallway that branched to the left. It was nowhere near as spacious as the grand hall, but still comfortably wide. Half a score of students could walk abreast down this hallway. The thought of the myriad of feet treading this very hall gave Keeree pause. What had happened? Why was this place no longer used? Was there danger here that they had yet to discern? For a moment, she panicked. Was this place like Phyr's house or the sanitarium? Was it going to affect her just as those places had?

Along the hallway were tables. Heavy carved wood, the legs of each one bore carvings of mythical creatures intertwined with one another as they wound their way around the stout wood. A dozen chairs flanked each table, five on a side and one on each end. They were as intricately carved as the table, upholstered in rich red velvet.

They stood in perfect lines. Most of the tables bore stands where students could prop their tomes. Beside each was an array of inkwells, cut glass and crystal, no two alike. Beside some of the inkwells, were quill pens and even a fountain pen. Keeree had heard of those, but she'd never seen one. Had the students been in such a rush that one of them abandoned it? And why have so many inkwells? Was it to allow the students to copy spells? Make notes? Keeree had no idea what the students did in the great library, no more than she knew what went on in the academy.

She drew a deep breath worried that the magic going to affect her as it had before. Would she be embarrassingly ill? She took a breath and searched herself. No queasiness. No turning of her stomach. Perhaps she was safe.

Phyr called from down the hall. "Over here. I found the library."

"Come on." Daraya yanked Keeree's arm, dragging her along until they reached a large set of double doors that stood open.

"We should be able to find something here that might help my mother. There must be healing spells here. Maybe even some the healers don't know about."

Above them were symbols in the wizard's script. "What does it say?" Keeree had learned a few symbols before Garyll stopped Sama from teaching her, but not these. Not that she recalled many. She had been very young.

"It says *library*," Phyr explained.

Keeree asked, "Why are there so many symbols? I thought each one was for a single thought or idea."

"Well," Phyr said, "if you read them as written, they say *'room for many books filled with great wisdom'* — or maybe *knowledge*? I'm not sure of that last one."

"But you said it was a *library*," Keeree corrected.

"It is."

"Then why doesn't it say 'library'?"

"There's probably no single character for library. It's like that. There are characters for most things, but not everything, or maybe there are and hardly anyone knows them all. I know a lot, but I'm not yet considered literate."

"That seems strange to me." Keeree wasn't so excited about the wizards' script. How was one to master spells written in such a strange manner? No wonder the academy had a reputation for grinding its first summer students into dust with work. Learning even a handful of those characters must be a chore. For the first time Keeree felt relieved she had not been chosen for the academy, or else at this very moment, no doubt, she would have been studying these obscure characters in the hopes of one day being able to read as well as someone like Phyr.

"That's just the way it is," Daraya said.

"Quiet," Keeree said. "I thought I heard something."

"It's just the gate." Phyr stood beside a hallway closed off by a locked gate made of gold and silver. Behind the gate, a floor-to-ceiling bookshelf stretched into the shadows. On the shelf were books, each one facing inward with a chain attached to the cover. The chains were threaded over a rod to lock each book in place.

The tomes varied in size from small notebooks to massive affairs that would certainly take more than one person to carry them. They were spaced apart on the shelves. Heavy chains bound each book to the shelf upon which it sat. From what Keeree could see of the books, many bore intricate locks that would prevent anyone without the key from opening them. Why? Did they contain knowledge that was dangerous?

She yanked on the gate.

"It's locked," Phyr said. "Do you think I didn't already try that?"

"Just checking," Keeree said. " Maybe it's only stuck. Throw your weight into it." Phyr's face fell, and she immediately regretted her words. "I didn't mean to offend."

"You didn't," Phyr said. But it was clear he was lying.

"I think I can climb over it," Keeree offered. "There's a gap at the top."

"You won't fit," Daraya said.

Bickering was going to get them nowhere. Best change the

subject. "You come across any ideas in those books you already read?" Keeree asked.

"None that we could use," Phyr said. "They all require magic and I don't have any magic."

"How *did* you lose your magic?" She asked. "We know what happened to Daraya, but not to you. Did someone attack you?"

"No." Phyr blushed. "It's not like that."

Whatever happened, he seemed ashamed to admit.

"You're not helping." Daraya was kneeling beside the gate. She had something in her hand and was wriggling it in the lock.

"What are you doing?" Keeree asked.

"Unlocking the gate."

"With what?"

Daraya held out her hand. In her palm was a short piece of wire that had been bent into a strange shape. "How do you think I keep my hair in place like this?" She reached up and flipped a lock of hair from her face. It fell right back in place.

"I thought it just sort of did that on its own."

"I wish," Daraya said. "I use the pins to keep it in place. They come in handy for things like this."

"So you know how to open a lock without a key?" Keeree asked.

"Doesn't everyone?"

"Not me," Keeree said.

"Me neither," Phyr added.

"Someday I'll teach you both. It's apparent your education has been neglected. Now let me work." Daraya went back to poking at the lock.

Keeree watched fascinated for a while, then grew bored when it appeared as if Daraya was getting nowhere.

She glanced down the stretch of books, pondering the immense body of knowledge that lay before her. But for all the good it did, it might as well have been on the moon. Without being able to read the wizards' script, the books were no more than fancy firewood to her. Why had her father forbidden her to learn the wizards' script? He had been chosen for the academy but expelled. Certainly, he understood her desire to be selected. To excel at the academy and redeem the family name. He must have been well-versed in the wizards' script. Then why had he been against her learning it? To deny her magic? For a fleeting instant, she saw her hand reach out and slide down the side of one of the books lying open on the table before her. The wizards' script shifted and the cypher language replaced it. Was that what Sama had discovered? Was it something that she herself might do? She couldn't wait to try. But what if it didn't work? What if what she had witnessed was not a dream but a fancy?

"Why so glum?" Phyr asked.

"Because I may never be able to read these. The wizards' script is hard to learn and Garyll insisted that I not even try. No wonder they didn't select me for the academy."

"You're not a failure," Phyr reassured her. "And, you'll learn. It's not that hard." He paused. "Well, it is hard, but you're smart."

"I don't think so. I don't have a head for images. Numbers, animals, plants, and crops, those I can remember, but scribbles on a page? It was a struggle for me to learn the cypher language. How will I ever learn the thousands of characters I need to be able to read these spell books?"

"Not thousands, tens of thousands," Phyr said with a red face.

Before Keeree could come up with a suitable response, a screech sounded from the gate where Daraya knelt.

"I think she got it open," Phyr said.

"I'd never have believed it." Daraya pushed the gate open and waved them through. Keeree followed Phyr. He stopped at one shelf and pulled out a thick tome. The chain that secured the book to the shelf clanked loudly, echoing off the distant walls. He opened the book and peered inside. It was written in the wizards' script, just as she'd feared.

"This is useless," Phyr said. He slammed the book shut and shoved it back on the shelf.

"What is the book about?" Keeree asked.

"These are agricultural texts. How to plant. What to plant. When to plant. How to cultivate. Not a word about healing."

"Try another." Keeree picked one and pulled it free. She opened it to a random page and peered at it. She stroked the edge of the page just as she had seen in her vision. The characters swam before her eyes. The wizards' script became indistinct and blurry, as if it had been brushed over while still wet. Soon the characters were gone, replaced by neat lines of cypher script descending the page in parallel rows.

"How did you do that?" Phyr asked.

"I just picked it up and ran my hand down the page."

"There must be more to it than that. The writing changed. How did you do that?"

"I saw a vision of myself doing it and I tried it. I ran my hand down the page and it changed. Now I can read it."

"What does it say."

"You won't like this one. This one is all about animal husbandry. How to breed hogs to get a heartier drift."

Daraya came out from the stacks carrying a small tome. It had a gold-gilt edge and deep-maroon leather binding. On the spine was a narrow row of cypher scripts bearing the same words emblazoned on the cover. It also bore a thick leather strip that held the book shut with a stout-looking lock that would be no match for Daraya's hair pins.

"What does this say?" she asked. "I think this is the N sound." She pointed to the first character. "Is that right?"

"Yes," Keeree replied almost absently.

"Well, what does it say?" Phyr asked. "What is the book about, that it bears such an intimidating lock?"

Keeree traced the symbols, pronouncing each one aloud as her fingers ran over the gold-engraved markings.

"It says 'Nexus'."

26

SEALED

PHYR

*P*hyr watched with interest as Daraya shove her hairpin into the lock and twisted it one way and another. The chill of the great library was starting to take its toll on him. He wished he'd thought to bring warmer clothes. The place was musty and had the distinctive odor of a place that, once busy with people going about their business, had fallen into disuse. Hunger had crept into his awareness and he wondered if they would find food, or would soon have to abandon this place and seek out their next meal.

Lost in thought, he was caught off guard when a great flash of blue-green light erupted from the lock Daraya was attacking. A loud crack split the air, echoed off the distant walls, and reverberated for half a hand of heartbeats before falling silent.

He shook his head. He was sitting on the cold tile floor. He didn't remember sitting down. Had he been thrown down by the blast? What blast? Had the lock been enchanted to punish anyone who successfully defeated it? He shook his head to clear it.

His body ached as if he'd worked too hard the day before, but nothing appeared to be broken. His eyesight had gone all fuzzy for a bit, but soon began to recover. He could even make out that Daraya sat beside him on the dusty floor, her hair sprouting all manner of debris.

Did he look that bad? He ran his hand through his hair. Bits of dust and grit fell to his shoulders and bounced off to land on the surrounding floor. He coughed to clear his throat. That had been some show. What was in that book that it was so well guarded, and how had Daraya managed to open it?

He picked the book up from the floor and read the page that it had fallen open to. It was a spell for turning wood into iron. Not something to help with their immediate needs then. He thought the book was supposed to be about the nexus?

"What's in the book?" Keeree asked.

"This one is about transmutation," Phyr answered. "I was hoping to find more about the nexus. Or more about a triad and what they can do."

"We could really use a spell for healing." Keeree shot a glance at Daraya.

Daraya sat on the floor, slowly rotating her hand to take in both sides. Her flesh was covered in blisters, each tiny bump filled with gently glowing light. Was this from the book-defending magic? Had the protection spell done that? No matter what it was, it looked painful. Daraya had a haunted expression in her eyes. Her face was twisted in pain, but she uttered not a sound. Was that part of the spell that had been cast over her? It made Phyr cringe to look at her.

"Let's see what we have here." He flipped through the pages, searching for some organization to the book. It appeared to be a haphazard collection of spells, with no rhyme or reason to them. Spells for transmutation followed incantations to make weeds grow in an enemy's garden. How was he going to find a healing spell in this mess? And where were the spells about the nexus?

"That one," Keeree pointed at a page as Phyr flipped through them.

"This one? It's for draining a swamp." He squinted at the page. He wasn't certain about some of the characters. It might be a swamp or maybe low-lying fields. That was the problem with the wizards' tongue. You couldn't learn to pronounce a spell or form the words for it, even if you knew the character that described it. No wonder the academy was so sought-after. There was no chance anyone would learn to master spells like this without a lot of help.

"Let me see that," Keeree knelt beside Phyr. She stretched her hand out and gently glided it along the left-hand side of the page. A line of cyphers appeared, glowing with a soft green light. In a few heartbeats, they vanished.

Phyr copied her movements.

Nothing.

"Do it again," he said.

Keeree swiped her hand along the edge. Once more the cyphers appeared, then slowly faded.

"What did it say?" Phyr asked.

"I don't know, but I get a strong feeling it might be a healing spell. Not that the words mean anything to me. I just get that feeling." She jutted her chin at Daraya. "She may not be crying out, but she's in pain."

"Do you think we should try this spell on her?" Phyr wasn't certain it would work, but what was the worst thing that could happen? If it was a spell intended to be used to drain a swamp or a field, what effect would it have on Daraya?

"Daraya. Come over here," Keeree said.

Daraya sat still, gazing at her hand as if she had not heard Keeree call her name. She clearly was in pain. She should have been crying out.

"I don't think it's just her hands," Phyr said.

"Me neither. Let's try the spell. What's the worst that could happen?"

Keeree took the book and held it open on her lap. She passed her hand along the edge of the book, and the cyphers sprang to life.

Keeree spoke the word in a voice barely more than a whisper, "Vos zinc aquagym."

A violet light rose from the book and snaked its way to Daraya, spreading out to form smoke-like fingers that caressed her flesh.

Daraya let out a scream.

"Stop!" Phyr shouted. "You're hurting her."

Keeree slammed the book shut.

The violet light faded.

Daraya continued screaming.

"What happened?" Keeree asked.

"I think the spell only worked partway," Phyr said. "Whatever made those blisters must have also prevented her from crying out. I think maybe you broke that part of the spell, but not the rest. Try again. Try something else."

Keeree opened the book.

From what Phyr could see, it was the same page. But this time when she brushed her hand over the spell, the cyphers were different.

Keeree spoke aloud this time. "Vos hinc papulae."

Again, the violet light rose from the book. Glowing fingers stroked Daraya's hands. But this time, as the smoke passed over her flesh. The blisters diminished, if only slightly.

Daraya's screams stopped, but she continued to sob, sometimes pausing to gasp for breath.

"I think it's working," Phyr said. "Try again. Try harder."

"Vos hinc papulae!" Keeree shouted the words this time.

The violet smoke tendrils thickened, becoming more and more substantial. The ghostly fingers brushed at the blisters on Daraya's hands. This time, where the finger passed over her flesh, the blisters vanished, leaving only light-red rings to remind one that only moments before her skin had been tortured.

"It's working," Phyr said.

As if to dispute Phyr's words, the smoke began to diminish, and the blisters returned.

"More," he said. "Keep trying."

"Vos hinc papulae," Keeree said. "Vos hinc papulae."

Phyr felt a strange tingling come over him. Keeree was doing something different this time. It was as if his eyes had clouded over. She appeared to be indistinct, almost as if a cloud of violet fog surrounded her, but everything else was sharp and in focus. A whistle rose from her, gentle at first, but rising in pitch and intensity until it hurt his ears.

He leaned in to get a closer look.

The hairs on his arms rose.

"What's going on?" he asked.

Keeree ignored him. "Vos hinc papulae," she repeated. "Iam hinc abire papulae."

At her words, the floor thumped once, twice, three times, as if something deep beneath the earth had shifted. Dust rose from the shelves, filling the air like tendrils of smoke, choking Phyr. He blinked to clear his eyes, but what he witnessed was not due to dust. Keeree was shrouded in the violet light that had come from the book, only this time it shrouded her, as if she had summoned it and wrapped herself in it like a cloak. Her hand was stretched out to Daraya: the violet light leapt from her fingers to touch the girl.

Daraya screamed once more, then fell silent.

The violet light vanished.

An eerie silence fell over the room. A ghost image of the light that had enfolded Keeree faded from Phyr's eyes as his ears struggled to take in the slight sounds of Daraya's labored breathing.

Daraya blinked. "What happened?"

"You were covered in blisters," Phyr said.

"Was I?"

"You were," Keeree said. "One moment you were trying to unlock the book, the next you were sitting there in the dust staring at your hand as if you'd never seen it before."

Daraya examined her hand. "Looks fine to me."

"It wasn't. Not until Keeree healed you." Phyr glanced over at Keeree once more. Gone was the violet glow that had surrounded her. Gone, the piercing sound of her magic. She looked much as she always had.

Funny how that thought came to him. She had just performed a powerful spell, yet nothing appeared different. Something about her should have changed, but it didn't.

"How did she heal me?" Daraya asked.

"With a spell from the book," Phyr explained. "She can translate them into that cypher language and then speak the words. It's amazing." Phyr was having a hard time containing his excitement. If the healing spell worked, maybe there was something to help restore his magic.

He rifled through the book. Growing trees overnight. Magic beanstalks. How to animate a centaur. How to reveal a hidden truth. Or was that hidden wealth? It was hard to tell. The characters were so much alike.

"What about this one?" He pointed it out to Daraya. "It's a spell of revelation. Perhaps we could use it to find something to help my parents."

"How will finding wealth help?" Daraya asked.

He pointed to the symbol. "I thought it was the truth."

Daraya touched a line in one of the characters with a fingernail. "This one means wealth. Truth is more like this." She scratched a line at an angle to the one she had indicated.

"Keep looking," Keeree said. "There must be something here to help. Otherwise, why have a library?"

Phyr flipped through the pages once more. Eradicating fungus, creating fungus, finding water, creating a well, sweetening a sour well. No revelation of truth.

"Wait." Daraya placed her hand on his as he prepared to turn the page. "This one is for revealing secrets."

"Are you sure?" Phyr squinted at the page. The characters were unfamiliar. He'd learned a lot, but not these. How did Daraya know these when she came from a family that despised magic?

"That's the one," Daraya said. "Farm girl, can you do your magic with this spell and tell us what the words are?"

Keeree threw Daraya a glance that told Phyr she was less than enthused about the moniker. But she held her peace and waved her hand over the book. The glowing cypher characters appeared once more, only this time there were two rows. One set was similar to those Phyr had seen before, but not the second one. They had the look of hands making gestures instead, tiny lines forming fingers and palms held in a specific shape.

"What are those?" he asked.

"Those aren't sounds," Keeree said. "They're hand gestures. Like the ones I use with my sister."

"So this is for those who can't hear?"

"I think the hand movements are to supplement the words. I think they help form the spell, shape the magic."

"Real wizards don't use hand gestures, or speak spells," Daraya interjected.

Phyr threw her a look that he hoped would encourage her to keep silent on the matter. What they needed now was Keeree's help, not a lecture on proper wizardry.

"Can you understand them?" Phyr asked Keeree.

"You don't have to understand them. I think you say the words *and* make the hand motions."

"Go ahead," Phyr said. "Try."

Keeree turned to Daraya, but the girl held up her hands. "Not me, farm girl. Do him first."

"Afraid to reveal your secrets?" Phyr asked.

Daraya turned red and Phyr felt his face go hot. Maybe she *did* have secrets she wanted to keep hidden.

"Do me," he said. "I have nothing to hide."

"Stop me if you feel at all uncomfortable," Keeree said.

"I will. Go ahead." Phyr drew a breath and let it out slowly. He closed his eyes as Keeree began intoning the words described on the page. He opened his eyes a slit to see the girl creating complicated hand gestures in the air as she spoke.

"Ostende rimatur, vera vestigate." Her hands inscribed a complex path in the air, leaving behind a faint vermillion glow. It faded almost as soon as it appeared.

"It's not working," she said.

"Keep trying." Phyr urged. She was making progress. Why was she so unsure of herself? Was it because she'd grown up without magic?

Keeree made the motions once more. She accompanied them with the same words.

Once more, the vermillion light appeared in the wake of her gestures.

This time it remained hanging in the air.

The glowing symbols floated toward Phyr and wrapped themselves around him. His stomach lurched. It felt as if he'd stepped outside of himself. He saw three people sitting on the dusty floor in the deserted library. One of them, a young man, was encircled in brilliant light. The young man rose and walked backward without moving. It was as if he were a projection of the image of Phyr moving back in time without moving in space.

As the figure backed away, Phyr got the impression of his house. The way it had been before the quake turned it to rubble. The specter of his body settled into his bed. It was the night before the examination. This was the night his magic had been sealed away from him. The night his mother had tested him and fled as if she was afraid to be around him.

At first, nothing seemed out of the ordinary, then someone appeared in his room. The intruder was tall and slender but their face was blurry, as if some magic prevented Keeree's spell from revealing who they were. The stranger passed a hand over Phyr's sleeping form as if searching for something. Nothing happened for several heartbeats, but eventually a faint glow rose up and enfolded the sleeping form.

Phyr's body rose from the bed. This was *the moment* his magic had been sealed away from him, and this was the person who had done it. If only he could see their face.

"I can't make out who it is," Phyr said. "Can you do something?"

"Can you strengthen the spell?" Daraya added. "Get a look at their face?"

Keeree ignored their words and kept mumbling.

Phyr watched as the image of himself was enveloped in glowing light. It wavered for a hand of heartbeats then vanished. His sleeping form sank to the bed. Darkness returned.

The figure crept from the room.

"Follow them," Phyr shouted.

The vision lurched and turned to follow the fleeing form. Phyr expected the person to leave the house, but they did not. What sort of person attacks someone in their own home and doesn't flee? He had a sinking feeling in the pit of his stomach. His father was in charge of pursuing and punishing those who violated the academy's rules. Was this his father? Was it Teil who had sealed away his magic? He could barely believe it, but it made sense. He would have words with his father if that was the case, but he had to be certain.

"Try harder, Keeree," he urged.

Keeree ignored him, increasing the urgency of her chanting.

The figure lowered itself into one of the chairs that sat before the fireplace. A hand extended from one sleeve and twitched. The fire sprang to life. The flames crackled warmly.

"Come on. Show your face," Phyr said. "Keeree do something."

"Ostende te," Keeree shouted.

The air wavered, and the face became clear. The person must have dropped the spell that masked their face, unaware that Keeree was pressing all her magic into the spell that witnessed what they had done.

As the fire flared to life, the face became visible.

It was Phyr's mother.

27

MUMBLIES

DARAYA

*D*araya laughed at the sight of Phyr's mother as the vision faded. Phyr's own mother had sealed away his magic. The wizard boy was no better off than she was. He had been treated no better than she had at the hands of her father, in fact. Her father had beaten her, but he hadn't taken away her dream, not directly. Phyr's own mother had killed his dream. Somehow that thought made her feel a bit better about herself, even though she knew it shouldn't. "I guess I'm not the only one with a messed-up family," she said.

Phyr's eyes watered as he blinked back tears. "You think you're special," he said. "You think you're the only one. Your problems are so much greater than ours, but you're no different. Keeree's father got kicked out of the academy in disgrace. My parents treat me like an afterthought, an embarrassment. My own mother had to trickle power into me to help me light a candle in preparation for the academy. She didn't think I could handle it on my own, and now I come to find out it was *she* who sealed my magic away. And she herself was a focus. Unsealed. How could she do such a thing?"

Daraya's insides knotted. Phyr appeared so confident and sophisticated, especially compared to Keeree. Phyr had it all. Nice home, nice parents, nice life. Only he didn't, and she'd completely missed it.

She put a hand on his shoulder. "I didn't mean it like that. I just thought I was the only one who had it bad. It turns out that I'm not alone. Everyone has to deal with something they would rather not. I'm sorry, but from what you say, your mother wouldn't hurt you. There must be some reason for what she did. Let's go ask her."

Phyr shook off her hand.

The knot in Daraya's stomach tightened. Had she offended Phyr to the point he was no longer going to be friends with her? She hoped not. She would find a way to make it right.

"Let's go see Issur," she suggested. "At the Sanitarium. See what she has to say for herself. No one wants to hurt their own child."

They climbed the long stairs in silence. Daraya worried that the great door might be too heavy to open, but it swung back without effort. It felt as if they'd been deep in the earth forever, but it was only late afternoon when they emerged. How long had they been down there? It could only have been a few glasses.

The gryphon was nowhere to be seen. Perhaps it had fulfilled its function when it encouraged them to solve the puzzle.

Daraya noticed that Phyr barely spoke as the three of them made their way to the sanitarium, even though it was a long walk. They reached the stark white building just before nightfall. It was quiet. With the sunset, patients were encouraged to sleep and family members were being ushered out. At the junction of the corridors sat the woman in white, wearing her cap emblazoned with a red cross. She looked up as the trio entered the hall.

"Visiting is closed for the day. It's time the patients quieted down for the evening." She favored them with a pleasant smile that Daraya recognized as one that brooked no argument. "Come back in the morning."

"Please," Keeree said. "Phyr's parents are both here. We'll be quick, but he's worried about them. He won't sleep well, not knowing how they fare."

"I'm sorry. No visitors past sundown."

Daraya glanced over at the shadows on the wall. "Sundown isn't for at least half a glass."

"In the morning," the woman repeated.

Daraya glanced at Phyr. His face said it all. On top of the hurt she'd caused him, this was too much. And it was her fault. She stepped closer to the woman, trying to appear intimidating. "Listen here, healer woman. This young man has been through a lot. Both his parents are here. They were both injured. He has no home to go back to and no one to look out for him, except his friends, and as his friend, I'm willing to break a few rules so he can see his mother. If you have a problem with that, then let's go see the chief healer. I'm sure that the thought of a boy wishing his parents a good sleep won't hurt them, in fact, it'll probably help."

The woman glanced up at Daraya, paused as if preparing to speak, then glanced at the doors. She sighed. "Be quiet then, and don't give the attendants any of your grief, or I'll have you thrown out."

"My mother. She's still all right then?" Phyr asked.

"Were you expecting her to have suddenly become better? That's not going to happen."

"No. I just thought..." He let his words trail off.

Daraya caught Phyr's face out of the corner of her eye. He was biting his lip and stood slumped over. He must have been worried about Issur ever since they'd seen the burned-out door in the corridor. He must have feared something happened to her sanctuary, or to her. She could only imagine how relieved he was to hear she was safe.

Daraya straightened up and took Phyr's arm in hers. "Come on."

Neither of them spoke as Daraya led them through the double doors to the bed where Issur lay. The woman was in no better shape than the last time they'd seen her. Her face was still lopsided, and drool spilled from her lip.

"Mother?" Phyr rushed to her and stood beside the bed, hands on his hips.

Her eyes turned to take him in.

"Did you seal away my magic?" he asked.

"Ph... sn..." Issur's lips worked, but the sounds that came out of her mouth were indecipherable.

"It's no use," Phyr said. "This was a bad idea."

"No, wait," Daraya said. "Maybe we can find her, in that place."

"The door's burned out," Phyr said. "We can't go back there."

"Maybe it was just the door. Maybe the construct is still there. There must be another way there. We have to try." Daraya turned to Keeree. "I've seen you work your magic. Try. See if you can't find a way to get to her."

"Me?" Keeree looked uncomfortable.

"I've seen what you can do. Don't you want to help?"

"Of course I want to help." She grasped the rails of Issur's bed as if to steady herself.

Was she going to be ill again? Best to get this over with. Daraya gestured to Issur. "Take her hand. See if you can't find a way to reach her."

Keeree reached for Issur as Daraya stepped back.

"Do you think she can do it?" Phyr asked.

"If she can't, then no one can. You saw what she did back in the library. Is that what a focus is? Is that why they're afraid of us?"

"Afraid of us? What makes you think that?" Phyr appeared confused.

"Because they sealed our magic away," Daraya said. "They're afraid of it. I don't know why, but the more I see of Keeree working her brand of magic, the more I realize that we're missing something. Something important."

"No one's been afraid of me. Ever," Phyr said.

"I wouldn't be too sure of that." She took Phyr's arm in her own and drew him close. "Let's hope she can get some answers."

"Why would my own mother do this to me?" Phyr asked.

"You're asking the wrong girl." Daraya rested her hand on Issur's bed. Mothers. Fathers. She was beginning to see that all families were complicated, not just hers, and that made her feel just a little bit less alone. She still could not believe her own father had been a focus, or that he had been close with Issur.

"She always wanted me to be a wizard," Phyr was saying. "It's all she ever talked about. How she would be so proud of me. How she looked forward to having her son join her at the academy."

"Maybe she was protecting you. Isn't that what mothers do?"

The wizardling looked at her as if he was formulating an argument. She steeled herself for an insult, but what he finally said spoke more about Phyr than about her. "Do you think Keeree was able to reach her?" he asked.

Keeree stood straight, eyes unfocused, Issur's hand in hers.

"She's doing something," Daraya said.

Keeree let out a cry.

Her hand went to her face.

"What happened?" Daraya asked.

"She slapped me. She was very upset. Angry with me for intruding on her sanctuary. I asked her why she did what she did. She didn't even deny it, just started screaming at me. She told me to stay away from her son, to stay away from magic, to go back to the farm I was raised on and forget the whole thing, just like my father had. She said if I kept this up, I would very likely end up dead. She said I was an abomination who should never have been born. When I pushed her about Phyr, she slapped me and ejected me from the construct."

Phyr's expression fell.

It was clear to Daraya that Keeree's words had hurt him. He still loved his mother, even after what she had done to him. Even though Issur had done worse to Phyr than Adrylt had ever done to Daraya. Yet, he was ready to defend her even now. He felt ready to take Keeree on in a physical battle.

"How about your father?" Daraya asked. Better to defuse the situation than to let Phyr and Keeree fight over what his mother had or had not done. Clearly, she had done something to Keeree. How strange. This wasn't the sort of reception Daraya had expected they would receive. "Let's find a healer."

Daraya quickly located the healer. It was the same woman they'd met the first time they visited. She glanced at Phyr, then Keeree. As her gaze took in the farm girl, her eyes narrowed. Was there something about Keeree she despised? Was it her attire? The faint odor of beasts? Or was the healer just naturally bitter?

"My father?" Phyr asked.

"He's sleeping," she said tersely, eyes still focused on Keeree.

"Maybe we could talk to him for just a moment," Daraya offered.

The healer favored her with a sickeningly sweet smile. "He's in a lot of pain. I'm not waking him. That would be cruel."

"Phyr," came a muttered and muted word from behind the curtain.

The healer turned toward it. "How can he be awake? I'd better strengthen my spell."

"Please," Phyr said. "He may be able to explain what happened to me."

"He should be asleep, but if he has something important to say, I can wait a few moments. But not much longer than that. He needs his rest. You can speak with him, but just for a moment," the healer said. "I'll be right here, and if it's too much for him, I'm putting him back to sleep."

"Thank you for your kindness." As Daraya spoke the words, the healer drew aside the curtain to reveal Teil. Both of his legs and one of his arms were held fast by plaster casts. A bandage covered his forehead. His breathing was slow and deep.

The healer bent over the bed, extending her hands above him.

She passed them from head to toe, once, twice, three times.

Teil gasped.

She touched his cheek. "Your son is here to see you."

Teil's eyes turned to Phyr.

"My son." He grimaced as if in pain. "My Phyr. I'm sorry."

Phyr stepped up to the bed and laid a hand against his father's cheek. "Father?"

Teil spoke through parched lips. "How is your mother?"

"She lives," Phyr said.

Teil's countenance softened for the briefest moment, then he let out a sigh.

"She can't speak," Phyr added.

"That's for the best then." Teil gritted his teeth, the momentary relief at hearing his wife was alive turned to pain.

"Father, I know she sealed away my magic," Phyr said.

Teil groaned. "She was protecting you. Don't be too hard on her."

"Protecting me from what?"

"From everything." Teil winced and cried out, "It hurts."

"That's enough." The healer pushed Phyr out of the way and leaned over her patient. "He's in pain. Can't you see that? Is that what you want?"

"No, I want answers," Phyr said.

"Well, you're not going to get any tonight." She passed her hands over Teil once more. "He needs to sleep if he's going to heal."

The grimace faded from his face, but his eyes remained wide.

He turned his gaze to Keeree.

When he saw her, he blinked. "I see you've found them."

"Found who?" Phyr demanded.

Teil's eyes closed for several heartbeats. Was he asleep? Had they missed their chance?

"Who, father?" Phyr repeated.

Teil's eyes opened.

His gaze fixed on Daraya, then Keeree. "I thought to keep you apart. I should have known it wouldn't work. The last thing my son needs is to be part of a triad. But I see that I'm too late."

"You're torturing him." The healer shoved Daraya and Keeree aside and leaned over Teil. "No more talking for you."

She waved her hand over him.

His eyes fluttered. He attempted to speak but quickly fell silent.

His eyes closed.

"Please. He needs rest."

28

NEXUS

KEEREE

Keeree started to feel overwhelmed and off balance. Something about Teil made her anxious. He'd blurted out his words as if it took great effort. Was that because he was in pain, or because he was lying and wished not to be questioned? What wasn't he telling them? She worried that much more was going on than she understood. She would have loved to ask Teil what he was talking about, but the healer had made it clear that she was not about to wake him again. It was a relief when Phyr begrudgingly linked arms with her and guided her out of the building. The sun was over the horizon. It would soon be full dark. She looked to the sky. The moon was just rising. It was full, red, and large. For some reason, that threw her. Had it only been a day since the examination? It felt like moons had gone by, yet they had not. Never in her life had she been through so much as these last two days. She felt exhausted.

"Where are we going?" she asked.

"To my house," Phyr said. "I want to see if there's anything there I missed. Maybe we can find some remnant of the spell my mother used on me. I don't know. I'm not really sure what to look for."

"I can feel something." Keeree had not been paying attention as Phyr led her through the streets. There was power here. No, not power. An echo of power. Like a fire that had burned to embers. It had once been a raging fire but now it was only hot ash. Strange. It felt almost the same as she'd felt when she took Phyr and Daraya's hands the day they had all met. As if power were surging from the earth and up through her. How could she explain it? "Not far from here," she said. "It's as if some invisible field or force was drawn from the earth." She glanced at the sky, expecting to see the lines of magical force radiating as they made their way up into the aether.

"Here?" Phyr asked.

"Yes. Here, but not anymore," she said. "It's moved, but there's a shadow here. As if the rocks remember."

"But it's gone now?" Phyr asked.

"Not long ago," Keeree said. "The rocks are still all tingly." The hair on her arms stood tall. Gooseflesh rose along her arms and made her shiver.

"You're standing on the threshold of my house," Phyr said.

Keeree gazed down. Sure enough. She'd been so preoccupied with her own discomfort that she'd barely paid any attention to their progress. Phyr's house had been built where the lines of magical flux rose from the earth. But now the power was gone. It was as if whatever created the magical force far below the earth had been moved. How was that possible? Could a piece of the earth move? And just what generated that magical force to begin with? It reminded her of the feel of the library beneath the caretaker's cottage. That place too had once teemed with power, raw power. She could feel it. That's what made her uneasy. With a sudden realization, she understood. The magic that had once been here left a shadow behind. An emptiness. "The nexus. It was here," Keeree said.

"You house was built on a nexus? That explains so much," Daraya said.

"The fount processed it. The stones absorbed magic and we, well my parents, could tap into that power. No one is supposed to be able to touch the raw power of magic. It would burn them to a crisp."

"But you did. Didn't you?" Daraya asked. "That's what it means to be a focus."

"How is it that you know so much about magic when your father despises wizardry in any form?" Phyr asked. "And how did you come to learn to read the wizard's tongue? That's not something you pick up on your own."

Daraya shuddered.

Just what was she hiding?

"I had an aunt," Daraya explained. "The sister of my father. She was a wizard. She taught me, but hid it from my father, or else she would never have been allowed to spend time with me. She read me stories of the wizards and the amazing things they had done. She taught me to read. She taught me everything she knew about magic. She said that she felt it in me, even as a little girl. That one day the magic would waken and that I would need to know how to control it.

"I would stay with her sometimes. She did magic. Real magic, not just the small magic everyone does. She made the broom clean the house. Made the dishes scrub themselves. One day when I was ill, she came to my house. She sat by my side until my father left, then she called up the magic to heal me. She saved my life. I was so sick. I coughed up blood. I was sure I was going to die. My mother begged my father to call a healer, but he refused. Said if it was my time to die, I'd have a clean death and not be contaminated by magic.

"Soon after that, my aunt died. I fear my father figured out what she'd done. He was upset. He struck my mother for letting Rodaso heal me. He knocked her to the ground and kicked her. I was so scared. I thought he was going to kill her. He screamed at me, too, but he didn't hit me. Not then. He didn't start that until later. When I started to become a woman. That was when *my* beatings began. He said I was a witch and that I couldn't hide it from him. We were never close, but since those days, I've lived in constant fear. That is, until two days ago. Now I only worry about where I'm going to sleep. And who's coming after us."

"You never have to worry about where you're going to sleep," Keeree said. "You're always welcome with us. And we've managed to beat them back every time they attacked."

"How can you not be scared silly?" Daraya asked.

"I've never had magic. I guess losing it doesn't seem all that horrible to me. And I trust Garyll."

"Well," Phyr said, "for me it's been a rough few days. And for my family. Come on inside. Maybe there's something here to tell us who's behind this. It's not Socha and Skeli. They're just pawns. Someone powerful wants us out of the way."

"And when we know who it is, then what?" Keeree asked.

Phyr shrugged. "Once we know who it is, then we can figure out how to stop them."

Phyr rummaged through the ruins of the house, muttering under his breath. Keeree tried to help, but she had no idea what to look for, and the longer they remained in the house, the more she felt the effects of whatever was there. Her stomach roiled as if she'd eaten something off and her sense of balance was failing her. She stumbled against one wall, knocking a painting to the floor.

"What's wrong?" Daraya asked.

"I'm not feeling well." Keeree stretched out a hand to steady herself, her sweaty palm coming into contact with a white marble figure that jutted from the floor opposite the fireplace. As she touched it, her head swam. There was still power there. Raw and untamed. It no longer flowed through the crystals attached to the marble, but it was there. She could feel it, and it made her uneasy.

As her hand came to rest, her vision swam before her. She recognized it now. She was seeing something that Sama had experienced.

The house vanished, and Keeree was once more standing on the hill near the academy.

A young Issur struggled to stand. The jewel on her forehead glowed as did her eyes. She gestured to the slight rise where two figures approached.

It was Bannwor, looking as he did today, and a much younger version of Teil.

"Help me up." Issur stretched out her hand. "I'll meet my fate on my feet, not lying in the dirt."

Garyll helped Issur to her feet. The two women stood on either side of him. Keeree could feel the defiance.

Bannwor and Teil brushed past them, Bannwor muttering, "I'll deal with you later." He strode up to Adrylt, who sat in the dirt. Daraya's father cradled the strange girl's head in his arms.

"This is all your doing." Bannwor accused Adrylt.

Adrylt shook his head but made no argument.

"You don't deny it?" Bannwor demanded.

Adrylt remained silent.

Bannwor stepped back and raised his arms, Teil, standing at his side, mimicking his movements. "Adrylt, you have been found guilty of wielding the wild magic and forming a triad in violation of academy law. For this crime, the punishment is to live a life without magic. From this day forward, you will possess no magic. Not the small magic, not the wild magic. Nothing. You will be a mundane for the rest of your days."

Adrylt made no move. It was as if he'd heard nothing.

Bannwor nodded to Teil.

"Inde tollere atmet," Teil intoned.

Brilliant strands of violet raced from his fingertips, encircling Adrylt. They wrapped themselves around him in ever-tightening bands. The magic stream broke itself into pieces, each piece forming a circle around Adrylt. They constricted until he gasped for breath. With a crash like thunder, they vanished.

"It's done," He said. "Adrylt. Go. Practice no more magic."

Adrylt ignored him.

Bannwor stood silently for a hand of heartbeats then turned to Garyll, Sama and Issur.

"The three of you have committed the same crime. What do you have to say for yourself?"

"We had no choice," Sama spoke first. "Adrylt attacked us. It was our only defense."

Bannwor peered into her eyes. "You speak truth, but there is no room for judgement. The laws are firm. You three pose a great danger to the academy, no less than Adrylt."

"Have we not demonstrated that we could resist the temptation to use the wild magic?" Sama asked. "We only joined our magic because we would have been killed had we not." She glanced over at Issur. "And do you really think we would form a new triad with her?"

"It matters not what I believe. It only matters that the rules have been broken, and the punishment is clear." He stepped back. "Prepare yourselves."

"If you seal away her magic, you'll be killing her." Garyll nodded at Issur. "Death is not the punishment specified."

Teil stepped up and touched the headband Issur now wore. It glowed with a gentle light that pulsed like a heartbeat. Teil touched her face beside each glowing eye. "They speak the truth. The headband is powering a spell she maintains. Removing her magic will cause that spell to fail. Without the headband and her magic, Issur's heart will fail and she will die."

"The punishment is clear," Bannwor said. "Unless they are all sealed, they could form a new triad. That must not be allowed."

"Seal those two." Teil nodded to Garyll and Sama. "I will keep an eye on Issur. You can not condemn her to death and allow the others to live."

"And if another focus arises?" Bannwor asked.

"I will deal with them," Teil said.

Bannwor turned to Issur. "Do you agree to this?"

She glanced at Teil, distaste clear on her face. "You leave me little choice."

"I take that as a yes?" Bannwor said.

"Yes." Issur spat.

"Step aside." Bannwor stood before Garyll and Sama. "I'm not sure that sealing away your magic is enough. You understand the prohibition of the triad extends beyond simply forming a union. There are greater risks a pair of focuses pose than a triad."

Garyll drew a breath but Sama squeezed his hand, and he remained silent.

Bannwor shrugged. "I think a second spell will be required if I let you two live. You must not bear children."

Garyll glanced over at Sama. "We're not bonded. I just lost Endwa. How could you think such a thing?"

"Stranger things have happened. We can't take a risk that you do bond and bear children." He raised an eyebrow at Sama. "You understand why?"

"That's never been proven," she said.

"Nor will it. There will be no child. No focus coming their into magic with the full memories of two talented wizards."

Bannwor stepped back and raised his hand. "Hoc autem solo puer." He spoke with a deep voice accompanied by the sound of rushing wind as the magic encircled Sama. Keeree held her breath. Sama was fighting Bannwor, but she was losing. Before she knew it, Sama had relented. The spell sank into her flesh and came to rest in her womb. There was a great feeling of emptiness that accompanied the spell.

"And now the sealing." Teil stepped up, leaving Issur standing alone. "I'm sorry."

Teil raised his hands. "Inde tollere atmet." As he spoke the words, fire erupted in Keeree's chest. It felt as if her heart had burst into flames and was about to burn its way out of her chest. Is this what Daraya had felt? Great bands tightened around her and it grew difficult to breathe. For half a heartbeat, she thought Teil had decided to kill them, but the sensation vanished, and with it, the magic she had come to rely on since it had come awake in her.

"Go," Bannwor said. "Make whatever life you can for yourselves."

"Go where?" Garyll asked.

"Anywhere but here," Bannwor replied almost absently. He had done what he came for and dismissed them. It was as if he cared little what happened to them.

"Come." Sama pulled Garyll's hand. "I know a place where we can go."

A hand shook Keeree, and the vision faded. While she had been lost in the vision, it had begun raining. Her hair was wet, and she was cold.

"Are you all right?" Phyr asked.

"I saw them. Your parents and mine. I saw them have their magic sealed away."

"My parents never had their magic sealed," Phyr said.

"No. Not yours. Mine. And Daraya's father. I saw it happen. Just like Garyll said, but it was so real." She tried to stand, but her knees wobbled and she collapsed.

"We need to go," Phyr said.

"You're going out in the rain?" Daraya asked.

"Rain doesn't hurt." Keeree was starting to feel more like herself.

"But it's cold and wet," Daraya protested.

"You'd rather stay here?" Keeree wasn't eager to spend another heartbeat in this place. It made her skin crawl.

"It's wet. Aren't you worried you'll catch the chills? Do you want to catch the chills?"

"That's an old wives' tale. You don't get sick from being out in the rain. I like rain." She held out a hand. "Not this sort, but rain in general."

"Well, I'm not accustomed to being wet."

"You won't melt," Keeree said.

"Says you." Daraya looked as if she indeed feared the rain. The more Keeree learned of her, the less she felt she understood her.

"Here," Phyr had found blankets somewhere in the debris. He handed one to Keeree and one to Daraya. He took the last one and swung it wide, letting it settle onto his head.

"You look like an old washerwoman," Daraya remarked.

"But I'll stay dry," Phyr said.

Keeree slung the blanket over her shoulder. She stepped into the street and turned for home. "Coming?" She called back to Phyr and Daraya, who were standing on the threshold as if waiting for an invitation.

As they made their way through the now-deserted streets, the sky grew dark. Black clouds obscured the moon until it was almost impossible to see where they were going. The rain picked up, driving heavy droplets through Keeree's clothes and blanket until her skin was wet and cold.

"We're never going to make it." Phyr said. "We need to find a place to shelter, at least until the rain passes. Maybe we can beg a room."

"Beg a room?" Keeree asked. "From a stranger?"

"Yes. From a stranger. That's how it's done. What else would you do if you were caught out in the rain?"

"Get wet," Keeree said. "Unless there's lightning. Then you lay down."

"Lay down?" Phyr asked.

"Lightning strikes the highest point. If you're standing in an open field, then it will strike you. If you lay down, you're no longer the highest point. The lightning will strike something else."

"So you seek out a tree and hide beneath it," Daraya added.

"Believe me. You don't want to hide beneath a tree in a thunderstorm."

If only there were a way to see where they were going. They weren't far from the edge of town, and not far from the homestead after that. But without the moon to light their path, they might just have to do as Phyr suggested. The thought of begging a room from a stranger was something that made Keeree uneasy. She'd never felt comfortable around strangers and was certain sleeping in a strange place with strange people was not something that would provide rest. Best they were getting home. But how?

"I can shield us. I saw the shield in my vision. I can call up a spell my mother learned." She concentrated on the spell and let the vision come.

She was sitting in the library, a large tome open in her lap. She'd been paging through it and had chanced upon just the spell she needed. It wasn't one she recalled seeing before, but it felt right. She rubbed her hand along the edge of the page and the cypher characters appeared. By now, the words they called out were beginning to sound familiar. Her mother had used this spell to protect the triad from the attacking gryphon, but it would work just as well for mere rain.

Did she dare?

Why not?

What could go wrong?

The vision faded and Keeree found herself huddled just out of the rain. "Iniecta patrocinium tempastatis." Off in the distance, thunder rolled, but she kept up the words, stretching her senses for the magic. It was so close. She could feel it. Her feet tingled, then her legs, then her body. Power channeled through her and out her fingertips.

"Ut nos excluatur," she added.

The air burst to life. Uncounted shimmering points of light

formed a canopy over their heads. The rain struck it and rolled off the edges.

"See? No more rain." By the eerie light of the canopy, Keeree stepped into the street. "Come on."

"Are you certain it's safe?" Daraya asked.

"Look at me," she said. "No rain. Nothing. Do I know my magic, or what?"

She twirled, letting the rain spatter from the canopy overhead as she did. It felt exhilarating to wield magic. It made her feel alive, as if she were drawing life energy itself from the earth. The power she channeled made her flesh pucker. The hairs on her arm stood on end. The air smelled off, as if it had a metallic taste.

She turned to Phyr and Daraya. "Are you two coming or not?"

Before either of them could say a word, a loud boom struck her. The air filled with light so bright she was blinded. Power coursed through her, setting every hair standing straight.

Every muscle in her body clenched then relaxed as darkness overtook her.

29

REACHING

DARAYA

Daraya knelt over Keeree. The steady rain beat down on her, drenching her through her clothes. It was hard to see. Daraya's vision had been washed out by the bright flash, and her flesh tingled as if she'd suddenly been exposed to cold. Keeree lay on her side in a puddle of water. A long, thick, red, line forked into a network of fine lines running along her arm and branching out along her fingers as if something had burned its way across her flesh. Despite her injuries, Keeree was breathing. At least she was alive.

"What happened?" Things were a bit fuzzy. Keeree had raised magic to protect them from the rain, and then?

Flash.

Bang.

Keeree lying in the street.

Thank all that was good she wasn't dead. Had she been struck by lightning? It sure seemed that way, but she was alive, so maybe not. Maybe it was something else, something more sinister. Was this a new form of attack by someone with greater power than Socha and Skeli? If so, who?

"We have to get her to a healer," Daraya said.

"We can't. It's raining even harder now." Phyr stood beneath an awning. Rain ran off the roof, digging a shallow trough in the dirt at his feet.

"Come help," Daraya said. "She's too heavy."

"What if it happens again?"

"You know what they say. Destruction never returns. We should be safe."

"What if we're not?"

"Stop being such a child. Come over here and help me."

Phyr stepped from beneath the awning, his gaze traveling to the sky as if he would be able to see the lightning before it struck. He knelt down and hauled Keeree's arm around his shoulder, lifted her to her feet and dragged her under a nearby awning. The wizard boy was stronger than he looked, or simply very desperate to get out of the rain.

"I don't know what to do," Phyr said.

"What would your parents do?"

"They would use magic. I can't."

"Maybe you can," Daraya said. "You know how you helped Keeree by showing her what to do? Maybe you can draw on her magic. Use it to power a spell. If you can open a doorway to the void, we can take her to the sanitarium. They'll be able to help her. Try."

She knew even as she spoke that she was grasping at straws. Phyr had no more magic than she did. But, more than once, he *had* been able to direct Keeree's magic. Maybe he could do it again, even without Keeree's help. Without a healer, Keeree might die. The thought of losing the friend she had just discovered was terrifying. More terrifying than the idea that without Keeree, she had no place to live, and nothing to eat. Keeree had shown her a different way to look at the world.

Keeree's world was populated by good folk who helped one another. Cared about one another. Even those they barely knew. It was a new way to live for Daraya. Keeree was genuinely happy, no matter that she worked like a dog from dawn to dusk and should have been miserable.

"Come, try, wizard boy. Show us what you've got."

Phyr threw her a glance that would have melted snow, then turned to Keeree, placed his hand on her forehead and closed his eyes.

Daraya tried to sense what he was doing. She called to mind the way it felt to touch her magic, but when she did, the imaginary band around her chest tightened, and it grew hard to breathe. No. There would be no magical help from her. "Curse you, Socha. If she dies, so help me, I'll hunt you down and remove your skin while you watch."

"I can sense the magic flowing through her," Phyr said. "It's strange. In our house, the stones absorbed the magic, and we tapped into that. But, Keeree is doing something different. She's..." Phyr pulled his hand back as if he had touched a flame.

"What is it?"

"She's filled with raw magic. Unfiltered. Straight from the earth. Even while she's unconscious. That's unheard of."

"I thought all magic came from the earth. Isn't that how it works?"

"Yes, and no. Magic does come from the earth, but no one touches it directly. It's dangerous. Magic is like molten rock that flows from the fire mountains. It's hotter than anything you can imagine and burns everything. When it cools down, it forms rocks that you *can* touch. That's how magic works. We draw it from places where it's cooled down. Where it's been absorbed into the earth or the stones. That's why we had a pair of large gemstones in the house. In the fount. To absorb the magic. Let it cool off until it was safe to touch."

"And?" Daraya asked.

"She *is* a focus. She's not letting the magic cool. She wields it straight from the earth. Concentrates it. But there's something strange about the way it feels. I think I've felt it before. When my mother dampened my magic. I was able to reach for it beneath my feet and draw it forth. But that couldn't be. It would have burned me."

"It's not burning her." Daraya glanced at Keeree. It was as if the lightning bolt had seared the path of a river delta on her arm. The currant-red line branched and forked to extend to each of her fingernails. "It didn't burn you," she said. "Keeree's a focus. So are *you*.

Maybe you could do the same thing. Try it. See if you can touch that magic, or draw it forth the way she does."

"And what if it burns me?"

"Are you afraid to risk yourself to save her? What sort of wizard are you?"

"You're just as much a focus as she is. Why don't you do something?"

Daraya shuddered at the thought of trying to touch the raw magic. She saw what it had done to Keeree, and it terrified her. But Phyr had used Keeree's magic before. Was he afraid now? She could see that. But after all they'd been through, how could he refuse to help?

"She would help you," Daraya prompted. "Maybe you should take a hint from her. Please, Phyr: Try." Daraya had no idea what else to say. She couldn't make him do it.

"If I die, I'm coming after you," Phyr said.

"I'll look forward to it." Daraya held her breath.

Phyr placed his hand on Keeree's head.

Daraya tried to imagine what he was feeling. Was it like she felt when she raised fire in the caretaker's cottage? Was that what she'd done? Tapped into the nexus? Garyll said all three of them were focuses. Maybe that's what they did. And maybe that was the key to breaking the spell that sealed away her magic.

She was so focused on her own plight that she almost missed it.

In the air before Phyr, a faint light appeared. At first it looked no more than an illusion, but it grew brighter, taking on a rich rose color and expanding. Soon the light had formed the image of a door, the knob glowing gently, the hinges pulsing with light as if asking to be opened. Hovering in the air before her was a sturdy oak door. The wood had been carved by an expert. The panels were perfectly straight. The glass as clear as air. Who had wrought such a thing? Or was it purely magic? She grasped the handle and yanked the door open.

"Quick," she said. "Get Keeree through it. Drag her if you have to."

Phyr draped Keeree's arm around his neck. Half carrying, half dragging her, he stepped through the door.

"Wait for me." Daraya followed him and let the door slam shut behind her. She rushed to grab Keeree's other arm.

They were once more in the long corridor filled with doors. Daraya was starting to feel almost at home here. She wondered if the wizards routinely used this place to move from one location to another. If they did, why was it always empty? She would have expected the void to be crowded.

"Which one goes to the sanitarium?" Daraya asked. A chill wind wrapped around her ankles and she shuddered.

They were not alone.

"This is the one you want, but you're not using it." Skeli leaned against a door, her arms folded across her chest. "You brought me the prize, I see."

"Don't be so sure," Daraya retorted. "We bested you before, who's to say we can't do it again?"

"I say. You may have figured out how to open the doorway, but once I seal *her* magic, you're done. No more games. No more threats. No more damp-wicks that need to be trimmed. Step aside."

"No. We're in this together."

Skeli shrugged. "Suit yourself, but this is going to hurt."

As Skeli began her incantation, Daraya's guts wrenched. She cramped up, fire shooting through her even as she doubled over in pain. This was even worse than when they'd sealed her magic away. She cried out. The pain went on and on.

Just when she thought she could take no more, she felt Phyr's hand slide into hers. His fingers worked their way up her arm until he was grasping her forearm.

Suddenly, color drained from the world.

Phyr had the talisman!

He'd draped it over their joined hands.

The pain receded.

Daraya hadn't worn the medallion before. Not for long. It had not affected her then. This time was different. The world was sepia, yet it was not totally devoid of color. Faint lines of gold and silver wove through everything. Tiny flashes of color appeared and almost instantly disappeared along the intersection of the gold and silver strands.

Her mouth fell open.

This was the raw magic, the sort Phyr was talking about. The medallion suppressed the small magic. The magic that the likes of Skeli employed. This magic must have been what Keeree had used back in the library. She reached out her hand to examine one of the threads, but it drew back from her touch.

"Don't," came Phyr's words.

Daraya pulled her hand back. The magic had a strange attraction for her. She longed to touch it. To wield it. Yet she knew it was not for her. Not yet. But, what if she was wrong?

Skeli stretched her hands out, fingers twisting in strange patterns. The magic she wielded was weak and insubstantial in comparison to the magic that coursed through the gold and silver threads. Almost too weak to bother with.

"Go away. Leave us alone." Daraya grasped a single thread of the wild magic coursing through the surrounding air. She shaped it into the form of a spell of protection her aunt had once used. Words came to her as if from nowhere. It sounded like Sama's voice.

"Discedre molestia diutius," Daraya repeated the words that the voice provided. As if the words themselves had power, the door beside Skeli burst open and a great wind whipped up, driving her garments through the open door. Daraya knew it was trying to force her through. The spell was working.

Skeli held on.

"Phyr, I need your help," Daraya shouted.

Phyr laid his hand on her shoulder. "Try again."

Daraya concentrated. She reached for the power. "Discedre molestia diutius," she screamed. The wind increased in intensity. The door rattled, but Skeli hung on.

"Just a little more." Daraya focused her senses on the magic flowing through her, for it *was* flowing through her. From where, she had no idea. Best not to think about it.

She relaxed and let the magic flow.

This time she whispered the words, "Discedre molestia diutius."

A fierce wind lifted Skeli off her feet.

She screamed as she was swept through the door.

It slammed closed.

They were alone.

Daraya shook.

Her words had power in this place, if nowhere else. For the first time, she realized just how much power she could have wielded had they not sealed away her magic.

"Come on," Phyr said. "Let's get Keeree to the sanitarium."

"I thought that was the door we needed," Daraya asked. "The one Skeli was standing next to."

Phyr shrugged. "Perhaps."

He frowned. "Does that mean Skeli's at the sanitarium with my mother?"

Daraya shrugged. She pulled at Phyr's arm, dragging him and Keeree toward the door where Skeli had just vanished. "Let's find out."

She opened the door.

On the other side was not the sterile sanitarium they had been expecting, but a deep wood full of conifer trees. The wood ended at a lake that stretched toward the distant mountains. It was day here, not the cold, rainy night found in the real world. This was not the sanitarium as they had hoped. Daraya knew this place. She'd been here before.

She emerged to see Phyr standing in the path facing someone. Someone in a hooded cloak.

"Hello, Mother," he said.

30

NODES
PHYR

*P*hyr studied his mother. In this place she was whole, but this place was an illusion. His mother lay in a bed in the sanitarium — unable to speak or move. He breathed with purpose. In and out. She was his mother. He still loved her, but it wasn't the same. They had both done things they could never take back. He was her son, but he would never be her little boy again.

"I see you figured it out," she said.

"How could you do such a thing to me?"

"To spare your father."

"Spare him from what?"

"He is in charge of protecting the academy from people like you." Issur's gaze took in Phyr's companions. "All of you."

Issur sighed. She stood still for a long moment before speaking. "You three represent a threat to the academy. To the stability of the entire wizarding world. Your kind can never be allowed to flourish. Since it's your father's duty to find people like you and seal them away from their magic, he would have had to do it. I'd hoped you hadn't inherited the curse from me, but you did. When you lit that candle while I was blocking your magic, it broke my heart. It meant your father would have to seal you. I knew he couldn't do it. He would *never* have done that to you. He loves you. He would have become an outcast to save you."

Phyr closed his eyes and inhaled. "So you decided to do it yourself."

"It's not like that." She took a step toward him. "If your father had been the one to seal away your magic, it would have been irreversible."

"So you can reverse it?" Phyr paused. Keeree needed help. He was being selfish. "We can talk about that later. Keeree's been hurt. Can you help her?"

"No. I'm not really here, you know. I'm confined to a bed. I have no access to magic. This place is just a distraction."

"What if we heal you?" Phyr asked.

Issur shook her head. "No. Phyr. I'm not ill. When my heart stopped, my body started to die. Parts of me *did* die. There's no spell to restore something that has died."

"But the healer said you might recover."

"Might," she said. "Most don't recover much beyond the ability to move their eyes and sometimes make a bit of sound with their mouth. Very few ever recover much of their former selves. You need to accept that. I'm not going to get better."

"Will you ever wield magic again?"

"I'm afraid not."

"Then what difference does it make who sealed my magic?"

"Phyr, I'm sorry. This is not what I intended. There are sometimes exceptions. Like my case. I wanted to buy time to present your case. I was trying to protect you."

"Did you think we wouldn't find out? That you're a focus?" He turned his back on her.

"Phyr. Wait."

"No more talking. I no longer care what you have to say." He whirled and headed toward the door.

"There is hope," Issur called after him.

He spun to face her. "Hope for what? If you can't lift the spell, no one can."

"That's not exactly true."

"What *is* the truth then?"

"How does a focus handle the raw magic without being roasted by it?" Issur asked. "Have you thought that through? You've already done it more than once." She gave him that look. The one that she used when tutoring him on magic, or reading, or his numbers. She was waiting for him to make the connection.

"I've hardly had time to ponder it since this all started."

"Think about how you lit the candle. I placed a shield around you. What did you do? All I saw was an immense burst of power. I have no idea what you actually did to call up the raw magic. How you guided it to light the candle, or even how you managed to pierce my shields to call it up, I can not imagine. What did you do? Do you remember?"

"I'm not certain."

"Try to remember. It may be the key to breaking through the spell I cast on you. The sealing spell uses your own magic against you. If you can get to a place where there is no magic, let yours run dry, then the spell will fade and you'll be able to ..."

She paused as if in thought. "Phyr, listen: the spell that maintains this place is growing weak. You have to leave. Take your friends and go. Let your magic bleed away. That's your only hope of reversing the spell." She paused, reached out and brushed his hair behind his ear. "And Phyr?"

He tensed. He didn't trust her the way he once had.

"Be careful." She glanced at Keeree. "There are powerful people after her. I don't want you to get caught up in it."

"She's a friend," Phyr said.

"No doubt, but a friend to whom?" Issur asked

The image of the surrounding woods wavered as if seen through the heat of a warm summer's day.

"You're depleting the magic that sustains this place. You must go." Issur reached into the air. A doorknob appeared, then a crack in the air that turned into a great oak door. Beyond the door was the sanitarium.

"Go now," she said. "All of you."

~

PHYR MOTIONED to Keeree and Daraya. This time he wasn't taking any chances. He would not let them get separated. They linked arms and stepped through the doorway as one.

"Ha! I knew it was you," the healer who'd been attending Phyr's mother stood facing them. Her fists were on her hips. Her lips pressed into a thin slash.

She grabbed Phyr by the arm and turned him toward the door. "Time to go. You're tiring her out. Do you know what it's like when she does that? When she's with someone in that place, her body tries to follow her mind. Her legs twitch, her arms twitch, and her mouth moves. Her tongue tries to form words. She chokes on her own spittle. I have to watch her closely the whole time so she doesn't die."

"Keeree needs help," Phyr said. "She was struck by lightning."

The healer turned to Keeree. "You must be mistaken. No one lives after being struck by lightning."

"She did. But she's injured. You're a healer, aren't you?" Phyr hoped to turn the healer's attention away from him and toward Keeree. She was breathing heavily, as if she'd run all the way from the farm to town. Her eyes were still unfocused.

"Put her there." The healer motioned to an empty bed across the room. "I'll tend to her myself."

Phyr helped Daraya carry Keeree to the bed and gently lowered her onto it.

Keeree's eyes opened. "Did you see?"

"See what?"

"I touched the magic," Keeree said.

Phyr's heart skipped a beat. "Shh. No one needs to know that." The last thing he needed was for Keeree to confess that she'd touched the wild magic. She could bring retribution not only on herself, but Phyr and Daraya as well.

He glanced at the healer, but the woman appeared not to hear what Keeree said, or if she did, she paid it no attention.

She stepped close to Keeree and glanced at Phyr. "Step back and let me work."

The healer bent over Keeree, passing her hands above the girl's body. She paused when she came to the burn mark that traversed Keeree's left side, fingers moving ever so slightly as they hovered above the mark.

For some reason, the burn mark reminded Phyr of the wine-stained girl who ran the cafe, Cheshi. There was more to her than he had at first thought. She had a deep understanding of magic for a damp-wick. He would have to ask her when next he saw her. That thought made him feel bad. He'd never thanked her for her part in saving Keeree, or even returned to check on her to make certain she was all right. She had attacked a wizard with no thought to her own safety. That girl was fashioned from strong metal, and he'd treated her rudely. He'd become caught up in his own troubles and had never even given her a second thought. Until now. He would remedy that as soon as he was able. He would go to the cafe and thank her. Express his gratitude. But how? He was homeless and had only a few coins in his pocket. Soon, he'd be in no better shape than Daraya.

"Wizard boy," Daraya interrupted. "She asked you a question."

Phyr turned his attention to the healer. "Sorry."

The healer pointed to the burn mark that stretched from Keeree's shoulder all the way to her fingers. "How did you say she got this?"

"She was standing in the street when the lightning struck," Phyr said.

"I've seen lightning strikes. This isn't one. If she was standing in the street and was struck, the burn mark would start on her head. That's why most folks don't survive. Fries the brain. See here. It starts on her shoulder as if she'd been standing beneath something."

Phyr glanced at Daraya.

Daraya shrugged.

"She was holding a shield," Phyr said. "A magical shield."

The healer turned to Phyr. Her hand rested lightly on the bedrail. Her fingernails clicked as she tapped out a light rhythm. "There is no such spell. If there were, no one would be struck by lightning."

Daraya jutted her chin at Keeree. "She had one."

"Hmm. Let me see." The healer bent over Keeree, passing her hand back and forth above Keeree's head. She paused. "You can go. I'll tend to her."

Phyr paused. Why did the healer want them to go? Keeree was their friend. Had she put the pieces of the puzzle together? Did she realize what Keeree had done? What she was? He suspected she did. He wasn't about to leave Keeree alone with her.

"We have nowhere to go," he said. "My house is ruined and Daraya can't go home. It's too late to find an inn. Can't we stay here? Keeree is here. My folks are here. I promise we won't bother anyone."

The healer looked at Phyr with her hands on her hips. Her countenance softened. "You can stay here. Sleep in a chair. Just don't bother my patients." She raised an eyebrow at Phyr. "Any of them."

Phyr pulled a chair up to Keeree's bedside and settled in. It was going to be a long night.

31

FOCUS

KEEREE

*K*eeree drew a breath. The air smelled of sage and sweet spices. She was covered with a heavy blanket, and someone had their hand on her head. That should have bothered her, but she couldn't think why. She should worry, but she simply couldn't. The sound of hushed conversation reached her ears, almost loud enough to overcome the high-pitched ringing, but not quite. She blinked. At first there was nothing but a blurry light, then after opening and closing her eyes several times, a face became clear. She knew that face, or rather she had seen it before.

"Good morn to you. You gave us all a bit of a scare, you did." The healer she'd met on her last visit to the sanitarium was bending over her. How had the healer gotten here? Where was here? The last thing Keeree recalled was raising a shield to keep the rain off as they made their way from Phyr's house to hers.

"Where am I?"

"You're in the sanitarium. You're recovering nicely. I used a spell to keep you asleep while the healing magic did its work, but now you're awake, so it must be finished."

"How long have I been here?"

"Half a moon."

Keeree sat up, shedding the heavy blanket. "Half a moon!"

"Well. Look at you. You do have a spark of life in you," the healer said. "I'm just funning you. You've only been here one night. You healed up real fast. Probably on account of how you're pure and all."

Keeree wasn't following. "Pure?"

"Your magic is pure. Makes it easy to heal you." She said that as if that explained everything. "You really don't know, do you? Come. Let's get you out of that bed and go somewhere we can talk. Your friends are due back from morning meal soon and I want you ready to go when they get here."

The healer helped Keeree out of bed and walked her down the hall to a small study lined with books. Everything was clean, as if someone had recently dusted.

The healer lowered Keeree into a comfortable chair facing a desk of carved mahogany. It was old and worn but shone as if it had been waxed just that morning. The woman waltzed around the desk, and sat in the chair facing Keeree. She folded her hands.

"You were saying?" Keeree asked.

"Your father didn't explain it to you? He's the one you inherited your condition from."

The healer held up her right hand, palm out. Her fingers were thin and clean, the nails polished to a shine with a natural color that hid the fact that they'd been polished. "Follow what I do and it will make sense."

Keeree stretched her hand out as the healer had.

"Now place it over your heart. Reach inside with your magic."

Keeree hesitated. How was she supposed to reach inside herself?

She took a calming breath, feeling her chest expand and contract beneath her hand. Her heartbeat was still discernible. Was that distracting her efforts? She ignored it, imagining her hand becoming insubstantial. The ghost of her hand separated from her flesh and slowly penetrated her chest. First it passed through her skin, a thin and almost insubstantial layer that was tougher than it appeared. Beneath her skin, muscle — not a lot — just the thinnest layer there. She flexed that muscle. Felt her chest move slightly, dragging her flesh and her real hand with it. But that wasn't what she was after. She needed to go deeper.

Next came the bones. She was familiar with bones. She'd butchered enough hogs to know how they were fashioned. Slender, curved, hard like wood, but flexible enough to bend under pressure. Bones were not all that interesting. It must be deeper.

She plunged on. Beneath the bones was something she hadn't expected.

It was small. Just a little larger than a crabapple.

She let her imaginary fingers explore it. It was hard. Almost like a stone. Branching out from it was a web of filaments. The web was finer than any lace she'd ever felt, but it was there, touching everything inside her, permeating her whole being.

"You feel it, don't you?" the healer asked.

"What is it?"

"That's what makes you a focus," she said. "It's something very few people have, thankfully."

"Thankfully?"

"Everyone has magic, yes?"

"I suppose so," Keeree agreed.

"And some have more control than others, yes?"

"That's what the academy teaches."

"Glad to see you can think for yourself. Where does that magic come from? The magic everyone employs?"

"From all around us," Keeree said. She wasn't sure about that. It was something everyone told her.

"Right. But not just everywhere. The magic comes from the earth. It radiates in invisible lines of force. That force permeates every part of your body. And as it does, it leaves behind a small trace of magic. That's what everyone uses when they perform the small magic."

"What does this have to do with me?"

"I'm getting there." The healer waved her hand in the air. "When you perform the small magic, you use up that energy and you have to wait for it to replenish before you can perform another spell. That's why they call it the small magic."

"What does that have to do with me?"

"I'm getting there. It won't be long now." The healer placed her hand on her chest where Keeree had felt the small organ. "You have something most people don't. The organ in your chest can be used to focus magic. Raw magic. Straight from the earth. Most wizards have a secret stash of stones, crystals that store magic." She touched a small pendant hanging around her neck. "Like this. It absorbs magic and stores it. When I need to perform a large spell, I can draw the magic out and use that. But when it's depleted, I have to wait, just as if I'd used up my own magic." She held her hand up. "I know. Why doesn't everyone have one of these?" She touched the stone again. "Because there's only so much magic, and more stones won't store more magic. They'd store less. That's just the way it goes, so we keep the stones a secret.

"That organ in your chest. It works sort of like the stones, but not quite the same. It can actually draw magic from deep within the earth, call it up at need. Almost limitlessly, from what I understand. That means you can call up magic in vast amounts. Mind-numbingly vast amounts."

"So why do I have this if it's so rare?" Keeree asked.

"It's inherited. Usually it skips a generation. Grandmother to granddaughter. But if both of your parents have it, then you'll have it."

Keeree held her peace. Garyll had explained much of it, and she had seen the rest in her visions, but she was still having a hard time accepting her parents as great wizards.

"I see, you never knew any of this," the healer said. "But we did. We knew this day would come, and to be frank, I'm glad it came today."

"I don't understand."

"Of course not. You were never trained. Your father hoped to protect you by raising you on that farm. The only place for leagues around where there's absolutely no magic. Not one line. Nothing. You lived your life without absorbing so much as a drop of magic, so the binding spell used on your friends wouldn't work on you. But that all changes today. Today, you're here sitting in my chair. You with your special ability. You with your unlimited access to magic. You, one who can bend the raw magic to her will with simply a thought."

"You say that like having the ability to wield strong magic is a bad thing," Keeree said.

"Yes. It's a bad thing. When you call up the magic, there is less of it for the rest of us. There's only so much magic to go around. When you squander it, as you've done several times in the last day or two, you bend the lines of magic toward yourself. Keep that up and you'll be the only one who can perform magic at all."

The healer stood and leaned over the desk. "But fortunately for the rest of us, you've been sitting in that chair. That special chair. The one I placed precisely there just for you." She straightened up. "Didn't you notice it? Didn't you feel just a tiny bit of a tingle while you sat there listening to me drone on about your family and how magic works?"

The healer stepped around the desk and placed a hand on Keeree's shoulder. "While you've been sitting there, you've been absorbing magic. Not a lot, to be sure, but enough to allow me to place the same spell on you as your friends have. In a moment, your magic will be sealed away just like theirs, and I'll be the one who saved the academy. I would never have thought it would be me, but when they brought you here, I could barely contain my excitement. I knew you'd come to my study if I asked nicely. Knew you'd listen intently as the magic worked inside you. Knew you'd be ready."

Keeree tried to stand, but the woman's hand tightened around her shoulder.

Fire erupted inside of her as if someone had taken a fireplace poker and jabbed it into her heart. No, not her heart. The other side. The place the healer had shown her. The place where she was supposed to be able to control magic, only she was not.

She was helpless, in pain and alone.

32

SOCHA
PHYR

*P*hyr led Daraya back to the cafe where Cheshi worked. They had to eat, and where better to eat than somewhere he knew he'd be welcome? Well, he hoped he'd be welcome. He'd never thanked the sisters for the part they played in saving Keeree, and he had no idea if any harm had come to them because of it.

The cafe was empty in the chill of the morning. Dew still coated the outdoor seating. Thankfully, the door stood open and the scent of baking bread said that someone was inside. If he had any luck, it would be Cheshi and not Omosa. Cheshi was shy and more to his liking than her older sister. Omosa was a touch too bold for Phyr's taste. She made him nervous, as if he somehow wasn't good enough for her and she was toying with him. Still, there was something about the two sisters that he had yet to discern. It was clear that neither of them possessed even the small magic, but he got the impression that they were both much more knowledgeable about magic and the workings of the academy than your average damp-wick. He made himself a promise to dig a bit deeper once he had the time, but he feared it would not be soon.

"How did I know you'd choose this place?" Daraya interrupted his reverie.

"I want to express my gratitude to the sisters for saving Keeree, and make sure nothing has happened to them because of us."

"And, you're smitten."

"And I'm smitten," Phyr admitted. "Is that so bad?"

"No, I suppose not. As long as you don't let it cloud your judgement."

Phyr stepped inside, glad of the warmth coming from the kitchen. "I won't."

"Won't what?" Omosa appeared in the doorway.

"Won't forget to express my gratitude for your assistance the last time we were in here."

"That wasn't me. That was Cheshi. She's the bold one. If it had been up to me, I'd have minded my own business, but she's the one with a nose for trouble."

"I'd like to thank her," Phyr said.

"Thank her by buying yourself a nice hearty morning meal. Meat pie, is it? And a rasher of salt pork, a couple mugs of strong tea." She raised an eyebrow. "And a sticky bun for the lady?"

"That sounds fine," Phyr said.

"Nothing for me," Daraya said. "I'm not hungry."

Phyr knew she hadn't eaten since the last time he himself had, and he was famished. Why then refuse food? She hadn't been shy about devouring a hearty meal when they broke their fast at Keeree's home. She must be destitute and ashamed to admit it. "Bring her the buns and tea," he said. "And the melon I see marked on the board." The worst that could happen was Daraya refused to eat, and he was hungry enough to eat everything he'd ordered.

"You don't have to do that," Daraya said. "I'll be fine."

"No, you won't. If you don't eat, soon I'll be carrying you to the sanitarium just like Keeree. Besides, didn't we agree that the three of us were friends? That's what friends do, they look out for each other."

"I don't need charity," Daraya said.

"And you're not getting any. Keeree's mother said anyone who happened to be at the farm during mealtimes gets fed. Regardless of who they are. Well, any of my friends around at mealtimes eat too, and I won't take any argument from you about it."

Daraya drew a breath, but Phyr stopped her before she could speak. "I know you can't go home. I know how that hurts. I know you feel lost and abandoned, but you're not. You have us. You're not alone."

"Don't think I won't find a way to pay you back," Daraya said.

"Of that, I'm certain. You keep associating with the likes of Keeree and me, and you'll have plenty of opportunities to pay us back — and then some. Now, here comes the food. Let's find something more pleasant to talk about."

Phyr glanced at Daraya to see if she was listening. Had his words managed to make her feel at least a bit better about her situation?

She wasn't listening. She was staring at the open door, her hand resting on the knife that Omosa had brought with the food.

Socha entered and took a seat near the door. He appeared to be unaware of the two of them. He seated himself beside a pair of young townsfolk who seemed so intent on each other that they didn't notice a student wizard had taken the seat beside them.

Phyr caught the look in Daraya's eye. "I don't like what you're thinking," he said.

"How do you know what I'm thinking?"

"By the way you're holding that knife."

"We were just speaking of repaying our debts. I think it's time I repaid this one."

Phyr placed his hand over hers. Carefully, he reached out and removed the knife from her hand. "This is not the way. We're not like that."

"Maybe you aren't, but I am." She shoved her chair back and stood. "He needs to pay for what he's done."

Across the room, Socha looked up. When he saw Daraya, his eyes went wide. He rose and started for the door, but Daraya was too fast. She bolted across the room and knocked him to the floor before he could take three steps.

The young couple took notice and rose from their table to crowd the back wall of the cafe.

"Why do you keep following us around?" Daraya demanded.

"I was looking for Keeree. They want me to distract her, just like I did with you. Do you think I have the sort of power to seal away someone's magic? I'm a failure. A nothing."

"I don't believe you!"

Phyr rushed over just in time to grasp her fist as she balled it in preparation to strike the hapless Socha.

She was stronger than she looked.

"You stay out of this, wizard boy."

"He's not the problem," Phyr said. "There's nothing to gain by beating him."

"It will make me feel better."

"Only for a while."

Daraya was still breathing hard, but the crazed look in her eyes was fading. She hadn't given up on Socha, though.

"Daraya. You're better than that. Did violence ever solve anything in your life? Think. Was there one time where violence made matters better?"

"What are we supposed to do then?" Daraya demanded. "Let him go?"

Cheshi appeared in the kitchen door. The blood spatters on her apron matched the blood on the large carving knife she held casually at her side. The wine-stain on her cheek was more pronounced than Phyr remembered. "Is there a problem here?" she asked.

"No. No problem." Phyr gave Daraya a nudge, hoping she would choose the correct course of action.

"This one," Daraya said. "He attacked me."

"It looks as if you are the one doing the attacking." Cheshi glanced from Socha to Daraya. "He's one of my better customers. Let him go."

Daraya brushed her hand through her hair and glanced around the cafe as if searching for an appropriate response.

Phyr followed her gaze. The young couple previously seated next to Socha had made their way to the door and hastily exited. The rest of the patrons watched her with varying degrees of shock on their faces.

"He needs to pay," Daraya said.

Cheshi remained standing in the door to the kitchen, but her muscles were tense, cords like rope showed beneath the flesh of her arms. "And no doubt he will, but not here. Not now."

"Fine." Daraya let go of Socha. She turned and shook a finger in his face. "One day I will make you pay."

Socha stood. Without a word, he turned for the door and ran.

"Coward!" Daraya shouted at his back.

"Are we done here?" Cheshi asked.

"We're done," Daraya spat.

Cheshi turned for the kitchen.

"I never did thank you for your help," Phyr called out.

Cheshi stopped and turned back to Phyr. "It was nothing. You needed help. I helped you. I'd do the same for anyone." She nodded to the door where Socha had fled.

"But, you put yourself in danger."

"Phyr. I was never in any danger. Magic doesn't work on me."

"I've never heard of such a thing."

"Of course you haven't. It's not something they want widely known. Some of us are not just mundane. We're immune. That girl had no chance of harming me with magic, and few can stand against my knife."

"Still. I am in your debt."

"Don't mention it." She glanced at the kitchen once more, as if in a hurry to get back to her tasks. "Are the three of you ready to settle down and enjoy your morning meal? I really need to get back to my work."

"Three of us?" Phyr asked.

"Isn't your friend with you?" Cheshi asked. "I presumed she was, from the amount of food you ordered."

"No. She's in the sanitarium," Phyr said.

Cheshi dropped the knife, the blade clattering as it struck the stone floor.

"You left her there? Alone?"

"She was struck by lightning," Daraya said.

"You foolish child." Cheshi pointed at the door. "Go to her. Protect her. You're all she has. How could you leave her alone like that? With them?"

Why was Cheshi so agitated about leaving Keeree with the healers? Did she have a grudge against healers? Because they couldn't, or wouldn't heal her?

"She's with the healers," Phyr said. "They're caring for her. They told us to go get something to eat and she would probably be awake when we returned."

"They wanted you out of the way," Cheshi said.

"Of course they wanted us out of the way," he explained. "They're busy healing her."

"They're not healing her. They're *sealing* her. How could you not realize that? The sanitarium is part of the academy. Whoever wants her magic sealed is probably there right now."

She gestured to the door. "Get going."

33

SANITARIUM
DARAYA

Daraya raced ahead of Phyr as they made their way back to the sanitarium. She burst through the doors with a resounding crash and dashed down the hallway, skidding to a stop before the desk. The healer from the night before was sitting behind it, eyes half closed. "Where is she?" she demanded.

"Quiet." the healer said. "We have patients resting."

"Where's Keeree?" Phyr demanded. "What have you done to her?"

"She's still asleep. She's suffered serious harm. She may need to rest for a few more days, but with luck, she'll be whole once again. She may suffer some long-term loss of memory."

"I want to see her," Daraya said.

"That's not advisable."

"I don't care what's advisable. Where is she?" Daraya took a step toward the healer, balling her hands into fists. The woman was no taller than she was and probably not accustomed to being accosted by anyone. So much for violence not solving anything.

"Step back," the healer said.

"Or what?"

The healer reached up and fingered a small crystal hanging around her neck. "Or else you'll force me to use magic on you."

"You can try." Daraya launched herself at the healer. She was unaccustomed to fighting, but it seemed that these days, there was no other way to get what she needed. It wasn't her way to be the one doing the hitting. It had always been the other way around. Her hands were her defense— not her weapons, but she was learning.

The woman went down under Daraya's fierce blows, landing on the floor with a huff.

Daraya straddled her, clamping her knees against the woman's ribs. "What have you done to Keeree?"

A cocky smile spread across the healer's face. "Last chance before I use my magic."

Daraya clamped her knees tighter.

The healer let out a breath and closed her eyes.

Her face went slack.

Her lips moved silently.

Fire engulfed Daraya.

Searing pain.

Daraya had burned herself on a hot stove when she was a child. She remembered the pain more than anything else about that day. How the flesh on her arm had blistered, the water beneath her skin accumulating until the blisters burst. The pain had been excruciating.

This was worse.

Far worse.

Every square digit of her body was on fire.

She glanced at her arm, expecting to see the blisters she felt rising there, but there was no sign of the fire she felt. It was magic. How could she defend against magic?

She screamed.

The healer shoved her.

Daraya tumbled to the floor.

"Soon, you'll be locked away just like your friend, Issur. If you're well behaved, I might even lift the fire spell when I lock you up," the healer said. "In a moon or two. By then, you may be more cooperative."

Daraya curled into a ball. The pain was excruciating. She barely heard the words of the healer, barely heard the footsteps echoing off the polished marble tile, barely felt it when the healer's body crashed on top of her, barely realized it when the flames subsided, barely heard the ear-shattering crack as the crystal hanging about the healer's neck exploded sending shards of amber skittering across the floor.

Daraya lay still, a heavy weight across her chest.

It was hard to breathe.

The flames were gone — but not the memory.

She shuddered.

"Daraya?" It was Phyr.

"I'm alive."

"Thank the stars." Phyr knelt down beside her. "Are you hurt?"

"Just my pride," she said.

Daraya kicked at the healer, who had collapsed on the floor. The pendant at her neck was gone. The thin silver chain sported a twisted bit of metal where the amber crystal had been. The woman's face was slack and a bit of white foam escaped from her mouth.

Around her neck was the talisman.

Phyr must have placed it there when he tackled the woman.

"I guess I'm even more in your debt," Daraya said.

"No debt between friends." Phyr helped her to her feet. "Where's Keeree?"

"She never said."

"We have to find her."

"Not before we get answers." Daraya knelt beside the healer and positioned the woman's head to look into her eyes. "Where's Keeree? Who put you up to this?"

The healer's eyes glazed over. Her parched lips parted, a touch of white remaining on them as they moved silently.

Daraya slapped the healer's face. "What did you say?"

Phyr knelt beside Daraya and grabbed her hand before she could land another blow.

"That's enough. Give her a chance to speak."

"Who put you up to this?" he asked the healer.

Her lips moved, but no sound came out.

"Who?" Phyr leaned closer.

"Bannwor," came the breathy word.

Bannwor?

Daraya recalled how Bannwor had sealed Garyll and Sama. It was Bannwor who had taught Teil to do the same. Was Bannwor out to get them now that Teil was incapacitated? She wanted to torture the healer the way the woman had tortured her, get more from her, but she didn't. Phyr was doing a much better job of getting information than she had. Perhaps he was right. Violence wasn't the answer.

"Where's Keeree?" Phyr whispered. "What did you do to her?"

"The farm." The words were almost incomprehensible so softly they were uttered. Daraya almost missed them.

"The farm," Phyr was saying. "Keeree's not at the farm. She's here."

The healer closed her eyes.

She kept them closed.

Phyr waited.

"Where is Keeree?" he whispered in her ear.

Nothing.

"She's not going to tell us anything," Daraya said.

Daraya looked at the healer. The woman's face was slack, and her breathing labored. Was the talisman having an effect on her? Was she dying? Daraya felt a surge of guilt. Phyr had placed the talisman on the healer, expecting to block her magic. To save her — Daraya. But it had done that, and so much more. The crystal pendant that the healer wore around her neck had exploded. Was it something that sustained her, and now that it was gone she was dying? Phyr's mother had a pendant like that. It carried a spell that kept her heart beating. Was the healer dying from some unseen malady now that her source of magic was gone? Was Phyr killing her, even though that was not his intention?

Phyr reached for the talisman.

Was he thinking this through?

What would happen if the healer had access to her magic once more? Maybe this wasn't the best course of action.

"Don't do that," Daraya said. "She used a fire spell on me. It was agony. We don't need her accessing her magic while we're here."

"She's dying," Phyr said.

"All right. Take the talisman off, but be ready to put it back." Daraya shuddered, the memory of the flames still vivid. "I don't need any more of her magic."

Phyr lifted the talisman from the healer. "Are you going to cooperate now?" he demanded.

She panted to catch her breath. "What do you want?"

"Where's Keeree?" Daraya demanded.

"She's in the bed. Beside Phyr's mother."

"What did you do to her?"

"She's bound, just like Phyr's mother. When I burned out her door, I sealed her into that place. Now Keeree has her own place too. There's nothing you can do."

"Take the spell off her."

"I can't. You destroyed the pendant. The spell is permanent now."

Phyr grabbed the healer and shook her. "Tell me how to break it, or so help me, I'll put the talisman back on you!"

So the wizard boy had some anger inside of him after all. For all of his talk of violence not solving anything, he was prepared to hurt the healer to get his way no less than she was.

"The spell was powered by the crystal," the healer said. "When you broke the crystal, the spell transferred to the stones that power the sanitarium. So long as she's here, or anywhere there's magic, the spell will hold. It's out of my hands."

"Take it off her," Phyr demanded.

"I can't." The healer smiled triumphantly. "And neither can you."

Phyr shoved the woman to the floor.

"Come on," Daraya said. "Let's go get Keeree."

"And then what?"

"Take her home. At least she'll be safe there."

"Do you think she'll be safe anywhere?"

"Better the farm than here," Daraya said. "There's no magic there. Perhaps the spell will fade when she gets there. We have to try."

34

BUCOLIC
KEEREE

eeree woke in her own bed. It was comfortable, warm, and safe. How had she gotten here? She vaguely recalled standing in the street inviting Phyr and Daraya to come with her. It had been raining. She'd raised a shield to keep them dry. She reached for another memory. The sanitarium. The healer. A spell. A place of loneliness. A place of solitude. She'd been trapped there. Like Phyr's mother. Only the place she'd been trapped wasn't a cabin in the woods with a light sunny breeze. She'd been lost in a place where moss grew on damp rock walls and stagnant water pooled on the floor. A place of dark and cold. A place of despair.

But now she was in her bed.

"She's awake." A voice intruded. It was Daraya.

She brushed the hair out of Keeree's eyes.

"How did I get here?" Keeree asked.

"We carried you." Phyr's head appeared beside Daraya. "Lightning struck you and we took you to the sanitarium, but Cheshi told us that you were in danger, so we rushed back. The healer had placed you in a spell like Phyr's mother, but Daraya beat her until she admitted what she'd done. Then she told us it was Bannwor who's been behind all our troubles. We couldn't wake you, so we carried you here like a sack of flour. Your father said we did the right thing without knowing it, but you didn't wake up and we were so worried that something bad had happened to you, but now you're awake."

"All right. That's enough." Garyll entered the room. "Why don't the two of you take a seat."

"Will she be all right?" Daraya asked.

"Thanks to you."

Garyll sat on the bed and placed a hand on Keeree's forehead. "You gave us quite a scare, young lady."

"I'm sorry. I didn't mean to cause any trouble."

"I see you've had quite an education in the past few days."

"More than I ever wanted."

"If your friends hadn't gotten you back here in time, things might have been much worse. Your magic was weak. Weaker than the healer thought. And your ability to absorb it is almost nonexistent. That," he said, "is the real reason you were raised here. If not, your magic would be sealed away just like your friends. I take it by now you've discovered what we've been hiding from you, and what we've been hiding *you* from?"

"I think so," Keeree said. "I didn't mean to bring trouble home."

Garyll shook his head. "You didn't bring trouble here. I did. From the moment you first quickened inside your mother. I knew this day would come. I thought I could keep you safe. But we can see how well that turned out." He ran his finger along the brilliant red mark that ran from her shoulder down her arm. The angry red line ran along her arm, then branched and forked across each finger to her fingernails.

"You couldn't know I'd be struck by lightning," she said.

"This wasn't left by any lightning strike."

"They said I was struck by lightning."

"It might have looked like that, but that's not what this is. This is from something stronger than lightning. It's the track of raw magic running through you. You called it up. Directed it. And from the looks of it, you almost lost control of it. You're fortunate to still be with us, but sad to say, you still have a trial ahead."

"Trial?" Wasn't the farm safe? She knew there was no magic here. That's why her own magic had never developed as others' had. Why she was never able to raise fire like almost anyone else. What harm could come to her here?

"I'm afraid you've stirred the hornets' nest. They won't rest until you're safely sealed away. All three of you. You threaten the entire world of wizardry, my dear daughter. Just by being who you are."

"Me? I'm just a girl."

"You're far from just a girl," Garyll said with a smile. "Have I not taught you that? The reason they're so intent on getting to you has to do with your own special brand of magic. When a triad forms, they can all access each other's magic. The wild magic. In order to defeat the triad, you need to seal them all. Or kill one of them. As long as you three live and you remain unsealed, you're a threat to the academy. Only the death of Endwa stopped Adrylt from wielding the wild magic. It's why Bannwor allowed Phyr's mother to live. The threat had been removed, or else she would have been sealed and she would have died."

Garyll glanced at each of Keeree's friends, then back to her. "Only you three can save the wizarding world. With you gone, Bannwor will be the most powerful wizard in the land. He's already tried to move the nexus, make it his own personal supply. Think what would happen if he had access to its power."

"But, what can I do?" Keeree asked. "They had to carry me here. I wasn't even able to make it home on my own, and now you tell me I have to save the wizarding world? I thought I was a threat."

"Only a threat to those who would keep people like us down."

"I don't understand." Nothing her father said made any sense. There was so much she didn't know.

"I explained about the triad." Garyll turned to Keeree's friends. "And how we were sealed away. What I didn't explain was what Sama did. She knew what was coming. She researched and found out that by keeping Keeree away from magic, she would be immune to most forms of it. Keeree was never allowed to develop any magic on her own and never permitted to learn anything that might have caused her to accumulate it when she did leave the farm. It wasn't until recently that the magic came awake in her on its own. The spell Bannwor put on Sama faded after summers away from any source of magic."

"If you stay here," Garyll explained. "The magic will bleed out of you and eventually the spell that binds your magic will fade. All of you."

Garyll paused as if offering an opportunity for Phyr or Daraya to voice their thoughts.

They remained silent.

"You might think that is the best course of action, but it's not. You threaten the power structure of the academy by your very existence. That's dangerous. They will come for you. Maybe not today, or tomorrow, but come they will, and they won't be easy to defeat."

"I thought this was an anti-node," Phyr said. "There's no magic here."

"That's true, but there are plenty of places where there's no magic. It's not a problem for those who store magic in their bodies, or someone who carries a crystal as Phyr's mother does. When they come, they will carry their own store of magic with them. You will not be able to stop them."

"So we're doomed," Keeree said.

"You're frightening the children." Sama stepped from the bedroom where Ersa slept. If what Keeree had been told was true, then the child had also inherited the organ that Keeree had. Did that mean her sister was in just as much danger as she was?

"There is hope. And there is someone who can help," Sama said.

"Fat lot of good that did us," Garyll said.

"It wasn't his fault." Sama's voice was wistful, as if she were recalling a time when things were different, a time she still secretly longed for. "Perhaps this time things will be better."

"Is our life so bad?" Garyll asked.

"No." Sama glanced at the bedroom. "If these can do what we couldn't, then we won't be having this same conversation in a half a dozen summers when our next child reaches her awakening. Do you just want to put it off? Is this the life you want for both your daughters?"

"It's not a bad life," Garyll said.

"It's not. But there's so much more. Don't they deserve a chance?"

"How can you be so confident?" he asked.

"How can you not? This one," she glanced over at Keeree, "has more fire inside of her than I ever did. She's stronger and smarter. You've seen to that. Have a little faith in your daughter, and yourself."

With that, Sama turned to the back bedroom.

Keeree stared at her mother's back as the woman left the room. Keeree had never thought of her mother as someone who had once been caught up in the sort of intrigue Keeree had become embroiled in. To Keeree, she had been simply her mother. Caring, encouraging, hard-working and focused on raising her daughters. But today, she had shown that there was more.

Keeree turned to Garyll, whose gaze was fixed on the back bedroom door as if he could see the woman and child behind it. He bit his lip and swallowed. "Before I start, I want you to know that there is a risk to what you may be undertaking, and no one would fault you for saying no."

Keeree glanced first at Phyr, then Daraya. Phyr seemed worried, but he nodded. Daraya appeared ready for a fight. Was that because she was more accustomed to violence in her life than Keeree or Phyr, or was she simply brave where Phyr was timid? Usually it was Keeree who jumped in with both feet before thinking.

"The three of you working together can wield the wild magic," Garyll said. "But you need training. It's dangerous. Not all who attempt it survive. There is one who can teach you how to work as a triad. It's dangerous, but it's the only way you can end this threat." He glanced at each of them. "I'll give you some time to consider. I don't want to push you. It's too important."

He shoved back his chair and left for the bedroom where the rest of his family waited.

35

SACRIFICE
DARAYA

Daraya's head ached from thinking about what Garyll had told them. Was she up for the challenge? Keeree's parents had been sealed from their magic to such an extent that not even a life drained of magic had been able to undo the spell. It wasn't the sort of life Daraya imagined for herself, but it *was* a life. A harder life than any Daraya had ever imagined.

She sat on the bench beneath the shade tree outside Keeree's home. The breeze was warm, carrying the scent of clover with it that she had only recently been able to sort out from the ever-present aroma of hog and kine droppings. The sun warmed her back.

Keeree and Phyr had been debating the merits of the course of action Garyll laid out for them. They needed to find the only wizard who could teach them the skills to survive the coming onslaught. Yet how could they succeed where three of the most-promising students at the academy had failed?

Yet, the prospect was intriguing. If they did succeed, and that was by no means assured, they would emerge as powerful wizards, well on their way to the fame and fortune she so desperately desired. But there was more than just surviving. Leaving the farm, even for a short time, meant subjecting herself to magic, the magic that would strengthen the spell that sealed away her power. Every day she spent out in the world would add a moon or more to the time she had to spend here in order to break the spell. Was she willing to take that risk? How much longer was she willing to spend isolated on this farm?

Not one heartbeat longer than necessary.

"I say we do it," she told Phyr and Keeree.

"How can you be so cavalier about it?" Phyr asked. "There's real danger here for us. What's to stop Bannwor from killing us? Or simply killing one of us?"

Daraya shrugged. Phyr was right, but he was in no better state than she was. His parents were in the sanitarium. He was alone, just as she was.

"I'm in if you are," she repeated. "I can't do it alone."

Phyr turned to Keeree. "What about you?"

She plucked a long stem from the grass beside her, folded it between her hands, and brought it to her lips. She bent her thumbs, placed them against her mouth, and blew. The sound she made was eerie and ethereal, shifting in tone as she opened and closed her hands.

"I grew up here without magic," she finally said. "The life of a mundane is all I've ever known."

"So you say no," Daraya said.

"I didn't say no. I'm just still thinking it over."

"How can you not want to repay those who ruined your parent's lives?" Daraya demanded.

"Revenge is never a good motive for taking action, especially like this." She leaned back and peered up into the sky as if searching for the answer there. "I'm not afraid if that's what you're thinking. But I know that we're not safe here. If we don't act soon, things can only get worse."

"So, it's a 'yes' for you?" Daraya asked. She wished Keeree were a bit more decisive, but it sounded like she'd come around.

"It's a yes for me," Keeree said.

"How about you, wizard boy? I can't believe you're even thinking this over. If we don't try, who's going to save your parents?"

"If we fail, who's going to save them?" Phyr asked.

"Exactly," Daraya said. "We fail, or we wait until Bannwor comes for us. Either way, it's the same. We should take the fight to him."

"You're so ready to fight," Phyr said.

Daraya shivered. Was she? "It's in my blood," she said. "I can't help it."

"You know what this will cost us?" Phyr asked. "Leaving the farm."

"I know. I'm prepared to spend a bit more time here than I might like. Especially if it means I'll eventually get my magic back. And besides, I'm starting to enjoy the smell. It's sort of growing on me."

"Grown *on* you and *in* you," Phyr said. "Wait till you get around someone who's spent their time in the city. They'll wrinkle their nose at you even though they're too polite to say anything."

Daraya thought back to when she'd first met Keeree. The girl carried the smell of the farm wherever she went. Daraya sniffed at her own shirt, wondering if Phyr was right. Did she carry that same odor? What would people think of her now? Still, if it meant getting her magic back, she was willing to put up with it.

"So, you're in?" Daraya asked again.

Phyr threw her a glance that said he was tired of her badgering.

"Come on, wizard boy. This is your chance to show everyone what you've got. If we succeed, we'll all be admitted to the academy. How could they not accept us after all we've been through? Then you can throw that back in their faces. Show them who's a wizard."

"All right." Phyr stood and brushed the grass from his robe. "Let's do this."

"Now?" Keeree asked.

"Of course, now." Daraya stood and brushed the grass from her own clothes. Now that they'd decided, she was less certain about it than when she'd been trying to persuade Keeree and Phyr. Why was that? Because now it was real. Before, it had been an academic argument. Now they were committed.

She only hoped they were ready.

~

Daraya and her friends set out immediately. Garyll had explained how to *find* the wizard's lair, but not how to enter it. This particular wizard lived close to town, most preferred to be near to the academy. And some never left the grounds. The path that led to the wizard's abode was hidden by magic, but with a bit of effort, Keeree had been able to locate it the same as Daraya had located the path to the academy.

She wondered what it would be like to wield the wild magic. She'd had a taste of how to draw the small magic forth and control it. It had made her euphoric, heady. She wondered if the wild magic was anything like that? Could they control it? If they did, could they stop? Garyll had said as much. The wild magic was addictive. Extremely addictive, and had consumed her father. Had Adrylt been an angry and bitter young man, or had the magic made him that way? What would it do to her? Would she succumb to it as her father had? Would it consume her? Would it leave her an angry and bitter shell of the woman she had hoped to become?

She shook off the thought. No reason to invite problems where there were none. She turned her thought to the wizard they were to locate. What if they weren't welcome? What if the wizard they sought was in no mood for company? What if Garyll had been wrong?

Off in the distance, she heard the screech of a raptor. It reminded her of the gryphon. Just the sound of it sent a shiver up her spine. What if they encountered that beast again? What if it guarded the wizard's abode? "What if he doesn't want to help us, or he can't?" she asked.

"Getting cold feet?" Phyr asked.

"No, but what if Garyll was wrong? How do we know we can trust this wizard? How do we know he's not in league with Bannwor?"

"Isn't it a little too late to be asking those sorts of questions?" This time it was Keeree's turn to challenge her.

"I'm just worried, that's all," Daraya said. "Aren't you?"

"No." Keeree said. "Not anymore. Fear doesn't help anything."

"You can't tell me you're not just a little afraid of what we may be asked to do?"

"I'd be a liar if I said I wasn't," Keeree said. "Fear and worry are not the same thing. There's nothing to do but push onward. We're committed to this. All three of us — or none of us. Don't tell me you want to back out now."

"No. Not back out, but maybe take it a bit slower?"

"It was you who said not to wait," Keeree reminded her.

"I'm just thinking." Daraya muttered. Why was she feeling like this? Was there more to it than just reluctance to put herself at risk? If they failed, would her father welcome her back? Surely not after she'd raised the ire of the academy. Losing her magic might have been something he would accept, but with the wizarding world dead set against her, there was no way he would ever take her back. Especially not after what Garyll had told them.

It was hard to believe that her own father had been friends with Phyr's mother. Was it just a coincidence then that the three of them had become friends, or was there some sort of destiny at work? Were they meant to become friends? Did that mean they would succeed? She hoped so, but she feared not. There was no guarantee they wouldn't all end up as Keeree's parents were. Mundane, with no hope of ever touching magic again. It made her sad to think of a life without magic. The elation she'd felt when she raised fire still haunted her. She would give anything to feel that power once more. Even risk her life.

She picked up her pace, letting the afternoon breeze blow her hair around her face. "Come on, you laggards, what are you waiting for?"

She glanced back to see Phyr, and Keeree stopped dead in their tracks.

She turned her gaze to see what had startled them. A distant screech drew near as the mighty gryphon circled overhead. That was the last thing they needed. The gryphon barring their way.

Daraya threw up an arm to ward off a shower of sparks as the gryphon settled to the ground, looming over her. So the wizard was not as welcoming as he'd been portrayed. Or was there another puzzle to be solved? She hoped not.

The gryphon seemed agitated. It stretched out a paw.

The smell of brimstone and ash bit at her nose as massive claws closed around her. Sparks and flame dropped to the ground as the gryphon lifted her and held her out as if examining her. It opened its flaming beak and let out a screech that was so loud it hurt.

His talons were sharp as he tightened his grip.

It became hard to breathe.

Painful.

The gryphon let out another piercing scream, and the air filled with the stench of brimstone and decayed flesh.

He tossed Daraya in the air, caught her by the leg, and dangled her over his open mouth. For half a heartbeat, she wondered what it would be like to be eaten alive.

Talons loosened, and she fell straight for the maw filled with flames and sparks.

36

FOUNTAIN

PHYR

Phyr watched in horror as Theored tossed Daraya in the air and swallowed her. Before he had a chance to think about running, the beast grabbed him as well. The grip of the talons was bone-crushing, the breath hot and putrid. As the gryphon tossed him into the air. He had barely a heartbeat to wonder what his parents would think of him being eaten alive.

As the great fiery beak closed about him, heat flared. Phyr felt it on his face, hotter than the noonday sun. The smell of brimstone was almost enough to choke him. He muttered a farewell to his life. It hadn't been long, nor had it been distinguished, but he'd miss it.

He landed with a thump on a hard, cold floor. Before him stood the short, balding wizard, Charyl. He was motioning Phyr forward. "Make way for your friend."

Daraya stood beside the wizard, brushing her clothes straight.

No sooner had Phyr vacated the spot when Keeree appeared.

She was screaming as she landed, but soon began laughing hysterically.

"Come, come," Charyl said. "It took you long enough." He raised an eyebrow at Phyr. "I trust you were not followed?" He waved a hand in the air. "No matter. Theored won't let anyone bother us. Not unless I tell him to."

"Where are we?" Phyr blurted.

Charyl's fingers touched his parted lips. He paused as if in thought, then placed his hand before his chest, fingers splayed out. "Why you're in my home. This is where you were headed, was it not?"

"Can we do that again?" Keeree was bouncing up and down like a child on her name-day.

"You sure are a strange bird," Charyl remarked. "Most people find being eaten by a gryphon rather unsettling, but then you do remind me of your mother. She, too, found it to be rather enjoyable."

"We're not here to talk about your mother," Phyr reminded Keeree. "We're here to learn how to protect ourselves."

"Protect yourselves?" Charyl asked. "I suppose that would be possible. I never thought about it just that way before. Protection," he muttered. "Yes. A possibility. Quite an interesting possibility."

"Garyll said you could teach us," Phyr explained.

"He did, did he? Well, I suppose he'd know. He's had a lot of time to think about it."

"How are you going to teach us to use magic? Ours has been sealed away," Phyr said.

The short, balding wizard let out a bark like that of a dog. "Teach you magic? Why would you think such a thing?"

"Garyll said you were our only hope. He said they're coming for us, and without your help, we may not survive."

"They've already gotten to two of you," he said. "From what I can see."

This was growing tiresome. Phyr was losing patience. His parents were stuck in the sanitarium, his home was destroyed, his friends were in danger, and this doddering old fool wasn't even paying attention to the conversation. He glanced at Keeree and Daraya. Daraya shrugged. She seemed happy to let Phyr lead the discussion.

"Can you teach us how to defend ourselves? Why else would we be here? Garyll said you could teach us what we need to know." Phyr's sighed. Was this their great hope? A senile old man who was lost in his own thoughts?

"I don't teach magic," Charyl said. "I don't teach anything."

"What do you do then?" Phyr asked. "You're one of the ones who evaluated prospective students for the academy. You're a professor or a teacher there, aren't you?"

"Evaluate. Advise. Provoke. I don't teach." He paused as if in thought. "I facilitate learning."

Before Phyr could say another word, the wizard turned his back. He raised a hand in the air as if to guide them. "Follow me, if you would be so kind."

"Where are we going?" Phyr asked.

"Somewhere you *can* learn," Charyl said.

Phyr glanced at Keeree and Daraya. Neither one of them looked inclined to argue. They were already following.

"I thought you weren't going to teach us anything," Phyr said.

"Precisely." Charyl strode off at such a pace Phyr was hard-pressed to keep up with him. He led Phyr and his friends along a dim tunnel that swerved madly, as if constructed by a drunken miner. At one point, he turned so sharply Phyr was afraid he would lose sight of the wizard and become lost in the maze of tunnels, but soon they arrived at a chamber that looked more like a ballroom than a mine. The floor was fabricated of tiles, no two the same size, shape, or color. Sitting in the middle of the floor was a carving. It appeared for all the world as if it were a standard lavatory basin on a pedestal.

"What is this?" Keeree asked.

"Please. Join hands around the fountain." Charyl took Keeree's hand and placed it in Phyr's. The wizard carefully intertwined their fingers and then grasped them as if he were holding them in place. He glanced at Phyr and then Keeree and nodded. He moved over and did the same with Daraya's hand.

Phyr felt foolish standing there holding hands with Keeree and Daraya. He felt acutely aware of the two hands in his. Keeree's strong and rough, Daraya's delicate and trembling.

Charyl thumped his chest. "You three have something the likes of us do not. It allows you to guide the wild magic. To command it. To bend it to your will. Only your will isn't enough. You need the small magic to guide it or else it will burn you where you stand." The wizard thumped his chest once more. "You understand?"

"Yes," Phyr said.

"Good. Since two of you no longer have access to your own magic, it's going to be up to this one to get things started." He placed a hand on Keeree's shoulder.

"Show them the way, farm girl." Charyl imitated Daraya's expression.

At first, Phyr felt nothing. The room was silent. No lights and no sound intruded. What was Keeree supposed to be doing?

She squeezed his hand. Once, twice, three times, then stepped back as if expecting the fount to erupt.

Phyr followed suit as Daraya also took a step back.

Their arms were stretched wide now, hands holding tightly.

A lump formed in Phyr's chest, right where the organ was that controlled the magic. Was that it? Was Keeree doing something, or was it him? He was uncertain. It felt as if his own thoughts were flowing through his outstretched arms and mingling with those of his two friends. He caught echoes of their own confusion even as he struggled to make sense of what he was experiencing.

In the center of the bowl, a faint light appeared. Just a spark that shot upwards as if escaping from some unseen fire. Then another. And another. Soon there was a steady stream of sparks leaping from the bowl, rushing toward the ceiling. It was as if a snake had sprung to life, formed of fire like the gryphon. Was this the lesson they were meant to learn? He hoped not.

As he watched entranced, the stream of sparks thickened, undulating wildly as it rose from the laver toward the roof.

Without warning, the stream arced toward him, shedding sparks that landed on the stone before him. Phyr felt the heat of it.

"Don't touch it, and don't let it touch you," Charyl said. "Don't try to control it or use it, yet, just guide it. Keep the stream centered. Talk to each other. It takes all of you."

The stream of sparks drew close to Phyr. It was hot. Like fire. The sparks burned his flesh where they touched him. He panicked. He tried to push the stream away, but the more he thought about it, the closer it drew.

"Don't let it touch him. Call it to you, away from him," Charyl shouted. "Together. As one, or all of you will be lost."

The stream contacted Phyr's chest. It burned away his robe and scorched his flesh. It was fire. Not magic. Pain flared where it touched him. Worse than the pain was the attraction he felt for the magic. It wanted him, and he wanted it. To wield such power, what joy! He'd touched it before. He'd reached deep within the earth, grasped the power he needed, and drawn it forth as one drew water from a well. Unlimited power. It was glorious. Heady. He would drink it in, and he would know power. He would break the spell that bound his magic and he would be free.

"No. Not like that." Charyl's voice cut through the ecstasy, but he ignored it. Here was power. Here was everything he'd ever desired.

Here was pain.

Phyr's chest exploded in pain. Searing hot. He screamed. Keeree and Daraya screamed with him. Did that mean they felt it too? Was he causing them pain as well?

Shame overcame him.

Who was he to command such magic?

He relaxed, letting his mind go blank despite the pain.

The stream of sparks re-centered itself.

The pain receded.

Phyr's hands, wet with sweat, slipped from the grasp of his friends.

The sparks died out.

Darkness filled the room.

For a couple of heartbeats, Phyr stood there, ashamed of how he'd behaved. Embarrassed at his own frailty, his own lack of control. He only hoped that Keeree and Daraya could forgive him for his carelessness.

A light burst forth, centered on the bowl.

Was this another test?

He wasn't prepared for another test.

Phyr glanced over at Keeree and Daraya.

They each had the same expression of shame on their faces, and they each had the same scorch mark on their chests.

Charyl took in the sight and smiled. "I see you've learned how to direct the wild magic. To focus it, you will need a spell, just the way you command the small magic. Find one. Learn it. Be ready." He waved his hand in the air. "Now off with you."

37

ATTACK

KEEREE

*K*eeree felt herself falling. She landed on soft grass, covered in dew. The familiar smells of the farm told her she was home, and the crowing of the cock told her it was just morning. How long had they been in the wizard's abode? It had been afternoon when they ran into the gryphon. Had their lesson taken that long? Or had it been a dream?

Her hand went to her chest.

The burn mark on her shirt, and the pain beneath it, said it had been far from a dream.

"Where are we?" Daraya had landed right beside Keeree. She sniffed the air, wrinkled her nose and scowled. "Never mind."

"You'll come to love it," Keeree said.

Daraya glanced at her, hand rising to her chest.

Her face reddened.

"Do you have an extra shirt? Something without a gaping hole in it?" she asked.

Keeree glanced down at her own shirt. She was showing more than she'd imagined. She glanced at Phyr, who was steadfastly ignoring both of them. Perhaps a change in attire *was* called for.

"Let's see what we have," Keeree said. "I don't have much, but what I do have, you're more than welcome to."

She led Daraya to the house and dug through the chest of drawers in her room. Most of what she had was homespun, made from the wool of their own sheep. What would a city girl like Daraya think of such shabby attire? She found the best shirt she owned, a faded brown homespun pullover, shook it out, and handed it to Daraya. "It's the best I can do."

Daraya held it up before her. "It's certainly better than what I'm wearing." She turned her back and stripped off the burned shirt. For the first time, Keeree saw the full extent of the scars on her back.

"How could anyone do that?" Keeree asked.

"Do what?" Daraya turned back to Keeree.

"Your back," Keeree said.

Daraya's face went red but quickly regained its normal color. "It used to bother me, but now it's just a part of who I am."

"It's never going to happen again." Keeree stripped off her own shirt and replaced it with another one, not near as nice as the one she'd given Daraya, but serviceable. She tucked it into her trousers. "Ready?"

"More than ready," Daraya replied.

Keeree reached out, took Daraya's hand, and led her back to the common area of the house. They found Phyr dressed in one of Garyll's shirts. It hung from him like an empty sack of flour. Poor Phyr. He would need to split a lot of wood before he was able to fill out that shirt, if he ever did. But at least the burn mark no longer showed.

Garyll was smiling as the two of them returned. "I see you've all survived. A little worse for wear, but you all survived."

"It was a near thing," Keeree said.

"And how was my old friend?" Garyll asked.

"Evasive, exasperating, inscrutable," Keeree said.

"Glad to see nothing has changed."

Sama entered the room. She had Ersa's hand in hers, and a look of worry on her face. Ersa was glancing around the room as if searching for the source of her mother's distress. Her free hand twisted the loose fitting yellow dress she wore.

"He's here," Sama said. "Best we make ourselves scarce."

"Already?" Garyll stood and rushed to the door.

Sama held him back. "It's not your fight."

"But..."

"Not your fight." Sama cut him off before he could finish. She nodded to Keeree and her friends. "It's theirs. You'll only get yourself hurt, and I need you." She stroked Ersa's head. "This one needs you."

"Keeree is our daughter too," Garyll said.

"And well prepared to take care of herself. Come. Let's find some-place safe where we can still see."

Garyll lowered his head and followed Sama out the back door.

"Looks like we're on our own," Keeree said.

Daraya reached for Keeree's hand "On our own, but not alone."

"Not alone," she said.

The three of them stepped out into the morning air. It was crisp and not yet warm. A gentle breeze carried the scent of clover to Keeree, with just a hint of the flowers her mother tended beside the path.

Standing in the road just beyond the gate was the tall, wizened form of Bannwor. For an instant Keeree hesitated, but Phyr pulled her along. The sun was hot, the morning dew gone beneath its insis-tent rays. The air crackled with ozone the way it did after a thunder-storm. Keeree felt the hard dirt beneath her feet. It reassured her to know the land was there for her. That her connection to its magic was no less than it had ever been. Today was the day she would need it the most.

As the trio exited the gate that marked the border of the farm, the air grew cold as if a sudden shower were about to unleash itself.

Bannwor stood on the crest of the hill. The same hill where Adrylt had stood when he attacked Garyll so long ago. Keeree shud-dered and whispered a plea that history not repeat itself.

Bannwor raised his hand and called out. "Don't make this harder than it needs to be. Let me complete my business and be gone."

"You're not touching our friend," Phyr said.

"And you're not stopping me." Bannwor waved his hand.

Phyr was thrown to the ground. He rolled over and got to his knees, but the wizard made a pushing gesture and Phyr collapsed to the dirt.

"And neither are you." Bannwor repeated the gesture. Daraya was ripped from Keeree's grip and cast to the ground just as Phyr had been.

Keeree stood straight.

Her heart beat wildly.

Without touching Phyr and Daraya, how was she going to accomplish anything? Even touching, it had been difficult to control the flow of magic.

"Are you going to submit to me?" Bannwor asked, "Or does this need to become a fight?"

Keeree folded her arms across her chest. "Fight."

Bannwor shrugged. "Have it your way."

Keeree gazed intently at the wizard. She expected him to mouth words, or move his hands to form his spell, but he stood silent and unmoving. Only after it was too late, did she recall that an accomplished wizard used neither words, nor gestures. She was a fool. She should have known better. A strange tingling arose in her feet, as if she were standing on sand that shifted around her.

At first it was so slight that she pushed the feeling aside, better to concentrate on the wizard, but the earth beneath her feet was growing insubstantial.

She glanced down.

She'd sunk half a digit into the ground.

She tried to move, but she was stuck. "Rabbit turds." How had she let herself become ensnared like that?

"How quaint," Bannwor said. "Rabbit turds. Haven't heard that one in a while." The smile on his face was lopsided and self-satisfied.

She wanted to punch it.

Shake it off. Keeree told herself. *He's just trying to get under your skin.*

The ground beneath her feet grew warm as it engulfed them. At first it was almost welcome. Nice warm sand enfolded her cold feet on a chilly day, but the heat increased, then began working its way upwards. It was as if the sand had become a snake and was slithering up her leg.

She tugged at her foot.

She was stuck fast.

"Daraya. Phyr." She reached for her friends, but they were both struggling no less than she was. So that was it? The wizard had defeated them by simply separating them?

The sand beneath her feet took on the form of a snake and wrapped itself around her legs.

It squeezed.

Keeree lost feeling.

She would have tumbled to the ground, but the snake was constricting too tightly. She couldn't bend her knees.

She yanked at her leg. It was held fast.

The snake wound itself around her middle, squeezing so tight she thought she was going to burst.

She let out a scream.

The snake tightened.

She tried to breathe.

The snake tightened.

She tried to inhale, but couldn't. Was the wizard trying to kill her? She'd thought he only wanted to seal away her magic. *That* she could have lived with. Perhaps she could still surrender. A life without magic was certainly better than dying. But she had no words.

Stars formed before her eyes.

She threw her hands out as if her sheer strength of will would let her reach Phyr and Daraya.

More stars appeared, but something else. The snake had burrowed into her chest. It had a firm grasp on the center of her magic. It bit down.

Pain flared.

It would all be over soon.

As Keeree tried to shriek. She felt a hand slip into hers. One on either side. Not the physical hands she was familiar with, but it was unmistakable. Daraya and Phyr had reached out to her. They were in contact.

For a moment, she panicked.

Was she simply dragging them to their doom as well?

No. She had this. She probed for the wizard's magic. Where had he hidden it? Garyll said Bannwor would bring his own magic with him. The farm had none of its own. If only she could find the source. Subvert it. Tap into it.

There wasn't much time. The stars were growing brighter, her vision was narrowing. It was little more than a pinhole.

She turned her gaze on the wizard, relaxing, trying to ignore the stars that swirled around her. Slowly it became clear. A stream of sparks flowed from over the hill behind Bannwor. It threaded its way through the wizard and reached out toward her.

Not like the raw magic she'd handled in the wizard's abode.

This was something else. Something tame and weak in comparison. She laughed. She could handle this. She reached for it, guiding it away from her just as she'd done to the wild magic with Phyr and Daraya's help.

The stream of sparks flared.

It was fighting back.

She tried to draw it aside, but every effort she made only tightened the snake's grip on her.

Her approach wasn't working.

She panicked.

The snake tightened its grip.

"Relax," Phyr's words came to her like a whisper in her ear.

Daraya's whisper joined Phyr's. "We have this."

The pressure in her chest lightened just a bit. She felt the force that Phyr and Daraya were exerting on the snake, on the wizard's own magic. It fought them no less than it had fought her, but they were making headway. She could breathe again.

Without warning, the snake released her.

The shower of sparks cracked like a whip to ensnare Daraya. Thick bands of embers encircled her, pinning her arms to her side.

Daraya cried out in pain.

"No." Keeree screamed. That wasn't supposed to happen.

She pulled at the magic.

The stream shifted toward her.

"Not so much," Phyr's calm words came to her.

She relaxed, but only a little.

The stream of sparks unwrapped from Daraya and darted toward Phyr. The crimson snake flared as it jumped from one of her friends to the other. The crack of the whip was unmistakable. It must have hurt Phyr no less than being struck by an expertly wielded strap of leather.

"No, you don't," Keeree shouted.

She grasped for the magic, seizing it as she would have seized a venomous snake.

It fought her, sapping the strength from her muscles until she feared she had nothing more to give, but with Phyr and Daraya's help, she held it firm.

What to do now?

Maybe give the wizard a taste of his own medicine?

She nodded at Phyr and Daraya. They might not know what she was thinking, but they would help. That was it then. Let the wizard feel his own spell.

She wrestled the shower of sparks off of Phyr and directed it toward Bannwor. It was a careful balancing act between the three of them, but as they moved, Keeree gained confidence in her skill. Slowly the three of them guided the snake.

Bannwor took a step back, his hands coming up to ward off the flaring magic that Keeree directed at him. He stumbled, dropped to his knees, and scrambled quickly back to his feet.

Keeree took advantage of his momentary distraction. She guided the great coils around him as he struggled to rise. Thick black coils wrapped around his legs, then his waist. They pinned his arms to his side. But there was a flaw in her thinking. How would she hold this spell? Would the snake remain coiled around the wizard, or would he recover and take back control? What would happen when the magic ran out? Would Bannwor come for them again? How would she ever be safe? Was there any place safe for her? Anywhere in the world?

That was it.

Keeree recalled the carving from the cafe.

'The worldwyrm devours itself' it had been captioned.

She guided the head of the magical snake to its own tail. It snapped greedily and swallowed. Soon the snake had consumed half of its own body and constricted on the wizard of its own accord as it struggled to consume even more of itself.

Bannwor screamed in pain.

He cursed.

He spoke the words to a spell that had no effect on the snake, or Keeree and her friends.

His face grew purple.

His breathing halted.

His tongue protruded, and his eyes bulged.

A great shower of sparks appeared where the wizard stood and with an earsplitting bang, vanished.

Not a trace remained.

Keeree drew in a deep breath. She could feel the difference. The small magic surrounded her once more. The wild magic had returned to the earth where it would become diffuse and cold. Cold enough for every washer woman and kine heard to handle it once more.

A sudden wave of guilt washed over her.

She'd killed animals before, but this was different. She'd just killed another person. It made her feel dirty, contaminated. She'd been forced into it, but it left a stain. She wondered if that feeling would ever fade, or was it a part of her now, just as wielding magic was?

38

PASTORAL

KEEREE

Keeree stood in the road looking toward town as the dust rose into the still morning air. It had been a moon since they'd dispatched Bannwor, but Daraya and Phyr's magic were still not back. Not completely. Garyll had told her it might take another moon, possibly two or three, and that was only if they remained on the farm. Every day they spent off the farm was another moon they would need to wait.

It wasn't a bother for Keeree. She knew no other life, but for Phyr and Daraya it was more of a challenge. Garyll had made Daraya a pair of wooden shoes when she complained that the constant exposure to cow and pig manure was destroying hers. She made it clear that under no circumstances was she going barefooted. Garyll painted dainty flowers on them, saying it made her look ladylike. She'd grumbled, but had soon taken to wearing them everywhere but in the house. She'd adopted a pair of piglets and was quite protective of them. Keeree warned her not to name them, but she had anyway. The two of them followed her everywhere, something she would surely come to regret when she was being nudged by a thirty stone porker looking for affection.

As the puff of dust drew closer, Keeree rushed to the barn.

Phyr was busy collecting eggs and carefully stacking them into a crate.

"Better hurry. She's almost here," Keeree warned him.

Phyr brushed the straw from his shirt. It had once belonged to Garyll but had been cut down to fit his frame. He'd taken to life on the farm much quicker than Keeree expected, and as hard as he worked, that shirt would not fit him much longer. A shy smile erupted when the door opened and a face peered in. The light streaming in the door fell on the red wine-stain that graced the cheek of the girl who had taken to visiting the farm for eggs and the occasional hen or hog.

There were places closer, and places cheaper, but she made the trek out to the farm almost every day. Keeree had her suspicions that these regular visits were responsible for Phyr's interest in the workings of the farm. He was still worried about his folks, but Cheshi brought him regular reports on their condition. Teil was almost ready to be released and soon Phyr would be reunited with his father, at least for a while. But, until Phyr had his magic back, there was little he could do for his parents. Leaving Keeree and Daraya alone would have exposed them to whatever fresh mischief the academy might throw at them. Until they were all restored, things were best the way they were.

Keeree smiled. She had gone from no close friends to two.

What could be sweeter than that?

THE END

ABOUT THE AUTHOR

James A Eggebeen began writing at a young age, but it was only after he was disillusioned by a college course in poetry, and switched to a creative writing class, that he was bitten by the fiction bug, and never looked back.

Born into a Dutch farming community in rural Wisconsin, James served in the Navy, then as an executive in the high-tech sector. It was when his wife spent three months abroad that he began to think about writing professionally.

He now works from home as a software architect, something he says avoids the daily Southern California commute. He has met many new friends as part of the writing community and loves working with new writers to help develop their voice.

With his next series of novels already well under way, his goal is to just keep writing.

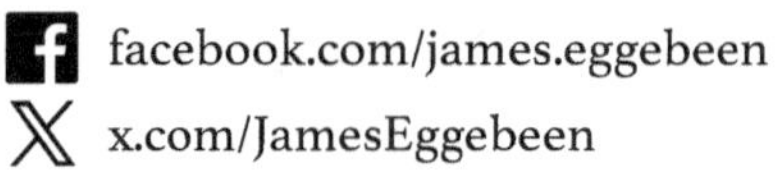

facebook.com/james.eggebeen

x.com/JamesEggebeen

ALSO BY JAMES A EGGEBEEN

Apprentice to Master Series

Foundling Wizard

Wizard's Education

Master Wizard

Wizard's Hatchling

Origin Series

The Priest

Dragon Lord

The Sorceress

The Healer

Flame Rider Series

Bonds of Fire and Fury

Angry Gods Saga

Contempt of the Gods

Stand Alone

Reluctant Wizard

Indentured Magic

Kalis

Gypsy

AUTHOR'S NOTES

I began writing Sufficient Magic as a young adult fantasy. It was a departure from my normal darker epic fantasy. I felt I needed a break, and to write something different. I planned to take the draft of the first few chapters to WIFYR (Writers and Illustrators For Young Readers). My first in-person writer's conference, but COVID had other ideas and instead, we did the conference via zoom.

I took a class from David Farland and received encouraging feedback not only from him and the class, but from my agent consult.

After the book was finished, I had it edited by my friend and mentor J.V. Jones. She pointed out several areas where I needed some polish, as she often does. I addressed those, then had David Farland edit the book one more time.

I was amazed that each of these professional writers had different things that they honed in on. As always, I learned a lot of lessons from both. I truly appreciate being able to work with such gifted individuals.

Shortly after receiving David's edits, he suffered a heart attack and died. It was a shock and a tragedy, as he had such a positive influence on my writing.

I abandoned the manuscript for a while, but decided it needed to see the light of day. I pondered querying it to several agents, but eventually decided that self publishing was the way to go. I edited it a few more times, got it proof-read, and what you see now is the culmination of several years of edits.

I hope you enjoy reading it as much as I enjoyed writing it.